Fawcett Crest Books
by David Morrell:

FIRST BLOOD

TESTAMENT

TESTAMENT

David Morrell

A FAWCETT CREST BOOK

Fawcett Publications, Inc., Greenwich, Connecticut

TESTAMENT

THIS BOOK CONTAINS THE COMPLETE TEXT OF
THE ORIGINAL HARDCOVER EDITION.

A Fawcett Crest Book reprinted by arrangement with
M. Evans and Company, Inc.

Copyright © 1975 by David Morrell

ISBN 0-449-23033-3

Printed in the United States of America

10 9 8 7 6 5 4 3 2 1

Part

ONE

IT WAS THE LAST MORNING the four of them would ever be together: the man and his wife, his daughter and his son. The son was just a baby, the daughter still in grade school. That didn't matter. In time, nothing did. It came upon them almost comically—the man sat at the breakfast table, his bare feet on the cold hardwood floor, and glancing over by the stove, he saw the cat slump into her bowl of milk. She was a very stupid Siamese. She liked to sleep on the television when the set was warm, but she kept rolling in her sleep and often fell off the back, pinned against the wall, her claws scraping to get up again, her blue eyes peering over the top in confusion. She was so fascinated by flames that she sometimes sniffed too close to lighted candles and set fire to her whiskers. Now she didn't even know how to drink milk anymore. He felt embarrassed for her, almost laughed when she tried to raise herself out of the milk, flapping her wet jowls. Almost. Her front legs buckled, she fell into the milk again, and suddenly all four legs were stiff, drumming.

Slowly they relaxed.

He frowned, walked over and looked down at her. She lay unmoving in a puddle from the upturned bowl. He picked her up; the bowl, released from her weight, wobbled hollowly upright. She was strangely limp and

6

heavy, head dangling, eyes open. His hands were wet beneath her sodden fur. Milk dripped into the puddle.

"My God," he said.

Claire hadn't noticed, too busy putting the baby in his highchair and heating his bottle. Now she turned, looked puzzled a moment and frowned just as he had. "But she was all right when I let her out this morning."

"Daddy? What's wrong with Samantha?" Sarah asked. He glanced at her, and she was peering over the back of her chair, still in her pajamas, her head cocked slightly to one side. "Is she sick? What's the matter with her?" She said it slowly, calmly, but she was squinting the way she did when she was worried. The cat was hers. They slept together. She had a jingle:

> I see Samantha's tail in the air.
> She hasn't got any underwear.

"You'd better go to your room, sweetheart," he said.

"But what's wrong with Samantha?"

"I told you go to your room."

He had a good idea what was wrong. He was thinking that the cat had been outside, thinking angrily of the old man two houses down the street who always confused this cat with two other Siamese nearby. They often killed robins and bluejays, and just yesterday the old man had stopped Sarah as she was carrying Samantha awkwardly down the sidewalk. "Listen, little girl, you keep your cat in the house from now on," the old man said. "She kills my pretty birds, and what I do to cats who kill my birds is grab them and throw them in a sack and tie the sack over my car's exhaust pipe. Or else I wait until they're in my backyard and then I shoot them." Sarah had come running into the house and down to the cellar, trying to hide the cat in a storage closet. The old man wouldn't even answer his door to talk with him about it.

"What are you doing?" Claire said.

"That old bastard down the street. I'm feeling for a wound of some kind."

But there wasn't any. And there wasn't any other sign that the old man had hurt her either. He couldn't understand it. What the hell had killed her?

"You don't have to blame the old man," Claire said. "It could have been anything."

"Like what? You tell me what."

"How should I know? She was sixteen years old. Maybe she just had a stroke."

"Maybe. Sure it's possible." But he couldn't stop thinking about the old man.

Sarah was beside him, crying; the baby started wailing in his highchair. He set the cat out of sight on the cellar steps, came back and held Sarah by the shoulders.

"Come on, sweetheart. Try to eat your cereal and forget about it."

But she wouldn't move, and when he lifted her onto her chair, she just turned to look toward the cellar door. He only managed to get her to fix her cereal by pretending he thought she wasn't big enough to do it for herself.

"Good girl. I love you."

The baby still hadn't quit wailing. His face was wizened and ugly as Claire took him from his highchair and sat at the table to feed him his bottle. She pressed the nipple against her wrist to check that it wasn't too hot.

"After breakfast I'm taking the cat to the vet," he

told her. "I'm damn well going to find out what happened." He couldn't stop thinking about the old man. Poison maybe. Could be the old man had left out some poisoned meat or fish or something.

Milk maybe.

Sarah was struggling to lift the heavy jug and pour some into her cereal, spilling a little on the table, and he wasn't thinking about the old man anymore, he was thinking about Kess, the meeting eight months ago and what Kess had said about poisoning people. Jesus, surely not. Surely not even Kess would have followed through on that. He lunged down, grabbing Sarah's hand to stop her from putting a spoonful into her mouth saying fast to Claire, "His bottle. No." But it was too late. She already put the nipple into the baby's mouth, and the baby choked once and stiffened.

"Poison," Kess said, "is a beautiful weapon. It's easy to obtain. The specific kind you need is probably right there on the shelves of your neighborhood plant nursery waiting to be distilled. It's convenient to administer. Everybody has to eat and drink, after all." He was ticking the points off on his fingers, his smooth pleasant voice sounding more and more involved as he went along. "It's certain and immediate. It doesn't require a proximate assassin: once you've mixed it into your target's mashed potatoes, for example, or his milk or coffee, you can be blocks away by the time he takes it in and drops. Plus, the best kinds are hard to trace."

HE KEPT GOING to the big front window in the living room, staring out for the ambulance and the police. Where were they? Why weren't they here by now? He paced, barely conscious of the soft feel of the rug beneath his feet; stopped as he heard a siren far off. Its wail came closer and closer, and he stared out the window up the street toward the corner. The wail peaked nearby, diminished, faded to the north. Another siren began behind it, crested, faded to the north as well. Ambulances to an accident. Police chasing somebody. God knows what. Why weren't they coming here?

He glanced across the living room toward Claire and the baby in the kitchen. She looked worse than before, catatonic now, staring blankly at the wide smear of milk across the black table. She was nearly always dark and smooth-cheeked and attractive, but for two months when she was pregnant, and after the delivery whenever the baby woke them in the night, her face played a trick, went grotesquely pale and gaunt like a skull, and it was like that now. He sensed something inside her winding tighter and tighter. He was afraid of what she might do to herself if the thing suddenly snapped and she became violent again. She had flung the baby's bottle across the kitchen while he was phoning for help. The bottle had shattered loudly, glass and milk flying against the stove, and Sarah had screamed

"Stop it! I don't want to hear anymore! I won't listen!" covering her ears, and then she had not been around. Where was she? Why weren't they coming? He was growing worried about what the shock of everything had done to her, wanting badly to go look, holding back, not daring to let Claire out of his sight, thinking— *Kess. He didn't have to do this. Not the baby. No matter what, he didn't have to kill the—*

Jesus, not the baby.

In the spring, a year and a half ago, he had almost gone away with another woman. She had been lovely and good for him, and she had sought him out at a time when his life seemed nothing more than work and responsibility to Claire and Sarah. It was an old story, and he should have known better. Because she was married and she had said that she wanted to leave her husband to be with him, but once she had moved out she said she wasn't ready to go away with him just yet, she needed time to be by herself and think, which meant that everything was finished. But he had already gone to Claire and told her he wanted out, and then he had discovered the fool that he had been.

This baby was their way of forcing themselves to stay together. He had even been there to see this child delivered. He had stood next to Claire in her hospital bed through four hours of labor, his hand in hers while she took a deep breath and held it during each contraction, letting it out slowly, breathing deeply again. Too thick, her water sac would not break. The doctor had to come and rupture it, flooding the bed. The doctor froze each side of her distended cervix with a foot-long needle. The nurses wheeled her off to the delivery room while he and the doctor went through a swinging door to a row of lockers and put on white caps and

gowns and face masks and shoe coverings, and then he
was in the bright, sharply antiseptic-smelling delivery
room where he sat on a stool by her head, watching a
mirror that was angled between her legs. He felt his
breath warm and moist beneath his face mask, faintly
suffocating. The nurses were arranging trays of instruments. The doctor was joking about the big surprise
the baby was going to have when it discovered there
was another world. He himself was laughing excitedly.
The doctor took a pair of scissors and snipped a long
slit down from the vaginal opening, blood pooling out,
and then in the mirror he and Claire could see the
baby's hairy brown-pink head, and Claire said "Come
on, baby, come on," proud, gasping, and it came, kept
coming with each contraction, the doctor easing out
one shoulder, then the other, the suspense of what it
would be and whether it would be all right, a nurse
saying "Come on, fella," himself saying "No, it could
be a girl," and then in one long easy slide it was out
into the doctor's arms, squirming to breathe with a
small thin grating wail, a boy well-formed, bloody,
covered with thick curds of mucus that looked like
brown porridge, the thick rubbery blue-black-veined
umbilical cord leading back into Claire as she had another contraction and the smooth slick red sac of after-
birth squeezed out into the doctor's arms as well.

And now Ethan was dead in his mother's arms. Because of Kess. He couldn't adjust to it, couldn't accept
it. Each time he turned from the window and saw
Claire hugging the child, her long black hair dangling
down touching the baby's face, the shock of what had
happened spread a new wave of numbness through his
body that left him dazed and shaken.

"Like breeds like," Kess said. "To get one you have to get them all, cut off the evil at its source, eradicate all the offshoots. You should feel privileged. I've never shown these files to any outsider before. They contain the names of more than one hundred and fifty thousand sympathizers, complete with microfilmed dossiers. Some of them are only your garden-variety camp followers, but most are genuine agitators, and a lot of them are in high places. If I give the order, in less than three hours I can have a rifle trained on every one of them. And after them their families."

No, he told himself and shook his head. No, not the baby. He tried to think about something else, about having some coffee to steady himself, and that was a mistake. Because when he had seen the cat slump into her bowl of milk he had just been about to pour milk into his first morning coffee. If he had not been busy with the cat, he would have sipped the milk in the coffee and died the same as Ethan. It had been a long time coming to him, so distracted by Ethan's death that only now was he fully realizing how very close he himself had been to dying. It came in a cold rush up from his stomach. The coldest he had ever felt it. Fear. He could have been dead right now, slumped across the table, sphincter and bladder relaxing, waste and urine emptying. They could have been burying him two days from now, lying softly, sealed in his coffin. Even more than two days: if Claire and Sarah had drunk the milk too and nobody had come around to the house wondering where they were, they could all have started to rot in here. The cold swirled around his heart and set it speeding.

Sarah. From the front hall he heard her coming

quickly down the stairs, her footsteps fast and even and muffled on the carpeting. He went to the archway, saw her trip down the last few steps and scramble to get past him into the living room.

"Where were you, sweetheart?" he said and barred her way.

"In the bathroom." She was staring anxiously past him, trying to get through.

"What's that in your hand?"

"Aspirins."

"Why?"

"For Ethan."

She looked so desperately sure the aspirin would bring Ethan back if only she got to him in time that he had to close his eyes to stop the pressure in them.

"No, sweetheart," he told her. His throat was constricting him so much that he could hardly talk.

"But maybe he isn't really dead. Maybe these will help."

"No, sweetheart," he said, his voice thick, cracking.

"For Mommy then."

It was all too much. He couldn't stand it any longer. "Jesus, why don't you ever listen to me? I told you *no.*"

3

THE AMBULANCE WAS BRAKING to a stop in the driveway. Throwing open the front door, he called out to the driver who was rushing across the brightly sun-lit front lawn toward him. "You didn't use the siren."

"Didn't need it. Traffic wasn't bad at all." He was hurrying across the front porch past him into the dark hall.

"But you took so long."

"Ten minutes. What the hell, coming across town, that's fast."

The driver was young—long hair, mustache, side-burns. The doctor hurrying inside behind him looked even younger, close blond hair parted perfectly. My God, he thought, surprised. I need somebody older. Why didn't the hospital send somebody older?

But they were already going through the living room to the kitchen while he tried to explain, and then they halted at the sight of her. The skin of her face was drawn even more severely, jaw and cheek bones standing out. Her eyes were frightening, glowing wide at them past the child held rigidly to her breast. When the doctor made a move toward her, she instantly came alert, and in the end it took all three of them to get the baby away from her. He felt sick fighting her. The doctor went through the motions of listening for a heartbeat with his stethoscope, of checking for eye movement with a penlight, but the baby was dead all right. "A body this small, rigor has already started," the doctor said. "Better get it out of her sight." But when the driver went to carry the baby out to the ambulance, Claire screamed and clawed to grab him back.

"Hold your wife," the doctor told him, swabbing her arm with a cotton ball soaked in alcohol.

His nostrils flared from the bitter smell of the alcohol. He hated struggling with her, gripping her arms so tightly he could feel her bones beneath her flesh. "Claire," was all he could say. "Please, Claire." He thought about slapping her to jolt her quiet, but he knew he couldn't do it.

Then the doctor was jabbing her upper arm with a hypodermic, and she swung so powerfully to get away that it seemed the needle would snap off in her, rip her arm, but already the doctor had the needle cleanly out, and they were forcing her across the living room and up the stairs to the bedroom where she clung to the doorknob, repeating, "My baby. I want my baby," while they pried her fingers free and dragged her to the bed, holding her down. She thrashed, moaning "I want my baby," slowly lost strength, rolled onto her side and started weeping, hands over her face, knees drawn up, and little by little they released her.

"No, don't fight it," the doctor was telling her. "Relax. Make yourself calm. Try not to think." He went over and closed the bedroom drapes, pale light filtering through, everything mostly in shadow.

The bed had not yet been made. She lay on rumpled sheets, weeping steadily, rhythmically, disrupting the pattern to shudder and breathe, beginning to weep again. She wore mostly washed-out jeans around the house, but today she had put on an orange pleated skirt, and now it was hitched up, showing one buttock covered by her silk underwear. The elastic of the underwear was loose, itself hitched up above a fold of white-skinned hip. Between her legs a few black kinks of pubic hair stuck out from under the elastic. He glanced at the doctor, and feeling modest for her, he reached to tug down the skirt. She thrashed to get away from the touch of his hand.

"I said, don't fight it. Give in, let it put you to sleep," the doctor bent close to her and ordered. His face was flushed from exertion, dark against his blond hair. He studied her, watching her weep and shudder and breathe. Slowly he straightened.

"It's working now. In a minute she'll be under." He ran a hand through his hair, and his part was destroyed. "How about you?"

"I don't know." He wanted to swallow, but his mouth was too dry. "All right I guess. Yes. I'm all right."

"Sure you are." The doctor reached into his satchel and came out with a clear plastic vial of pills. "Take these two with a full glass of water. These other two are for when you go to bed." The pills were long and yellow. "Here's one for your little girl. Remember. A full glass of water. Especially the little girl."

Reminded of Sarah, he suddenly wondered where she had gone to this time. She had twice been in the way downstairs, and then she had disappeared.

"Wait," he said. "These things aren't going to put me to sleep, are they?"

The doctor looked sideways at him. "Sure. Sure you're all right "

"I just don't want to be put to sleep."

"They're only to relax you. That's the truth, no need to look at me like that. They might make you dizzy, so don't try to drive, and don't drink any liquor after them. You'll wind up on the floor."

Claire was weeping slowly now, softly, almost asleep.

"I'll stay with her until I'm certain she'll be quiet," the doctor told him. "Better go and take the pills."

He looked down at her, lingered uncertainly, then did what he was told.

———————————————————————————— *4*

THE BATHROOM WAS DIRECTLY across the hall. Thinking of the poison in the milk, he stared uneasily at the glass of water in his hand. The water was clouded gray as it always was after several days of heavy rain. Still he could not stop thinking of poison. The pills maybe. But he knew that was crazy. Even if Kess *had* planned a follow-up, he would have picked another kind of man to deliver these pills, somebody older, who looked more like an experienced doctor; and Kess's man would have said a name, would have mentioned something about the hospital to establish his credentials. But this guy had not said anything; he had just gone right to work.

The water had a gritty earthen taste that obscured any taste the pills might have had. They wedged down his throat in two choking lumps, and afterward he left the tap running, cupped cold water in his hands, and splashed his face repeatedly.

You knew what kind of man Kess was. You knew even before you met him. What the hell was going on in your head?

The year before, in December, three of Kess's lieutenants had been charged with attempted assassination.

That was in Hartford, Connecticut—their target a third-term U.S. senator. They had attached a fire bomb under the stage in a hall where he was to give a much publicized speech, and it had failed to kill him only because midway through his talk he had left the stage to speak directly with his audience. Fragments from the stage had badly lacerated eight persons in the front row. The lieutenants themselves turned out to be from three Connecticut branches of the Kess organization, respected in their own communities: a policeman, a fireman, a high-school botany teacher.

One day later, six mortar rounds had hit an upper New York farmhouse and barn where a Children of Jesus youth camp was being set up for the holidays. Fifteen minutes of sniping had killed two girls and a boy; two other boys were burned by fires from the mortar explosions, and most of the others were almost torn apart by shrapnel. At nightfall, police had raided an isolated hunting lodge owned and used as a training ground by another of Kess's lieutenants; they arrested five men and seized eight machine guns, three bazookas, two mortars, one antitank missile launcher, two Browning automatic rifles, eight field radios, a variety of handguns, shotguns, and hunting rifles, and ten thousand assorted rounds of ammunition.

Both times Kess had denied any knowledge of what his subordinates were up to. He seemed genuinely shocked and annoyed by it all. But a week later on Christmas day police had raided his home in Providence, Rhode Island, and seized twelve unregistered Thompson submachine guns plus two cases of grenades, charging him with violations of the National Firearms Act. They had also charged him with organizing a conspiracy to attack and loot an Illinois National Guard armory.

Now in September, the water dripping off his face into the sink, trickling down the drain, he thought of how he had watched the news of Kess's arrest, how he had been curious to see what the man looked like, but there had been no pictures. He thought of how he had worked so hard, taken so much time to set up the meeting with Kess—and then he suddenly thought of Ethan again and fought to concentrate on the cool feel of the water drying on his skin. He toweled his face as roughly as he could. Anything to keep from thinking. Get busy, he told himself. Do something.

Like what?

Like find Sarah. Find out how she is.

He found her the first place he looked—down at the end of the hall in her room. She was sitting propped up against the headboard of her bed, pretending to be occupied. The book in her hands was upside down.

"I've got a job for you," he said.

She turned a page and peered at it. "Is Mommy going to die too?" she asked quietly from behind the book.

He had to close his eyes again. "No," he said. "She's just very upset and we have to do everything we can to help her. That's the job I have for you."

The pressure eased, and he opened them. She had the book down from in front of her face, squinting at him. "Did Mommy hurt when the doctor gave her the needle?"

"A bit." He felt his throat seizing totally shut, and he hurried to say it all. "Sweetheart, when the doctor comes out of the bedroom, I think Mommy would like it very much if you went in and covered her with a blanket and snuggled next to her. She'll be asleep and she won't know you're next to her, but when she wakes up, it's very important that one of us be there to say hello. Can you do that for her?"

She nodded her head sadly. "You screamed at me and pushed me."

"I know," he said. "I'm sorry."

5

THEY WERE STANDING in the sunlit open doorway at the bottom, watching him. The one was tall and big-hipped, the other was thin, and they both had their badges out. All the time he continued down the stairs, clutching the rail, they never stopped watching him.

"Reuben Bourne," he said his name was. He was sitting at the table in the kitchen while the tall big-hipped one asked the questions and the thin one glanced around at the spilled milk all over and the broken glass by the stove.

"My name's Webster," the big-hipped one said. "He's Ford. Do you know what kind of poison it was?"

"No." Their names shouldn't have seemed important to him. The pills were doing it, he guessed. He knew he had heard their names somewhere before, but the pills were clouding his mind so much that he couldn't place them.

"Well, do you know how the baby got his hands on it?"

"Yes. It was in the milk that came this morning."

"The milk?" Webster said incredulously. He and Ford looked sharply at each other.

"That's right. My cat died from it too. I put her over on the cellar steps." The pills were certainly fixing him. His voice sounded to him as if it came from somewhere outside his head.

Ford went to see the cat, stepping over the milk and broken glass by the stove. He seemed to take a very long time to cross the last few feet toward the cellar door. Tired of waiting for him to get there, he himself turned slowly in his chair, and from where he sat at the kitchen table he could see out the big front window in the living room to where the driver had backed the ambulance out of the driveway and parked it at the curb between the two fir trees. He could see the driver sitting behind the steering wheel out there, combing his hair in the rearview mirror.

"Mr. Bourne, I asked you a question," Webster was saying. "I asked you if you had any idea how the poison got in the milk."

"Kess," he answered, still looking toward the ambulance. The curtains on the side were drawn; there was a small object outlined behind them, but he couldn't be sure it was Ethan. He thought of the rough starchy white sheets that Ethan must be lying on but couldn't feel.

"How's that?"

"A man named Kess did it."

"You know this man? You know for a fact that he did this?"

"Not personally. I mean, I know him, but I don't think he did it personally. He likely ordered someone else to do it. I met him early this year for an article I was working on." His voice sounded even farther out-side his head. He was having trouble now getting enough breath to say all the words.

The driver was finished combing his hair.

"Mr. Bourne, please look at me," Webster said.

He managed to turn to him.

"What do you mean an article you were working on?"

"I'm a writer."

"Hey, no kidding," Ford said interested, coming back from the cellar door. That was the first he had spoken. "What do you write? Maybe I've read your stuff."

"Novels. Stories." It was all too complicated to ex-plain. Because of his writing, Ethan was dead, but he was losing the strength to tell them, and finally he had to fall back on the standard modest reply he always gave to strangers who asked him about his work. "I got lucky three years ago with a novel that almost made the best seller lists and was turned into a movie." He gave the name.

"I must have missed that one," Ford said.

Webster looked around at the kitchen and the living room. The place was more than a hundred years old, inside walls of brick and oak: the money from the book had meant that Bourne could afford to buy it and re-store its features. It had the feel of old photographs, of solid deep-grained dark wood and heavily mortared walls and things which were built to outlast the men who fashioned them. Webster obviously was thinking, Yeah, you got lucky all right. "What about this article?" he said.

"When I'm having trouble with a book, I sometimes let it rest and try an article. God help me, last Decem-

ber some things happened with Kess that made me
want to write about him."

"Who is this guy anyway?" Ford said.

It was all just too much to explain. He had the sen-
sation that his brain was slowly revolving inside his
skull, and when he concentrated to stop it, the kitchen
shifted on an angle. He stood off-balance, steadied himself, and made his way off the cold hardwood floor
onto the deep soft rug toward the wall of bookshelves
in the living room.

"What's the matter?" Webster said. "What are you
doing?"

"Getting you this," he answered, wondering if he
would be able to make it back and sit down again,
opening a copy of the magazine with his article in it.
"I don't know how to put it better than this."

9

*Chemelec is the base of Kess's organization, his com-
mand post. It stands in the middle of a large open field
on the outskirts of Providence, Rhode Island: a huge
sprawling one-story structure made of cinder blocks
that give it the appearance of an enormous bunker,
windowless, surrounded by a tall electric barbed-wire
fence with several armed guards patrolling the perim-
eter.*

The company manufactures chemicals and electron-

ics equipment, but its profit is due mostly to sizable subsidies from various large American corporations. After all, Kess has insisted from the start on the abolition of trade unions. His followers themselves contribute dues to the company. They have to keep it working: they need quick access to those chemicals and electronic instruments required for the kind of sophisticated explosives they plan to use in time of emergency, required as well for chemical warfare and the electronic jamming of enemy radio communications.

The company was founded by Kess in 1965, an amalgamation of two other companies that went bankrupt on him in 1964 because of what he insists was government pressure on his customers not to renew their contracts. That is only a sign of his difference with the government, not the cause of it. He was with those American forces that invaded Germany in 1945 and were ordered to stop while the Russians came in from their side. He was only twenty then, politically uneducated, but he could see what was going to happen between America and Russia in Germany, and he had watched so many of his friends die in combat that he insisted America had the right to take the country for her own. He insisted so much that he was ordered to keep his views to himself, and when he did not, was given a psychiatric discharge as a paranoid aggressive.

In 1963, he and five friends were deer hunting in upper Michigan when someone else in the woods took a shot at them by mistake. From all reports they enjoyed the scare; found cover, deployed and double-flanked the man, fired several intended near misses at him, forced him to surrender his rifle, then intimidated him for the rest of the day until they finally chased him *screaming from the woods. What delighted them most was their discovery that years out of the army they still retained their presence of mind under fire, recalled exactly how to trap a man, and did it well. They began talking about their war experiences and decided that if the country were ever attacked, a distinct possibility they thought, they would still be able to put up a good fight. Over drinks that night they warmed even more to the idea, figured how they would do it, camping in the hills, living off the land, sniping, hitting a patrol here, a supply depot there, backing deep into the woods before they could be pursued. Ideally, of course, the enemy could never be allowed past the coastline, but that required meticulous defensive preparations, and as far as they were concerned, the government was too weak to do so, riddled as they believed it was with the enemy or enemy-sympathizers. Kess himself supplied the name—The Guardians of the Republic.*

"Your wife is resting fine now."

He looked, and the doctor was standing at the archway to the kitchen. The living room rug had evidently muffled his approach. His hair was parted perfectly again.

"She'll be waking around six. She'll be groggy and she won't want to eat, but give her some soup anyway, and if she gets frantic again, here's two more of those pills. Is your foot hurting very badly?"

"My foot?" He peered down. His bare feet seemed very far below him, as if he were seeing them through the reversed end of a telescope, and he had to stop himself from peering too far down and falling. The nail on his right toe had been ripped half away from the flesh, thick blood clotted darkly under it. The toe was numb. He had thought that was because of the pills. "I didn't even know. It must have happened when we were struggling with Claire," he said. "I'll take care of it myself. After you leave. It'll be something to do to keep my mind off everything."

"I need your permission for an autopsy."

He wasn't prepared. He had a sudden image in his mind of the doctor slitting open Ethan's small chest, spreading the flaps, removing the organs. "All right," he said quickly, "yes," and studied the two long yellow pills in his hand to cancel the image of the open chest. "You lied to me about these pills."

"They're relaxing you, aren't they?"

"Sure. If you call wanting to fall off my chair being relaxed."

The doctor grinned and picked up his medical bag.

"A minute with you, Doctor," Webster said.

The doctor looked at him. "Certainly."

"No. Not here."

Bourne wondered what was going on. He watched the doctor look quizzical once more as Webster took him from the kitchen, crossed the living room with him, and disappeared into the hallway by the door. Then he heard Webster start talking in the hall, and he found out. Webster was talking very quietly, but his words were carrying back all the same.

"I would have assumed you'd check on this anyhow, Doctor," Webster was saying out of sight in the hallway. "But you've already removed the body before I could look and have pictures taken, so let me be direct. I want to know if there are any bruises on the body. We'll have our own man help you with the autopsy, and we'll have our own man go over the cat. No reflection on you, but this is all just funny enough that I want to have a double shot at it so nobody misses anything."

All the while Bourne listened he looked steadily at Ford in the kitchen, and the man did his best to act preoccupied, glancing embarrassed at the floor, shifting his glance toward the milk on the table and then toward the broken glass by the stove, as if there were something important there that he had not seen before. He finally got the idea of lighting a cigarette, and happy to have something to say, he asked Bourne if he wanted one. But he didn't wait for an answer. "Listen, Webster doesn't mean any harm," he said. "Really. It's just his way. The last time he was sympathetic was ten years ago. A guy had his eight-year-old daughter raped and killed, and Webster sat around with him, talking about how bad it was. The guy had a theory that one strange kid from the high school did it. So as soon as Webster left, this guy went after the kid with a shotgun and found him before Webster did and blew the top of the kid's head clean off. If that wasn't bad enough, it turned out that this guy and Webster were wrong, the kid wasn't the one."

"But I'm *not* wrong."

"No. Listen—"

But the doctor was just then going out, closing the door, and Webster was just then coming back into the kitchen, and Bourne said to him, "You don't need to worry about any bruises. I don't go around punching five-month-old babies."

"You heard?"

"Like you were announcing it."

"Well, I'm sorry."

"You should be."

"I mean I'm sorry you heard. I'm not sorry about

the way I'm doing this. I've tried to be delicate about it, but since you want to make a point, we might as well have it in the open. Poison in milk, that's new to me. But I've seen cases a little like it where the baby has accidentally got his hands on a bottle of bleach or floor wax or furniture polish. Except that when you check the child's body you find it's no accident at all. Because the kid is bruised from head to foot and maybe he's got ruptured organs and dislocated joints and the parents have just finished him off, crazy enough to think we won't notice he's colored black and blue. So you say this guy Kess is responsible, and I have no reason to doubt it. But I want to see this thing from a lot of angles, and you wouldn't think much of me at my job if I didn't. Shootings, knifings, those I can understand, those I can live with and treat as routine. But I've got two kids myself, and when I hear about a baby that's been poisoned by its milk, well Jesus."

7

THE AMBULANCE WAS long gone. The lab men, the police photographers, the fingerprint crew had been and left. There were women across the street, watching the final police car, watching the three of them come out onto the porch. Webster gave him a card with a phone number on it, and Ford stood there in the bright sunlight, holding the two plastic sacks with the half-full bottle of milk and the cat bunched stiffly, and Bourne still couldn't place their names. His toe felt like a knife blade had been rammed under it. Abruptly the names came to him. Of course. Webster and Ford. Elizabethan dramatists.

"What's that?" Webster said.

"Nothing. It's everything that's happened. These pills the doctor gave me."

"I think you'd better lie down."

"Believe me, I am."

He smiled and made his confusion look like a joke on him, but really he was worried. If he didn't even have enough control to know when he was talking, how could he handle Sarah, or Claire when she woke up? And he was worried too about his eyes. Before, the kitchen had started to cloud gray on him the way the glass of water had been. Now as he steadied himself against the rail of the porch and watched the two detectives cross the lawn to the cruiser, his eyes were pierced so sharply by the sun that even shielding them he had to squint in pain. He leaned dizzily against the rail and watched Ford pull the cruiser away from the curb, watched it recede up the street, and the moment it rounded the corner up there so he couldn't see it anymore, the phone rang.

It rang again. The front door was open; the nearest extension was down the hall. He did his best to hurry in and grab it before the extension upstairs in the bedroom could rouse Sarah or maybe even Claire. "Hello," he said, slumping on the bench beside the phone; the man's voice began to rasp and his fear returned.

"Yeah, there go the cops, but it don't matter if they stay or go, we're gonna get you, don't you worry none."

"What?" he said and straightened. *"What?* Who *is* this?"

"Just let's say a friend of a friend of yours, but then you two ain't exactly friends at that, are you? I see it was only your new kid they carried out to the ambulance. That's all right too, don't you worry none about that neither, we're sure gonna get all the rest of you too before we're done."

"No," he tried desperately to say. *"Christ, no more. You've done enough."*

But he never got the chance. There was an immediate click and then the phone was buzzing.

8

HE SAT on the bench, listening to the buzz of the phone in his hand for a long time. Just sat there. He didn't have the strength to stand or set the phone on its base or anything. He was cold. His hands were trembling, knees shaking, and he was certain that if he did try to stand he wouldn't be able to stay up. He couldn't stop the voice from continuing to rasp inside his head. It had been intentionally illiterate, he guessed; the way it had emphasized the faulty grammar. And for a reason he did not understand, that made him even more afraid. The cold became a warm liquid pressure in his bowels.

Christ, how had the guy known about Ethan in the ambulance and the police driving away? Where could he have been calling from? Close. *Very* close. But there weren't any pay phones around. Where could he be?

In a house on the street or up at the corner.

The front door was still open. He turned and looked out toward the house directly across the street. The women were still on the sidewalk over there, talking, watching. That was enough. The next thing he was over and shutting the door.

But none of the neighbors would have done this. He was sure of it. He knew them all. He was friends with a lot of them. Not even the old man down the street would have done this. Then he remembered what the guy had rasped on the phone about friends—and the other thing that Kess had told him months before.

"We're not alone in this. There are dozens of other organizations like us. We alone have twenty thousand trained dependables, another twenty thousand waiting to be trained. Put our members in with those in all the other loyalist groups in this country, and you come up with a figure that's just slightly under the present strength of the United States Marine Corps which was two hundred and four thousand the last time I checked. And they're everywhere, in industry and government, in law enforcement and the military. The guy you bought your car from, the quiet fellow who lives up the street, any of them might easily be one of us."

He stood where he had closed the door, and glanced up the stairs, and the sight of Sarah startled him.

She was holding her stomach. "Daddy, I'm sick."

"How bad?" he said, hurrying up the stairs to her.

"I have to throw up."

The pills from the doctor, he thought angrily and tried to calm himself. Things aren't bad enough. These pills have got to make us sick.

And then he suddenly wondered if he'd been right in the first place. Maybe the doctor was from Kess and the pills were poisoned, slow acting to give the doctor time to get away.

He almost panicked. Seeing Sarah's helpless face, he struggled not to. Slow-acting poison didn't make sense, he told himself convincing himself. When the symptoms showed up, there'd be time to get an antidote.

Sure.

He thought it through again.

Sure.

"It's all right," he said as calmly as he could. "If you throw up, you'll feel better. Come on."

And he put his arm around her and took her into the bathroom and raised the toilet seat.

"Let your stomach throw up if it wants to," he told her gently. "Kneel down here and I'll hold you. There's nothing to be afraid of."

And he waited with her.

"Daddy?" she said, kneeling before the bowl.

"Yes, sweetheart."

"Will I have one of those that Mommy said?"

"One of what, sweetheart? I'm not sure what you mean."

"One of those that Mommy thought Samantha had because she was sixteen years old."

He didn't understand. He tried to think back to when the cat had been poisoned and what Claire might have said. After Ethan and everything else, that seemed such a very long time ago.

"You mean a stroke?"

"Yes. Will I have one of those when I get to be sixteen?"

"Sarah, you know that Samantha was poisoned. I

want you to realize that. I don't want you to eat anything without asking me first."

"But when I'm sixteen, will I have one of those?"

"No. Cats age differently than people. With a cat, sixteen is like being eighty."

"Then you won't have one of those for a long time yet."

Suddenly he was holding her tight, hugging her, kissing her neck. "That's right, sweetheart. God, I hope to be around for a long long time yet."

She didn't react, just knelt there while he hugged and kissed her.

"Daddy?"

"Yes."

"Is Ethan in heaven with Samantha?"

He was beginning to understand now. Slowly he drew back to look at her.

"Sarah, let me ask you something."

She didn't answer.

"Are you really sick, or did you just want somebody to talk to? You're lonely, isn't that it? You don't understand what's happening, and you're lonely and worried?"

She lowered her head and nodded.

"You should have told me. Honestly I wouldn't have minded. This way you had me sorry you were sick."

She still didn't say anything.

"Listen, there's nothing to worry about. Everything is going to be fine. I'll tell you what. There's something I have to do, but first I'll take you back into the bedroom and tuck you in with Mommy and wait with you a while. Does that sound all right?"

She just raised her head and looked at him.

What he had to do was phone Webster and tell him

about the man who called. Maybe Webster would have the nearby houses searched. Something. Anything. He had put off phoning Webster almost as long as he could stand it, waiting for him to have the time to reach the station. Maybe Webster wouldn't even have got there now. But he couldn't make himself wait much longer.

He stood, and his knees felt sharp and stiff from kneeling. He had to tug Sarah gently by the hand before she would go with him. They went across the hall into the bedroom. Claire lay under a soft blue blanket, on her side, sleeping so deeply that in the pale light from the closed drapes she did not at first seem to be breathing. He waited impatiently while Sarah crawled next to her under the blanket, and then as he was stooping to kiss Sarah's cheek, deciding not to stay with her but instead to go right away and call, the phone rang loudly on the night table.

9

IT PARALYZED HIM.

"Daddy, what's the matter?"

He was suspended from kissing her, turned toward the phone as it rang again.

"Daddy, why don't you answer it?"

The voice that might be rasping on the other end.

It rang again. But maybe it was Webster back at the station by now, phoning to tell him something.

And maybe not.

But maybe. He took the chance and answered it. The voice sent chills.

"Yeah, motherfuck, calling the cops again ain't gonna help none either. We're gonna get the lot of you no matter what. You think about it. You try and think who we're gonna drop next. Your other kid? Your wife? You? Pass the time on it."

"Daddy, what's the matter?" Sarah said. "Your face."

He felt his skin going tight and cold. He couldn't stop the trembling in his voice. "Wait. Don't hang up again," he pleaded. "We've got to talk. Please. You can't go on like this. You've got to stop."

"Stop?" the voice rasped back at him. "Why, that just makes me regular disappointed to hear you say that. You're supposed to be a smart man, aren't you? I mean, you've written all them books and all, haven't you? Don't you see that we can't stop this now? Don't you see that we're just getting started?"

"No. Listen. You've got to tell me what it is you want. Please. I'll do anything. Just tell me. Is it money? Will that make you stop? For God sake, tell me."

"Friend, I'd say you've done plenty enough already. There is one thing might help though."

"What is it? Anything."

"Next time answer the phone a little quicker. I got tired of waiting."

Click and he was listening to the dial tone.

"Who was it, Daddy?" Sarah asked.

"I don't know, sweetheart," he managed to control his voice and say.

"Why were you talking to him like that?" She was sitting up in the bed, looking worried.

He couldn't let himself upset her anymore. Slowly, hand trembling, he replaced the phone.

"But why were you talking to him like that?" Sarah was insisting.

He looked from her to Claire asleep with her long dark hair spread over the side of her face; looked back at Sarah sitting up, her own hair short and sandy. He thought of Claire's brown eyes, her dark face. And Sarah with her blue eyes and light skin and freckles. They were so unlike that a stranger could not have guessed that they were actual mother and daughter.

His. When he had almost gone away with the other woman, there had been nights when he thought how simple his life would be if Claire and Sarah were killed in an accident. He had hated himself for thinking that. He had known how overpowered by grief he would be if they died. Still their deaths would have been no fault of his, and he would have been free to pursue his life. Now he thought that if they died he would not know how to go on.

"You stay here in bed," he told her. "I mean it. I've got to make a call downstairs, and I don't want you out of that bed."

10

THE SECRETARY STARTED to say good morning, that this was Chemelec and all that, and he cut her off. "I want to get a message through to Kess." It was ten o'clock. Where he lived was on mountain time. In Providence it was noon, and he had been afraid the secretary would be gone for lunch.

She didn't answer right away. Her voice was careful. "I'm terribly sorry. Mr. Kess isn't with us anymore."

"He's in hiding, but you know how to get in touch with him all right." The phone was warm and sweaty in his hand.

"No, sir, I don't. I don't know what you mean at all."

"But you remember me. Eight, nine months ago we talked a lot. Now you just get in touch with him. Tell him Reuben Bourne called to say he's been punished enough. Tell him I know I made a mistake, but my baby is dead now and that's enough. I'm angry and scared and this sounds like I'm ordering him, but I'm not. I'm begging him. Please. Tell him please leave the rest of us alone."

"I really am sorry, sir. I have no idea what it is you're saying, and there's nothing I can—"

"No. Please. Don't hang up."

"Good morning. Thank you for calling Chemelec."

"No. Wait."

The click again, and this time the static of the long-distance line. The whole conversation could not have taken more than thirty seconds. He had been hoping so desperately that this would save them all, and he hadn't even been able to say everything right, and all of a sudden it was over. He felt there was no bottom to his stomach.

What else did you expect? he told himself. Did you

really believe all you needed to do was phone and ask for mercy?

Christ, mercy isn't Kess's way.

11

"IT'S OBVIOUS WHY I can't search every house on the street," Webster said. "The judge would wake up from reading the Constitution, and right off he'd want to know what exactly I was searching for. So what could I tell him? That I was looking for a guy with a rasp in his voice that was plainly a disguise in the first place?"

They were in the living room, Bourne slumped down in a chair while Webster leaned forward on the sofa opposite him and explained.

"Even if the judge was crazy enough to allow a blanket search, the warrants would take too long to get processed," Webster said. "By then whoever phoned would be clear off, he probably is by now anyway, and whatever might be strange in any of those houses—guns, say, or poison, would be long gone with him. Besides, there's no need to assume he called from a house. It's my guess he was in a car that had a phone. He knew about your son being dead because he drove by when the attendant was carrying the body out to the ambulance. And he knew when Ford and I left because he was in a car parked close by, watching."

He listened hopelessly, lighting another cigarette

from Webster's pack. It had been three weeks since he had determined to quit smoking, but that didn't really matter anymore, and he sucked the smoke full-throated into his lungs, waiting for his brain to stop spinning.

"The other business," Webster said. "About your planning to call me and him phoning to say don't bother, that was just theatrics. He knew you'd want to get in touch with me about his first call, so he just waited until you thought I'd had time to get back to the station, and then he made his second call to tell you not to. That way it looked as if he was reading your mind. There was always the chance he would have been too late, that you would already have phoned me, in which case his second call would have seemed like he had a tap on your phone."

"At least my way we had a direction to hunt for him," he answered weakly.

"Listen to me. I could have said this when you called. I didn't have to come back out here to say it, but I wanted to see your face and make sure you understood. Finding him isn't your worry, it's mine. All you have to worry about is keeping control."

"What the hell good will that do? You see what I'm like. Supposing I do manage to get myself together, that won't stop them from coming for us."

"Them? We don't know it's more than one."

"It's anywhere between eight and twelve. That's the way they operate. In a cell. And they always work together."

"I've asked the FBI for a list of Kess's people from around here."

"That won't do any good either. Kess doesn't keep

membership records. His orders go from word of mouth down through his subordinates. The FBI might know about a few of them from this area, but there's no way to link any of them together."

"You ought to know; you were right about Kess anyhow. In February, when the grand jury indicted him, he did go underground. There's a rumor he's in the British West Indies. Another rumor that he's in Hawaii."

"Or right here."

Webster looked hard at him. "You just keep control. There are a lot of things I can do to protect you. A man will be here shortly to put a tap on your phone. If your guy calls again, we have a chance to trace him. I sent Ford out to the dairy you get your milk from. He's tracking down the delivery man. I should have a report soon on the kind of poison that was used, and with any luck we'll be able to trace that too."

"They got it from a plant nursery."

It was once too often he had told Webster his job, and Webster stiffened. "I *know*, Mr. Bourne. I'll *check* on it." He opened his mouth to say something more, paused uncomfortably, and glanced at the rug. "I had another reason for coming back out here. A message I got from the doctor when I reached the station. . . . I apologize. It's not often I let things get through to me. There were no bruises on the body."

"Sure." It was almost funny.

BUT WEBSTER MUST have had still another reason for coming back out, and it wasn't just the questions he started asking because the answers were all in the article Bourne had given him.

"That's fine. Tell me anyhow," Webster said.

Bourne took a deep drag that almost burned the cigarette down to its filter before he crushed it out. "All right," he said. "The first thing I saw when the guard showed me into Kess's office was a big magnum revolver weighing down a stack of papers on his desk. There was a handful of cartridges strewn across the desk blotter and a howitzer shell cut off at the base to make an ashtray."

"You know about guns? You know this was a magnum?"

"I do a lot of research for my books, and I'd recognize a big gun like that anywhere. The biggest. A forty-four. And the first thing Kess said to me when he came smiling from around his desk to shake hands was how sorry he felt that he took so long to grant me an interview."

"But if he'd stopped seeing reporters in the first place, then why did he change his mind and see you?"

"Because I think he was sure he'd be indicted and he was already planning to go underground. The interview was to be his last public statement, and he figured

I was the one to make him look as good as possible. Because of my books."

"If he read them, he was one up on me."

Bourne saw now what Webster was doing—trying to draw him out, to talk everything away and relax. Because the trick was working. His stomach still felt like it had a fist in it, and his arms and legs were still as cold and shaky as ever. But somehow he felt more at ease. Not alone.

"They're about fear," he said and lit the fifth cigarette from Webster's pack. "You'd better take some of these for yourself before I smoke them all."

"I don't smoke."

"Then why the cigarettes?"

"I always carry a pack with me for people I'm talking to."

The trick was working all right, and Bourne had to smile. He sucked the smoke deep into his lungs and held it there. When at last he exhaled, hardly any smoke came out. His throat was scratchy, mouth dry. "Chases," he said. "Men on the run alone, hunted down, driven to defend themselves. And Kess saw a lot of himself in that. It's like he wishes he were back in some rain forest thirty thousand years ago. It's his big dream. To take his men up into the hills once the enemy invades, and hit supply depots and snipe at enemy patrols, and run away from search parties. That's the joke of it. He saw himself in my books, so he figured I'd sympathize with him. He granted me an interview, and now I might as well be one of my own characters. Except that they always know what to do, and I can hardly keep from filling my pants."

"Another except: you're not alone. The man who's coming to tap your phone will stay here to protect you in case anything happens. I have squad cars circling the area to look for any cars or trucks that stop too long or come around too often, and I'll have a cruiser parked in front of the house very shortly. Don't worry. We'll get them before they get you."

Bourne almost believed him. But then Webster told him "Keep the cigarettes," and stood up to go, and all the ease that Bourne had come to feel drained from him.

"Wait a while more, can't you?" Bourne said. He sounded like an anxious child. He couldn't help it.

Webster studied him. "Have you got any guns around the house?"

"Three. A rifle, pistol, and revolver. Twenty-twos."

"You know how to use them?"

"My wife and I took an NRA course. An ex-Marine instructor taught us."

"Well, don't bother."

He said it gently, but it came like a slap all the same.

"This isn't like in books. It's for real, and I don't want you shooting one of my men by mistake or somebody else who turns out to have nothing to do with this. Were you in the military?"

"No."

"Why not?"

"College exemption."

"That just makes it worse. If you go out on your own after one of these guys, you'll find that writing about shooting a man is a hell of a lot different from having the guts to line up those sights and pull the trigger. You might as well shoot yourself and save the other guy the trouble. With those cap gun twenty-twos of yours, you wouldn't be able to hurt anybody anyway."

He had heard that before, seen it, written it, back when Kess had shown him through the classrooms at Chemelec. *"You've proved you can hit targets on the shooting range,"* the instructor was telling his men. *"But you'll find the real thing very different. First off, a live target can shoot back. Second, he won't oblige you by standing out in the open and waiting to be shot. When you go out on maneuvers next week, we'll be simulating combat conditions and we'll give you practice on concealed targets. In the meantime, go over the list of aiming · problems in the manual and memorize the solutions. Note the first item. Remember—when shooting at a target that is running uphill, your tendency will be to aim too low. He IS running up, after all, constantly rising out of your line of fire, so you'll have to raise your aim accordingly. If you want to hit him between the shoulder blades, shoot for the back of his head."*

Webster was already by the front door.

"Please?" Bourne asked, his voice thin and dry. "Wait a little?"

"For what?"

"The man who's coming to tap the phone. I guess I'm getting a little paranoid. How will I know he's really from you? Wait until he gets here, will you? So I can be certain?"

And then the phone rang.

Bourne jerked. The adrenalin scalded into his stomach as he stared down the hall toward the phone and then toward Webster.

But Webster wasn't there. He was already going down the hall, answering it.

"Hello," he said flatly. And that was all he said from

then on. He only listened. And Bourne was right next to him, watching his face which didn't change the whole time, and Bourne couldn't keep from asking, "What is it? What are they saying?"

But Webster just went on listening. Then he swallowed and set the phone gently back on its receiver.

"What is it?" Bourne said.

After a pause, "Nothing."

"But you were listening so long. They must have said something."

"No. Nothing. It was just quiet breathing."

"There was something else. I know it. Your face is very good. It doesn't give a thing away. But your eyes changed."

"All I heard was breathing."

"This is my life and my family we're talking about, and it isn't your right to hold back on me. Tell me what the hell it was that bothered you."

Again a pause. "I can't be sure. That's why I listened so long. It was just this quiet gentle breathing. But there was an extra tone in it that I didn't catch at first. . . . I'm still not sure I'm onto it right. But it sounded like a woman."

13

THE DOCTOR had been wrong: Claire didn't wake at six as he had said. Bourne pulled up a chair by the bed and sat and looked at her for a long time in the pale light from the closed drapes. She was breathing but that was it, and she didn't wake at seven either. The light got paler outside through the drapes, and if she didn't wake by seven-thirty, he was going to phone the doctor.

"Daddy, I'm hungry," Sarah said in the open bedroom doorway. She had been in her room for the last two hours, doing nothing. Once she had asked him to play a game with her, but he had no heart, and she had gone on doing nothing. He thought of her sitting on her bed, staring at the floor. Little girls weren't made to have that much patience.

"I am a bit too, I guess," he said. "Hungry. At least I suppose that I should try and pretend that I'm hungry. But I can't go down and make something for us. Mommy might wake up while I'm gone."

If she wakes up, he thought. She'll wake up. Sure she will.

But what can you fix to eat anyway? What in the house do you trust? Something on the back shelf in a can. He thought of soup—split pea with ham—and his mouth turned sour on the taste of it.

"I can make it myself," Sarah said.

"I'd like to let you, sweetheart. But I want you pretty close to me."

"Why?" She was still in the open doorway, her head barely even with the light switch.

Might as well come out with it. "Sweetheart, I'm going to tell you something that's hard to understand, but you'll have to believe me anyway. There's a man who thinks your father did something bad to him, and now some friends of his are out to hurt me. They want

to hurt you and Mommy too. They've already done
that to Ethan and Samantha."

"Killed them?"

"Yes."

"Why?"

"I just told you."

"No, why does the man think you did something
bad to him?"

"I wrote some words about him that he didn't like."

"Did you have to?"

"I once thought I did. Now—" Now you're not sure,
but you damn well had better be. If it cost you Ethan
and maybe everybody else, it damn well had better
have been worth it.

But it wasn't.

Claire turned, breathed hard and muttered "I want
my baby." Then she was motionless again. He was a
second before he realized he wasn't moving either.
He tried to relax but couldn't. His shoulders were so
tense they were aching.

When he looked, Sarah wasn't in the doorway any
more.

Then she was back.

"There's a man downstairs by the phone," she said,
puzzled.

The detective sent here to guard them. That made
him angry. "Did you go down when I told you not to?"

Her face lost its composure. "Just a little."

"You'd better get the hell in your room and stay
there."

He was sorry as soon as he said it. Her face drooped
worse and she looked again as if she were going to cry
and he wanted to say he was sorry. But he had to make

her realize this was serious. He had to make her obey, and keep on obeying. So he just stared at her and said, "Go on. You heard me. Get to your room." She turned, paused lonely at him, and went reluctantly away.

The room paled into darkness. He sat unseeing and listened to Claire turning restlessly, muttering, breathing hard, and at last he couldn't bear it anymore. He had to do something, went over and slid back the drapes and looked out at the night. The streetlight was not working. That bothered him. He could not recall the last time it was out. A match flared yellow in a car parked out there. He tensed even more, stepped instinctively to the side of the window. Then the spot of flame was gone, and he dimly recognized the shape of the dome light on top of what must be a police car.

All the same, he closed the drapes. The dark of the room constricted him. He switched on a dim yellow light in the corner that would not cast his outline through the drapes. He turned toward the bed, and Claire's eyes were open.

Blank. Unregistering.

But at least they were open.

Slowly they came into focus. "Reuben?" she said, and closed them and opened them. Her lips were thick and cracked and very dry. She edged her tongue along them. "Reuben?"

"Ssshh," he said. "Take a while to get awake. The doctor gave you a sedative and you've been asleep all day."

"The doctor?" she murmured stupidly. Her lips were barely open as she spoke. She raised her hands to her face and drew them down her cheeks and left them listless on her breasts. "What doctor?" she wanted to know faintly. "Where's Ethan? Were there enough clean diapers for him?"

He looked past her toward the shadowed wall.

"Oh dear Jesus," she whispered. "He's dead."

It swept through him again. The numbness when he saw Ethan choke and stiffen and die.

"How do you feel?" he said.

"How do you think I feel?"

"The doctor said I was to make you some soup."

"I don't want any."

"The doctor said that too, but he said I was to make you eat some anyway."

She didn't answer, just stared up at the ceiling. Every so often she blinked. Otherwise, her hands on her chest, she looked as if she were laid out in death. He sat there, watching her uncomfortably, and in a while he got up to go downstairs and make the soup. He didn't want to go away from her. All the same he felt relieved.

Her voice stopped him at the door. "Don't bring any milk." The strength in it surprised him. He stood rigid, his back to her, and looking out the open doorway he saw Sarah small and gray in the blackness of the hall. "What was wrong with it?" Claire said behind him.

He waited and turned. "Poison."

She was still staring at the ceiling. He didn't move.

"Natural or what?"

"Do you mean was it put in the milk?"

"That's exactly what I mean."

He couldn't understand it. She should still have been half-unconscious.

"Kess," he said. "Or some of his men."

"Because of the article?"

"It looks that way."

Slowly she turned her head to him. Her eyes had no whites.

"You killed Ethan."

Out in the hall he heard Sarah stop breathing.

"No," he said quietly. "It was Kess or some of his men."

"No, you killed Ethan."

The drug, he thought. It hadn't done any good at all. It had maybe even made her worse.

"Please, Claire," he said. "Sarah's listening out in the hall. You don't know what you're saying."

Her voice was even stronger. "I know you didn't have to write those things. You knew what might happen if you did."

"I didn't write anything Kess didn't say I could."

"That's not the way he wanted you to write them. You made a deal with him. Remember?"

He had to look away.

"Didn't he warn you? Didn't he say that if you treated him like all the others had—" she took a long breath "—and made him out to be some lunatic he was going to get you?"

He couldn't answer.

"Didn't he?"

"But he went into hiding. He was in so much trouble, who'd have thought he'd make good on his threat?"

"You killed my baby. I'm warning you myself now. Don't go to sleep. You go to sleep and so help me God I'll kill you."

14

HE SPENT THE NIGHT downstairs in the living room. He
tried to read but couldn't. Trying to write was impossible. He kept thinking of the phone, and it finally
rang at eleven. Even expecting it, he was frozen a
second before he was up and going down the hall to
answer it before Claire might be wakened. If she picked
up her extension and the voice started rasping, that
would be her limit.

The man on duty already had the reels turning on
the tape recorder.

"Who knows, maybe it's nothing. It could be just
your mother."

"My mother's been dead two years." He picked up
the phone, and it was a girl friend of Claire. That didn't
matter. He started shaking anyhow. "Claire isn't feeling
well. She'll call you back tomorrow."

"I hope it isn't serious."

"She'll call you back," he said and hung up.

He couldn't help wondering if she was the same
woman who had been breathing on the phone to Webster. No, he told himself. That's insane. You have to
stop thinking like that. She's Claire's best friend.

But he couldn't get the idea out of his mind.

"You look awful," Webster told him. He came at
seven the next morning with a new man for the phone.

But Webster didn't look good either. His big-boned face was slack and pale, and his eyes were for the first time dull, and he looked like he had been up all night himself. He even wore the same gray suit, out of shape now.

"It was ethylene glycol," Webster said. "And they didn't get it from a plant nursery, they got it from a garage. Some kinds of antifreeze and windshield cleaners have it in them. It's a little sweet, and if you'd swallowed some of it in the milk, you would maybe have noticed the taste just before it killed you. It only takes a drop or two. The trouble is, so many people buy those cleaners there's no way to trace them all."

"You came all the way over here at this hour just to tell me you can't trace whoever bought the poison?"

"At least you know I'm being honest. If I tell you the worst, then you'll know to believe me when I tell you something good."

"So for God sake tell me something good."

"Right now I haven't anything. You were right, the FBI couldn't help us much. The man who delivered the milk seems pretty straight, but we're watching him anyhow. He left the milk around six, so there was plenty of time for somebody else to slip the poison into it. The doctor is finished with the autopsy. You can have your child's body released to the undertaker."

At first he didn't know what Webster was talking about. Then he realized. A funeral. He had so little accepted Ethan's death that he hadn't even thought there would be a funeral.

"What is it?" Webster said. "What's the matter?"

He shook his head and phoned the church as soon as Webster left.

"I'm sorry," the housekeeper said. "The fathers are all out saying masses now. The rectory hours aren't until nine."

So he waited and smoked from the new pack of cigarettes that Webster had given him before he left. They tasted like musty cotton batting, hard to draw on, and he wouldn't have trusted them from anybody else but Webster. Even then he wouldn't have trusted them if he had not already without thinking smoked the others Webster had given him the day before. *"You take some slivers from this plastic. You slip them into your target's cigarette. One drag later and he's dead."* He had used that in his article, making certain not to mention the kind of plastic. But what was the difference? he thought emptily. Christ, wasn't there anything that couldn't be used to kill a man?

The priest said there was an opening for a funeral in two days. He looked in the phone book for undertakers, but there was no listing. *See* FUNERAL DIRECTORS, it said. Sure. Of course, he told himself. That's what I need. A God damn director. His instinct was to pick the first name on the list and be done with it. But he kept thinking of Kess and how the first name on the list was obvious, so he slid down to the next from the last. He knew it wouldn't take long for Kess or his men to find out which undertaker he was using, but at least this way he wasn't helping them any to set up some kind of trap. "There's been an extensive autopsy," he told the man on the phone. "I'm not sure if my son can lie in open state."

The voice was warm and smooth, like a minister on the radio. "If that is what you'd like, sir, we'll do our best to arrange it."

He thought a moment. "Yes. My wife will want that. I can't come down to pick out a casket or anything. Please give him the very best you have."

The voice was puzzled. "Certainly, sir. Whatever you wish."

"I can't go over to the hospital and sign the release papers either. You'll have to bring them here for me to sign before you can get the body."

The voice was twice as puzzled. "Well, yes, certainly, sir. May I say that we all of us sympathize with you in your time of mourning."

"Whatever you want. Go on and say it."

15

AN HOUR LATER a priest showed up at the front door. He was stooped and wrinkled. His hair was thin and white like spider's silk, his black suit specked here and there with dust. He said he was the pastor, but he himself had never seen him before and he had never heard Claire mention a priest like this either, so they sat in a triangle in the living room, the two of them and the detective from the phone.

The priest apologized for coming around so unexpectedly. He obviously didn't want to talk about what he'd come for. "It's a small matter, I'm sure," he said, fidgeting on the sofa. "But we really should discuss it. You can't imagine how I dislike bothering you in your grief." His voice was hushed and unsettling, as if he were straining to whisper in the vestibule before mass.

"What is it?" He still wasn't sure this was really a priest. He thought of calling the church to make sure. The detective had his hand near his shoulder holster under his jacket.

Again the reluctance. "I hardly think it's anything serious, I'm sure it isn't, but you see, I was checking through our records as a matter of course, and—well— you are Roman Catholic, aren't you, Mr. Bourne?"

"Yes."

"And your family?"

"Yes."

"Do you attend mass very regularly?"

"My wife and daughter go every Sunday."

"Yourself?"

"I haven't gone in ten years."

"Not even to make your Easter duty?"

"That's right."

The priest looked out the front window for a moment, as if he had seen Bourne in a state of exposure. He cleared his throat. "May I ask why you don't attend?"

"They changed the mass into English and then they brought in the guitars."

"A few of us very much regret those changes as well, Mr. Bourne. In spite of them, you should have completed your Easter duty so that you could remain in the Church and try to save your soul. You don't believe, is that it?"

"That's right." He sounded like he was in confession. "Not in the Church?"

"Not in God. Excuse me, Father, but what is it you want to say?"

"Perhaps I already understand. After I checked through our records, I phoned the other parishes, and I learned from the court house that your child was born here—but I find no record of his baptism."

Almighty God, you sent your only Son to rescue us from the slavery of sin and to give us the freedom only your sons and daughters enjoy. We now pray for this child who will have to face the world with its temptations and fight the devil in all his cunning. Your Son died and rose again to save us. By His victory over sin and death, bring this child out of the power of darkness, strengthen him with the grace of Christ, and watch over him at every step in life's journey. We ask this through Christ our Lord. Amen.

He saw now what was coming, and he knew what it was going to do to Claire. He didn't know how he could tell her. Principle, he thought. The things I have done for principle. "Yes," he said quietly. "The baby was not baptized." He was sure now that this was a priest. Not even Kess or his men would have thought of this.

"My dear man, was there a just reason?"

"The baby was very sick for the first two months and we couldn't take the chance of going outside with him."

"But surely—how old did you say he was on the phone? four months? five?—surely by then he was well enough to be taken to the church."

"I didn't want him baptized," Bourne said, "because I wasn't sure I wanted him raised Catholic."

"Baptism has no denomination. It admits anyone

to the possibility of Christian salvation, regardless of sect."

"If you believe."

"But it wasn't yours to bargain disbelief against the welfare of his soul. Are you absolutely certain that no one baptized the child? A nurse at the hospital perhaps? Or your wife when the child was sick? It doesn't require a priest. Anyone can do it, and with ordinary water."

I baptize you in the name of the Father, and of the Son, and of the Holy Spirit.

"No," he said. "I'm sure no one did it."

"This is very difficult."

"Go on. I know what you're going to say anyhow."

His words were formal, a refuge into the language of pronouncement. "Canon law forbids a funeral mass for your child. It also forbids his burial in consecrated ground. Since the child had not yet reached the age of reason, he could not have committed any sin and therefore he is not liable to the damnation of hell. He will repose in the state of limbo, free from the pain of the eternal fire, subject only to the great frustration of never being allowed to participate in the beatific vision of God's glory."

16

SO THEY WENT that night with two detectives to the funeral home. He had told Claire everything by then, expecting her to accuse him again, to scream and hit him, at least do something, but she had not reacted at all. She had been silent all the hours before, and she had not spoken after, and it was as if she were alone somewhere back in her mind, unaware of anything around her. One detective went in the car with them; the other drove behind to watch for anyone following. At the funeral home, the two of them got out first to scan the darkened tree-lined street before they said it seemed all right to go on in.

The place was soft rugs and muffled voices. There were rich red, thickly gathered drapes on all the walls. Rose light filtered through them, and from every wall an electric organ played thin muted minor chords that went on smoothly, never ending. Funereal Musak, he thought, feeling suffocated.

He did not like having Sarah along, but he would have worried leaving her away from him, even with the guard that stayed behind to watch the house, so he had some books for her to read, and cookies and milk from a grocery store on the way, certain these at least were safe to eat, and he asked an attendant for a place apart where she could take them.

"But I want to see Ethan. Why can't I see Ethan?" Sarah asked.

"Because he won't be like when you knew him."

The electric organ played on thinly.

"He'll look different?"

"No, but he won't be the same."

She mulled that over. "He'll look like a doll?"

The image struck him horribly. "Does that idea bother you?"

"No," she said. "I guess not."

"Then that's what he'll look like."

She was still mulling it over as the attendant led her away. One detective immediately followed, soft across the rug. The other looked in all the rooms, glancing repeatedly toward the front door.

Almost at once the undertaker silently appeared. It seemed his shoes barely touched the rug. His suit was black, perfectly fitting broadcloth. He was tall, his face was thin and gray and pursed with consolation— and like the priest he made Bourne nervous whether Kess had got to him or not. He looked past Bourne toward the detective watching the front door. Then he looked back at Bourne and held out his hand. "Mr. Bourne, our deepest sympathies." His handshake was soft and dry. "Your son is this way. I hope our arrangements have been to your liking."

They went down a hall past a room with a casket at the far end, a young man's face projecting from it while a black-clad woman knelt before it, shoulders heaving as she cried. Another woman stood awkwardly beside her, half-raising her hands, then lowering them, uncertain if she should interrupt to touch and comfort her.

They continued softly to the next room, and this time at the far end there was Ethan in his casket. He felt a chill that almost kept him from going in. The detective stood just inside the room, coat open, where he could still see the front door while they went over and the organ went on playing. The casket was rich dark oak; like the house, he thought, and short and shallow like a toy. In it Ethan lay on stuffed white satin, dressed in a blue wool nursing gown, his best, that Claire had spent hours selecting from his drawer and then had given silently to the undertaker to take down.

Bourne had been wrong when he agreed with Sarah. Ethan didn't look like a doll. He just looked dead. And the undertaker had used the wrong kind of make-up, the sort that fills in wrinkles on the face of an adult. But Ethan's face had already been smooth, so the extra surface made his skin seem thickly covered with pale wax. So small, so tiny featured. He turned away, glanced back, turned away again, and gradually he became accustomed to this stranger who once had been his son.

Claire looked, and kept on looking, and beneath her black veil her face was heavy and old. She had her long black hair tied severely back, her features stark. Cry, he thought. Why doesn't she cry and get this out before it all eats her away?

And what about yourself? he thought. He's your son. Why don't *you* cry?

The wreath of carnations he had ordered. The sickly

sweet musty smell of flowers going stale. Death. Everywhere death.

The organ would not stop playing.

He shook his head and turned entirely away, and the undertaker was still with them. What does he want? Bourne thought. A compliment? Don't tell me he wants a compliment on Ethan's face.

"Is everything satisfactory?" the undertaker said.

"The casket is very nice."

"It's our very best. You need never have second thoughts about that. You've done everything you can for him." The rug and the drapes absorbed his voice so that he sounded like he spoke from another room. "May I offer you and your wife some coffee perhaps?"

He thought of poison and said, "No."

"Some wine or perhaps something stronger? We sometimes find that helps."

"No. No, thank you."

"Anything you wish, please let us know." He sounded disappointed. Slowly, smoothly, he left the room.

At least as far as the door. The heavy man who stumbled past him had his tie open, red-faced, breathing hard, and Bourne no more than recoiled blinking before the detective was lunging over, pinning the man face to the wall. "Dear God," the undertaker said. "My God, what is it?" The detective had his revolver out, the undertaker gasping at it, and the red-faced man was mumbling, "What the hell? Hey Jesus," while the detective told him "Quiet," searching him for weapons, up and down his pant legs, at his crotch, under his arms, finished before Bourne realized what he was doing.

"What do you want?" the detective said.

"My friend."

"What friend?"

"He's dead. I've come to see my friend. They hit him with a train and now he's dead."

"Oh," the undertaker said. "That's in the next room."

"And now he's dead," the man repeated.

The detective smelled his breath and turned his face away. "Let's go find out about your friend. And while we're at it, let's find out how drunk you are."

"No," Bourne said. "Don't leave us."

"Only for a second. I have to check this out."

"But what if they sent this guy to distract you? What if while you're gone they come for us?"

"No matter what, I have to check him out. I won't leave this door out of sight."

The sudden fright had started him shivering. As he watched them go, he thought he was going to be sick.

Claire had seen it all, blank, and now she was watching Ethan again. Looking at Ethan made him sicker. Even when the detective came back in and shrugged, he didn't feel any better. He couldn't go and sit down and leave Claire standing alone. He had to wait with her, fighting to control his nausea, and ten minutes later when she spoke for the first time that day, her voice was thin and quiet, and she never took her eyes away from the body. "Oh, Reuben, why? You can't know how much I wish that you and your slut had gone away."

_____ *17*

THEN TWO DAYS LATER, in the morning, they had the funeral. The priest said that various general prayers were allowed, but no mention of salvation, and no holy water could be sprinkled on the coffin, nor any dust spread out in a cross upon the lid. The priest also said that unbaptized infants were not allowed past the ante-chamber to the church, and Bourne said "All the way in or nothing," and the funeral, what there was of it, was conducted at the undertaker's.

There were fold-down metal chairs arranged in rows. He and Claire and Sarah sat in front. Behind them, more friends had come than he expected. He wondered if any of them had been a part of Ethan's death. Two detectives were watching the door.

The priest read his salvationless prayers, closed his

book, and told them, "The death of the aged we can understand. They have lived out their time and done their work, and God in His wisdom has judged them ready to be called. . . . But the death of the young, that is one way of God that we find most difficult to accept and comprehend. We look at this child in his coffin, and we are heartsick at the waste, at his lost chance to feel joy in the goodness of living. Never to relish food and drink, to take pride in his body, to know friends, love his family. Never to have the chance to do great things, to be a good man, an example to his generation, a privilege to be with. All denied to him by God. The waste, we say.

"I could tell you to rejoice, that God has seen fit to call him early to eternal ecstasy. But for reasons we do not yet know, God did not permit this child to be baptized. The stain of original sin still makes up the character of his soul, and he now exists in limbo. That is another kind of waste, his lost chance to witness glory, and that waste we find even harder to accept.

"We sit at night in the silence of our rooms, and we ask why, hoping for solace, and we conclude—that God in His infinite foresight knew perhaps of this child's failure to achieve salvation and put him in limbo to save him from the fires of hell. Then too, if life can be joy, it can also be pain, and fear and sickness and grief, and perhaps we can find consolation in knowing that he never had to go through it all, that he never had to be like the rest of us, that his death was mercifully for the best."

Bourne looked at the old priest's white spider hair, and he thought how hair and fingernails continue to grow after death. And that's *all* that happens after death, he told himself.

The grave site was in a far fenced-off corner of the cemetery under a large sheltering chestnut tree, no crosses on any of the graves around, a deep hole with concrete walls and a floor. To keep the grave from sinking once the casket and the body decompose, Bourne thought. After they lower the coffin, they'll top it with a concrete slab and bury it all. Earth was piled by, covered with imitation grass. When I die, let them cremate me, he thought.

The day was hot and bright, and he smelled the warm moist air. The priest entrusted the body to the earth from which it came, which Bourne thought was a lie considering the concrete, and then the undertaker said next to him that it was time to leave now, but Claire would not budge.

"I'm staying until the end," she said, the only time she had spoken since the night at the funeral home.

"Whatever she wants," Bourne said.

So there was some discussion between the undertaker and the attendants, and just as they finally lowered the tiny casket by its straps into the man-sized hole, Sarah came forward and set a wreath of flowers on the lid. Bourne knew that was not her idea, that she would never have thought of that by herself. It was Claire. It was Claire who had made her do it. He looked at Claire, and she was staring at him through the veil. He looked at the casket descending, and when he could not see the small dark lid or the white wreath of flowers on it anymore, he turned away.

18

WHAT TOOK THE LONGEST was for Claire to let him sleep in the same bed with her again. She spoke to him now, but only to ask what pants he needed ironed, to say that supper was ready. They bought their food at a different supermarket each time. They stopped having milk delivered. They drove Sarah to and from school instead of letting her walk, and they never let her play outside without them. Even with the cruiser in front of the house, every car that slowed made them stare.

But nothing happened, and the more nothing happened, the more Bourne tensed in dread of answering the phone and hearing the man's voice rasp at him again. The abrupt harsh ring never stopped unnerving him. He concentrated to forget by working, but it wasn't any use: he knew all about the position he was in, he had written about it too many times. If somebody wants to get you bad enough, there simply isn't any way to stop them. They have too many ways to do it. It's all just a matter of time.

He went upstairs to the closet in the hall and arranged the rifle, pistol, and revolver on the second shelf, a full box of bullets next to them. Webster had warned him not to think like that, but Webster wasn't the one in fear of dying, and Webster didn't understand how years of researching this sort of thing had made him close to being an expert. The guns were normally kept in a small locked dressing cabinet in the bedroom, hard to get at, secure from any accident with Sarah. Now he had to show her where they were, tell her, order her not to touch them, and he believed her when she promised.

He came down early one morning from the bedroom, and there was no detective in the hallway by the phone. The tape recorder, the earphones, the lead-in wires, all the taping equipment was gone. He hurried to the front window, and the police car outside was gone too. He was suddenly conscious of the thin loose pajamas he wore. Immediately he stepped clear of the window.

"I tried to get over here before you found out," Webster came and said. "Understand I had nothing to do with it. The chief himself ordered it. Three shifts of men a day, one on the phone, two in the car outside, another two in three cruisers circling the district. Multiply that by the weeks we've been at this, he says, and figure the cost, figure the other places we need those men."

Bourne's face was burning. It was all he could do to control himself. "But you're supposed to be the police. If you can't protect us, what good are you?"

"I know how you feel, but—"

"You don't know how I feel at all."

"Well, listen to me anyway. The chief has a point. He says if Kess and his people haven't moved against you by now, it's either because they've lost interest or else they're waiting until we pull out. In any case, there's no sense in our sticking around. If they're really determined to wait for us to go, he says we could be here all year and still do no good. The day we left they'd be right back at you."

"So why not save time and let them come for us today, is that it? What is he, one of Kess's men or something?"

"Now you watch it. I spent all night arguing with him, and that kind of talk just makes me wish I hadn't even bothered. I've already talked to the guys who were out here guarding you, and they've all agreed to come around from time to time and make it look like we're still involved. You have my office number and my home. If anything happens, even if you think you're only imagining it, you give me a call. I don't care what time day or night, you call. With any luck, you won't even have to. The chief could very well be right. Maybe they have lost interest. Maybe they're satisfied now that they've scared you and killed your son."

"Maybe nothing. *They're going to come all right.*"

19

HE LEFT the car door open, running across the hot tar parking lot toward the entrance to the grade school. WOODSIDE, it said on top. Claire was hurrying behind him. "What is it? What's happened?" he shouted to the woman waiting nervously outside for them. She was pale in the sun, young like the doctor had been. Too young. Sarah's teacher. Short. Dull brown hair cut even with the bottom of her ears. Green dress stretched out. Five months pregnant, maybe more. "Tell me what it is," he called, running up to her ahead of Claire.

"I. She."

The building was new and clean and shiny, one long level of brick and glass. He swept past her, swinging open the bright front door, floors inside of polished marble. The place had the sharp sweet smell of turpentine.

"Which way?" he said, voice echoing. "Where have you got her? For God's sake tell me where she is."

"Down there," she said and swallowed.

To the right, and he was hurrying down the corridor, past open-door classrooms, past drinking fountains low on the wall for children, too beside himself to knock as he wrenched open the door marked PRINCIPAL, and there was Sarah weeping, wrapped up in a blanket on a corner chair, a white-starched nurse beside her, the principal rising off-balance behind his desk.

"It was a mistake," the man was saying. "You have to understand we had no way of knowing."

Bourne barely glanced at him: thick glasses on the desk, squinting eyes, open tie, rolled-up shirt sleeves. He was immediately over to Sarah, holding her. Claire was right behind. Sarah went on weeping. "Sweetheart, tell us what it is. Are you all right?"

She shook her head yes, she shook her head no.

Then he saw the blood on the floor.

"Jesus."

"You've got to understand," the principal was saying.

"Jesus, you're hurt, Sarah. You're cut. Who cut you? Where?"

He fumbled to open the blanket.

The nurse tried to stop him, stronger than she looked. "You keep out of this."

"You've got to understand," the principal was saying.

Bourne swung to him. The man's underarms were dark with sweat. The room smelled full of stale smoke, musty butts, one cigarette burning in the littered ashtray on the desk, another half-stubbed out, still smoldering. "All right then, damn it. Tell me. Tell me what it is I have to understand."

Sarah was weeping louder.

"I had her calmed down," the nurse said. "Now you've made her afraid again."

"That's a good idea," the principal said and tried to smile. "I'm sure we'd all accomplish more if we all calmed down."

"I've made her afraid of what?"

"The policeman," Sarah said and wept.

"What policeman?"

"Sweetheart, try to tell us about it."

"Oh, Mommy, the policeman."

"We did our best," the principal said. "You've got to understand that. I don't know what's been going on, but there's been a policeman watching her for the last few weeks while she's been back to school." He took a long drag from his cigarette, squinting without his glasses. "Today there was a different one."

"No."

"He told me he had to ask her some questions, that something new had happened and he had to ask her about it. How was I to know what's been going on? Nobody's told me anything."

"We wanted her to lead some kind of life."

"What?"

"It wasn't right keeping her at home all the time. She was going crazy. We wanted her to meet new children, play, do something to keep her mind off things. If we had told you what was happening, you wouldn't have let her come, or else word would have got around and everybody would have been staring at her. We figured the policeman was enough to protect her."

"What are you talking about?"

"The policeman. Just tell me about the policeman. I was wrong."

"He came this morning and asked to have your daughter taken out of class so he could talk with her." The sweat stain was spreading under his arms. "So I let him. You understand why I let him, don't you? The next thing, one of the teachers heard her screaming in the basement. She was bleeding and screaming and—"

"Where?"

"In the basement."

"No. Where was she bleeding?" But he already knew and his throat was gagging him but he had to hear for certain anyway, and then the principal was telling him how she had been assaulted and the logical thing that the armed policeman had used to do it and he thought he was going to be sick.

"No," he said. "No," he kept repeating.

20

HE DROVE HER HOME between Claire and himself on the front seat. The bleeding was finally stopped—the doctors at the hospital had stared at him when he explained. They stitched her where the barrel sight had ripped. They cushioned her with sanitary pads that were going to have to be changed, and they gave her a needle to stop the pain. He thought of poison again. Then they gave her some blood and they wanted to keep her there for observation, but he said, "No way. The next time it might be a doctor instead of a policeman. She's coming home with me." So now she huddled between them, clutching a blanket, holding herself, and her face was the gray of powdered cement.

"Why, Daddy? Why did he want to hurt me there?"

He had to think it through before he could explain. "Sweetheart, when your mother was getting big with Ethan, do you remember you asked how she got him?" The image of Ethan made him pause, the body stiff and senseless in his coffin in his grave. He realized he had started speeding and eased his foot off the gas pedal. "Do you remember you thought that a baby started to grow inside a woman as soon as she reached a certain age, or else as soon as she got married, and you wanted to know if that was true?"

She held herself closer.

"So I told you no," he said.

"Reuben, stop it," Claire said.

"She asked me a question and I'm going to answer it." Then to Sarah: "And I told you how your mother and I had gotten together, and what we had done to make Ethan. Well, that was a good thing to do. Your mother wanted me to do it, and I wanted to do it, and it made us feel very happy together. It's something special that you only do with someone you love, and if everything goes properly and you do have a baby, well that can be even more special."

"But why did he want to hurt me there?"

He rounded a corner and couldn't keep off saying it. "Sarah, not everybody will always be as kind to you as we have. There are some people in the world, bad people, who enjoy taking something special and abusing it. We don't know why they want to enjoy hurting us, but they like to do it anyhow, and we have to keep watching for them."

"Reuben," Claire told him sharply.

"I'm going to answer her question," he said. "Sarah, that's why we told you never to take anything like candy from a stranger, never to go for a ride with somebody you don't know. That's why I'm telling you now to be careful of every person you meet. They might be good, but they might be one of the bad ones, and there are a lot of them around, not just the people who are after us, but a lot of others too. They like to hurt you, tell you lies, cheat and steal from you and ruin your reputation out of jealousy. They——"

He rounded the corner into their street, and when he saw what was happening, his first impulse was to slam on the brakes, his second to rush the car down

to the fire trucks. There were sirens coming. There were
thick black hoses stretched out from the fire hydrant
on the corner down across the street to the house. He
raced the car thumping over them, past people standing
watching, toward the firemen in slick black rubber
raincoats struggling with the pressure in the hoses,
spewing water loudly onto the house, onto the garage.

Flames licked through the top of the garage, bright
orange in the black smoke rolling skyward, showered
with the heavy spray of water from the hoses. He
braked so hard that he and Claire and Sarah jerked
forward, and just in time he thrust out his right hand
to keep Sarah from hitting the dash, and then he was
out of the car, hearing the shouts and the truck motors
and more sirens coming, feeling the black sticky soot
drifting down on him, the air a fine cool mist from the
backspray of the hoses. And there was Webster in his
gray suit leaning calmly, hands in his pockets, against
the nearest fire engine.

He glanced at Bourne and came walking slowly
over, looking once more at the smoke and flames. "It's
just the garage," he said. "From what I'm told, the
house has a good chance to be saved."

Bourne couldn't answer. The wind changed and the
smoke came drifting over, burning his nostrils and
his throat when he breathed. He watched the bright
orange flames bursting through the black smoke on
top of the garage. He looked at Claire holding Sarah
in the car. He looked back at Webster. "So how did
they start it?" he managed to say.

"Don't know yet. I came just after the trucks got
here. One of the neighbors phoned in the alarm."

"Did they see who did it? Enough for a description?"

"I have a man checking on that. Actually I didn't know about the fire until I got here. The reason I came out was to say that the teacher at the school gave us a description of the man who attacked your daughter, and we ran it through the files, and there's no policeman on the force who matches it. I don't know where he got the uniform, but I know he wasn't one of us." There were big black flakes of soot on his suit and face. "What's the matter?" he said. "You look like you don't believe me."

"I can't tell who to believe anymore. My son is dead, my daughter assaulted, my home on fire. All that and the police won't protect us, and—"

"We'll protect you now all right. The chief admits he was wrong, and he's assigned a special detail to keep watch on you."

"Sure, and what if it's one of your men who lent this other guy his uniform? What if that one is on the detail?"

"You've got me there. We can't very well have police come out here to watch the police."

"Then I'm right back where I started. Only worse."

21

"YOU CAN SEE where it started," the fire chief said.

The back wall of the garage was burned through in the middle, circled by char that was blacker than any place else except the beams from the roof. The rim of the circle was uneven, black fingers splayed out in every direction. They waited while the firemen hosed down the smoking hissing wood once more, and then they stepped carefully in among the pools of water and the rubble. The heat from the wet cracked cement floor came up through the soles of his shoes. He burned his leg against Sarah's bicycle, its frame twisted and smoking, the tires melted. The stench was choking.

"There," the fire chief said. "You can see what I mean." He was pointing at the broken glass on the back floor, then up to the charred design around the hole in the wall.

Bourne took a moment, and then he saw all right.

Webster said it first. "Molotov cocktail."

Mix one-third liquid detergent and two-thirds gasoline in a large soft-drink bottle, cap it, and tape on a menstrual tube. Sure. They drove up fast, got out, and lit the tube and threw the bottle into the garage against the back wall. The bottle shattered. The detergent stuck the gasoline to the wall and concentrated it like napalm. That's why the hole in the wall and the charred fingers out from it. That's where the gasoline splashed and stuck.

But he wasn't only thinking it, he must have been saying it as well. Because the fire chief was looking at him and asking him, "How come *you* know so much about it?"

22

HE HAD no other choice: they had to spend the night in the house. If they were going to be attacked anymore, he couldn't let it happen in some friend's house, or in some hotel where he wouldn't know the routine and couldn't be warned by something out of the ordinary. He waited in the car with Claire and Sarah until the fire chief made certain that the fire would not start again. Sarah was in too much pain to walk. He had to carry her into the house, and Claire did what she could to make the place look like it used to be. The stairs, the upper floor were pooled with water. The walls were black and stained with water. He put Sarah on the bed in his and Claire's room. Her own room down the hall was a shambles after the firemen got through with it. He and Claire opened windows, but there was little breeze, and the thick acrid smell of the smoke was everywhere.

Then Claire disappeared, and when he went looking for her, he found her behind the unlocked closed door in the bathroom. She was sitting with the toilet cover down, face slack and tired, staring emptily at the bathtub. Her jeans were wet and black from cleaning up.

"Maybe that would help," he said. "Go on, take a bath, why don't you? Nothing's going to happen this soon after the fire."

"Reuben, there isn't anything will help."

"The police car is out front again, and the man is downstairs with the phone again. We're safe enough now. Go on."

"I don't even hate you anymore. That's how tired I am."

He had been smiling, and the smile froze on his face, and the little spirit he had left simply died just then. It was all he could do to go back across the hall and check on Sarah in their room. She was asleep. In a moment he heard the water start rumbling into the bathtub, and at least that was something. The best he could hope for at any rate.

By nine Claire was asleep next to Sarah, and he kept the house in darkness, wandering through it. He had a cigarette with the detective on duty by the phone, the tips of their cigarettes glowing red in the dark. He went back upstairs to try to sleep, couldn't bear the smell of the smoke anymore, and stood by the open window to clear his head and breathe.

It was raining, had been raining for an hour, a slow steady drizzle that came straight down whispering onto the grass and the pavement. He leaned his head into it, letting it soak his hair and trickle coldly across his neck, breathing the fresh cool air. The streetlight was out again. Except for a few rain-misted lights that were on in some houses at the end of the street, everything was dark and dripping wet.

The streetlight. He tried to convince himself that the busy anxious feeling in his stomach was just nerves, no reason for panic, but something was tugging at him from behind and something was pushing at him from in front and he panicked anyway, jerking his head back in through the window, cracking it smartly, as the explosions lit up the night like fireworks, like thunder and lightning that might have come with the rain. Five, eight, ten roaring flashes, he was never sure how many. A constant string of them from between the houses on the other side of the street, shotguns, downstairs windows shattering as he dove to the floor, and the window above him burst inward, glass crashing down on him, pellets whapping against the far wall.

Claire sat up startled, bewildered. Sarah started screaming. He was groping to his knees, heart racing, water from his wet hair running ice cold down his back. A blast hit another window, slashing glass over Claire and Sarah. Claire screamed, dragging Sarah out of the bed with her, huddling with her on the floor as another volley hit the house and more glass ripped across the room and Sarah was hysterical.

"Daddy! Daddy!"

And with that the shotguns stopped. He heard car doors opening, men shouting in the night. He was on his feet, trembling, peering out one corner of the window. The police. They were out of the cruiser, separating, running splashing through the pools of water and the rain toward the cover of the two big fir trees in front of the house. Webster, he was thinking. He had to get Webster. The police would have radioed for help. That didn't matter. He had to get Webster.

He swung round the bed to the phone, picking it up, trying to remember Webster's number, and there was no dial tone. The line. The line's been cut.

"Stay here," he told them. He was heading out the door toward the hall. "No," he told them. "Get in the bathroom. Get in the bathtub. Anything for cover." He didn't wait. He was already going down the hall, Sarah crying in the room behind him as he stumbled down the stairs, nearly bumping into the detective who had left the phone and was standing in the dark by the front door.

"The phone's been cut," Bourne told him.

"I know it."

He felt the detective's handgun glance against his shoulder, and realizing this might be one of Kess's men, he recoiled, falling back against the bannister of the stairs.

"Easy. For Christ sake don't get in the way," the detective told him thickly. "Get back upstairs."

"I've got to help. Tell me what to do."

"Get back upstairs."

Someone outside shouted.

"Me. They're calling me," the detective said. He went into the living room, crouching beside the big shattered window, calling out, "Fine! Everything's fine in here!"

The man outside shouted again.

He kept on. But Bourne couldn't make out the words. Then he heard the detective coming back swearing to himself into the hall.

"What is it?" Bourne said.

"A God damn mess," the thick voice came at him. "The shotguns opened up on the cruiser too. Our guys ran for those trees out there, but one of them was hit in the head, and now he's got blood coming down over his eyes so he can't see."

The detective unlocked the front door and opened it a crack, the night a paler shade of black against the dark of the hall. A slight wind came up with the rain, blowing coolly in.

"Wait a minute," Bourne said. "What are you doing?"

"I'm going out there. I have to bring him in."

Bourne listened to the rain outside drizzling on the pavement. "No," he said. "Stay here. Let the other guy bring him in."

"Can't. If those shotguns start again, we need somebody to shoot and cover us."

"But you can do that yourself from here. Please. There's no reason to go. Don't leave me."

"Have to. I don't have a clear line of fire because of those trees. The only way to do this is for me to get him while the other guy uses his better position to cover me."

The detective opened the door wider, and Bourne listened to him breathing nervously.

"No. Please," Bourne said and reached out to grab his arm.

"Don't you think I want to stay here?" the detective told him. "Don't you think I want nothing to do with going out there?"

23

AND THEN he was gone.

Bourne stood there in the dark next to the open doorway, listening to the detective's quick steps off the hollow wooden porch onto the wet sidewalk, onto the soft wet grass, and then in the monotonous spatter of the rain he could not hear him anymore. His hand was still outstretched from where he had grabbed at the man's arm. He imagined him, finger heavy on the trigger of his handgun, racing low toward one of the fir trees, diving flat onto the cold wet mud-spongy grass, seeing about the policeman hit in the head. Why wasn't help here by now? he was thinking. Where were more police cars? He couldn't even hear any sirens on the way.

Everything was doubling on him, building in circles. He was back to when he had first waited for the ambulance and the police after Ethan was poisoned, standing almost in the same spot, pacing, worrying why help wasn't there. The poison and the cat. Ethan. Sarah and the house. The calls. Why weren't any sirens coming?

Because Webster would leave them quiet, not to warn Kess's men.

And then the chill breeze from the rain creeping steadily in on him, he suddenly shivered as he realized the police in the cruiser outside might not have been able to radio for help. They might have been in such a hurry to get out of the car that they didn't have the time. He held his breath, trembling, counting one, two, three, straining to hear the detective struggling back with the wounded policeman over the wet grass through the rain toward the house. Where were they? What was taking them so long? He had a vision of Kess's men rushing the house and he wanted desperately to close the door on them, but he couldn't, he needed to leave it open for the detective and the wounded policeman coming through.

But what if it's Kess's men who come running through?

Lights were on here and there in houses across the

street, more lights coming on all the time. Maybe Kess's
men would go away now. Maybe they'd already gone.
Maybe nothing. He saw the flash of the shotgun across
the street, heard the simultaneous blast, the scream, he
didn't know whose, and that was the end, he had the
door shut, locking it, and one of the gunmen across the
street must have been using a solid high-velocity slug
for deer instead of the standard shotgun pellet load because pellets never would have ruptured through the
two and one-half inches of the door, deafening him,
reeling him back blind in the dark as something
slammed his shoulder, numbing powerfully, and spun
him.

The screaming outside wouldn't stop. But it wasn't
out there now. It was him, and he was braced somehow
on his feet against the archway to the living room,
clutching his senseless shoulder, screaming. There
wasn't any blood. He couldn't understand why there
wasn't any blood, and then he realized that the slug had
not been what hit him, just a bursting fragment from
the door, but that didn't make a difference. He just went
on screaming as the second slug came walloping
through the door, chunks and splinters flying, and then
the shotguns started up again, all of them at once,
sporadic cracks of handguns in return, then no handguns, only shotguns, and his mind went out of control,
they've finished the police, they're going to come for
me, for all of us, and he was charging up the stairs.

He stumbled, clutching his shoulder, reached the top
of the stairs, and rushed to where his guns were in the
closet. He couldn't find them in the dark. He had to
turn on the hall light. He still couldn't find them. Claire.
She must have moved them, afraid of Sarah touching

them. He heard Sarah crying hysterically in their room. Why hadn't they gone into the bathroom as he told them? "Where are the guns? Where did you put the guns?"

And then he found them. On the top shelf. Under some blankets. Which one? The rifle was too awkward in close quarters. Which one, the pistol or revolver? As if in answer, Webster's words came back to him. Shoot yourself and save the other guy the trouble. With those cap gun .22's, you won't hurt anybody anyhow.

He grabbed the revolver, a western-barreled Ruger. It was slow and had to be cocked each time before it was fired, but it came with an extra bullet cylinder, a .22 magnum cylinder. Once he pressed the button on the side and slid out the regular cylinder and slid in the one for the magnums, this was more like a .32. It couldn't slam a man flat. It might not even make him stagger, but it would damn sure let him know he was hit, and if even so it wasn't much, it was all he had.

He took that long to register the blood on his hands, staring at it in surprise. It was drying sticky, leaving traces on the Ruger. He checked his shoulder again. Just hand-print smears of blood on his shirt. It wasn't his shoulder, it was his hands. From the glass that had fallen on him in the bedroom. He hadn't even known that he was cut. Shoulder aching, swelling, he fumbled to load the bullets, scrabbling them from their box, dropping some, chambering the rest, hands clumsy, shaking. The shooting outside was stopped now. They've finished the police. They're going to come. "Claire," he said and rushed into the bedroom. "Get up. We're leaving."

But she made no move to stand. She made no sign

she even heard him. The scream outside was beginning again, a constant high-pitched strident scream that raised his skin and sent it prickling, and she was cradling Sarah, rocking her in the dim light from the hall, kissing her hair. "Oh my God I am heartily sorry," she was saying, "for having offended Thee. And I detest all my sins because I dread the loss of heaven and the pains of hell, but most of all—" And Sarah was crying, and he told them both, "Shut up. Get on your feet."

"Because I have offended Thee, oh my God, Who art all good and deserving of all my love. I firmly resolve with the help of Thy grace—"

"No," he said. "We're leaving." He dragged her up and shook her. "Do you hear? We're leaving."

The broken glass littered the room like shards of ice. The slap across his face was so sharp that for an instant he saw double, eyes watering. He blinked repeatedly. He staggered back and shook his head to clear it.

"Don't tell me to shut up," Claire was saying. "We're going to die because of you."

"That's right. If we stay here, we're going to die."

He lifted Sarah awkwardly, her tears warm and wet through his shirt sleeve onto his arm as he carried her out of the room, down the hall and the stairs, away from the light up there, darting past the front door in case of another slug, into the dark living room, toward the kitchen and the back door. How much did she weigh anyhow? She was so heavy that after struggling to carry her down the stairs he could barely walk a straight line with her. In the dark of the kitchen, he jolted against the sharp corner of the stove and had to set her down, holding himself and wincing, and Claire wasn't with him. She must have stayed upstairs. He had thought when she slapped him that she would be all right now, but he was wrong.

No, he wasn't wrong. She was a shadow coming in the dark. "What if more of them are outside in the back?"

But he had thought of that, and there was only one way to find out. He had to go out first himself. He unlocked the door and gripped the doorknob. The revolver was awkward and heavy in his hand.

And again Webster's voice returned to him. This isn't like in your books. It's for real. If you go out on your own after these guys, you'll find that writing about shooting a man is a hell of a lot different from having the guts to line up those sights and pull that trigger.

He couldn't turn the doorknob.

Have to.

Can't.

24

THE SCREAM OUTSIDE in front settled everything. It unmistakably died. In the expanding silence, he imagined his attackers rushing toward the front door. His stomach on fire, hands trembling, he wrenched open the back door, told Claire, "Lock it behind me," threw open the screen door and dove off the back porch into the bushes by the side.

They slashed his face, and he landed, twisting his

hurt shoulder wet in the mud, the rain drenching him, and he thought too late that somebody might be hiding in these bushes. The idea sent him rolling against the wall of the house, straining to see in the rain and the dark if anybody was there.

No one that he could make out.

He searched, crawling through the mud under the bushes. Webster had been right. He didn't know what he was doing. He had written about things like this and imagined himself in situations like this often enough, and here he was making too much noise, breathing too heavily, too loud. He was snapping branches, scratching them together, slipping awkwardly in the mud, and anybody around could tell easily where he was to shoot him.

That finally gave him confidence. He was so bad at this that he should have been dead by now.

Unless they were here and waiting for Claire and Sarah to come out as well.

Can't think about that.

He dimly saw the long stretch of his backyard, good cover for them everywhere, the trees and alcoves of bushes, the swing set for Sarah, and beyond everything he thought he could make out the white back fence and the gloom of the neighbor's yard behind it. The shotguns ought to have wakened the people in the house back there. Lights should have been on. He could see the reflection from lights in the houses on both sides of his, glistening off the rain-misted grass in their backyards. But none over there, and he thought maybe the people were away.

Or maybe Kess's men were in there holding them. Because of me.

Can't think about that either. Get moving.

He crept out of the bushes and crossed in the rain to the bushes on the other side of the back steps. His shoulder was in unmanageable pain now, and he had to shift the revolver to his left hand. It wasn't important that he was a poor shot with his left hand. If he came upon somebody in these bushes, he would never have a chance to get a shot off anyhow. The idea of him stalking anybody was a joke—he didn't know the first damn thing about it, whether to slip into these bushes or work along their edge or what. He'd only been fooling himself. He decided to try the edge, and his only reason for going on was simply now to make himself a target, to make sure the yard was safe for Claire and Sarah. Again something was tugging at him, and he turned, seeing no one. The rain increased, rushing hard, drenching him, clothes clinging coldly to him while he trembled. He turned back to the bushes and crouched, wiping the rain from his eyes to peer in among them, and reached the side of the house and there was no one.

He breathed, trembling so much that he couldn't continue.

Move, he told himself. Just a little more. Do it. Go on. It's almost over.

He still didn't move.

Come on. Hurry. Check that back fence, get Claire and Sarah and get the hell out of here.

It was only the prospect of them clearing that fence into safety that managed to start him going again. Halfway across the yard toward the fence he saw the shadow move. On his right. Behind the maple tree. Its dark trunk grew double; a figure dislodged from it. "God damn it stop!" somebody yelled, and as he bolted insanely back toward the house, his feet slipped out from under him on the slick wet grass. He fell face downward onto the sodden earth, sliding to try to stand. He fell again and heard "Damn it stop!" again behind him and the shots sent him worming quickly on his stomach toward the shelter of the bushes. There were three of them, bullets ripping through the air over his head, whacking into the wood of the house. "Reuben!" he heard Claire screaming in the house. "Shut up!" he was thinking. And then he was into the bushes, pivoting low to aim and fire, one two three four quick patterned shots, and then the shadow was gone and he didn't know where to shoot anymore and the night was silent except for the patter of the rain and the shouts of people in the front yard and the sirens coming. Far away. Faint. But at least they were coming.

"Reuben!" Claire was screaming in the house.

"Shut up," he thought. "Don't open the door." But he couldn't shout it because it might attract more gunfire to him, and then he heard the moan on his right, but he couldn't tell exactly where it was coming from so that he could shoot at it. That surprised him. That he had actually fired in the first place and was ready to do it again. Webster had been a little bit wrong after all. The sirens were closer, louder, and the moan kept on, strained, hoarse, and there was something else about it, something almost liquid as if the man had been hit in the throat.

These bushes were a joke, he realized. They only made him feel secure without giving him any real cover. Anybody out there must have seen him crawl behind them. Why didn't somebody riddle the bushes and kill him?

Because nobody was out there anymore.

The moan came again, coughing something bubbly, and he started crawling on his stomach toward the maple tree as the door behind him was opened, and he shouted, "Close that door!" He waited. "Close the damn door!" he shouted again, and whoever had it open closed it.

Then he was crouching beside the maple tree, and he saw the man stretched out groaning in the flower bed by the fence. The guy was faceup, blinking at the sky, drooling something dark that was dribbling down his chin in the rain. His hand was stuck out toward where his gun had fallen in the grass, and Bourne grabbed it before moving any closer. A magnum. Better than his own. He cocked it, aiming at the guy's forehead, but the guy wasn't blinking anymore.

The rain came gusting at him, lashing. The sirens were even louder. The next thing he was running, slipping in the grass, back to the house, up the stairs and opening the door. "Let's go," he told Claire.

"Are you all right?"

"I'm fine. Let's go."

"But the sirens. We're safe now. We've got help."

"We're going. Webster was the only one I trusted, and sometimes I wasn't even sure about him. The only way we'll be safe is if we go where no one knows we are. Not the police. Not anybody."

He felt her staring at him in the dark.

"Claire, I wish we had a choice. We can't stay here. They came once. In six months they'll come again. The only thing we can do," and he could hardly say it and he didn't know why but he was crying suddenly, "the only thing we can do is hide."

The last word came out as a sob. He wiped his eyes,

lifted Sarah into his arms as the sirens pulled up shriek-ing in front of the house, and started with her down the backstairs into the rain.

"I don't want to leave, Reuben," Claire said behind him.

It was complicated, but he knew what she meant. She would go. She wasn't saying she wouldn't. But she didn't want to.

"I know," he said, looking once more at their house. "Christ, I don't want to leave either."

And then they were going off in the rain across the backyard while he heard someone pounding on the front door. Sarah was in his arms, and he gave her to Claire while he climbed the fence, and then he took her again while Claire climbed over. He moved cautiously through the next yard, down past the side of the house, looking up and down the next street. Sarah was soaking wet, crying against his chest in his arms. His salt tears were mixing with the rain in his mouth. He ran awk-wardly with her, crossing the street, Claire hurrying be-side him, and when they went past the side of a house over there into the next backyard, as near as he could tell there was no one who had seen to follow them.

Part
_____

TWO

"IS THAT IT, DADDY?"

"No, sweetheart. Our place is just around the bend up here."

They were walking south along a dirt road parallel to the foothills, him and Claire and Sarah. To the left was low flat sweeping grassland. To the right were steep thickly wooded slopes of yellowed dogwood and aspen and poplar that rose up tier after tier to the evergreens and beyond them the snow-capped craggy mountains. The afternoon was bright and warm and pleasant walking. He reached up to touch the branches that hung down over the side of the road as he walked beneath them.

In the end he'd decided to go on in and talk to the real-estate man by himself. Granted the possibility of their being followed, a man, a woman, and a little girl were just too easy to remember and identify. There was always the risk that the real-estate man would remember him alone, but there wasn't any way around that and in any case he had a beard now and he wasn't using his own name anymore. The only other risk was that the guy wouldn't know what to make of his pulling out a down payment in cash and in twenties, so he finally pretended he only wanted a place to rent as a base for autumn hunting. That way he could pay him cash now and at the beginning of each month, and the guy would not think it too unusual. There were just three places. He was ready to take the first one, but he didn't want to seem too eager, so he went with the real-estate man to the others and then back to the office where he gave him the money and signed the papers.

"It's an exceptional place, Mr. Whittaker," the real-estate man had told him. "I can't understand why it hasn't been taken until now, and I'm sure you won't be disappointed. Incidentally, what's your pleasure?"

"Pardon me?"

"Hunting. What is it you like to hunt for?"

"Oh. Elk mostly. I used to try deer, but lately I've been wanting something bigger."

"I know exactly what you mean. I have a friend who won't settle for anything but moose, but there aren't too many of them now and you have to put your name in for a few tags that are drawn from a lottery and he keeps losing."

"That's why we don't have many to begin with."

"Excuse me?"

"It's all right. Nothing."

Then he had walked out of town to the rock-filled hollow where he had left Claire and Sarah, and they had bought some knapsacks and supplies and started down the road toward the cabin, and now five miles later they were rounding the bend and there was a half-hidden wheel-rutted road going up through the trees, long dusty grass growing up between the ruts, and they took it. Thirty yards later the trees disappeared and there was just a long windswept slope of grass on both sides, dotted here and there with rocks and sagebrush, and they stood there a moment smelling the fresh clean afternoon air, feeling the sun on their heads.

"That's something we forgot," he said. "Something for our heads. We spend much time bareheaded out of doors up here and we're just begging for a sunstroke."

"But where is it, Daddy? I don't see it."

"You will in a moment, sweetheart, and I'm pretty sure you're going to like it."

You'd better, he thought. Because this is it. The best we're going to get.

Then they were on the move again, working harder because of the steep angle of the slope, out of breath, kicking up dust, him helping Sarah as they neared the top and Claire said suddenly, "Oh, Reuben," and he didn't know how to take that, whether she was happy or disappointed or what. "You like it?"

"I love it."

And he was proud. It was on a level, back from the edge of the slope, hidden from the road below, a two-story cabin made of thick stones around the foundations and huge well-mortared logs above them and a porch and a well in front and even a little tower on top. There were windows on either side of the front door, each window subdivided into smaller panes of glass, and a shed to the left, and a path of stones, almost over-grown by the long grass, leading up to the front door, and Sarah was already running through the grass to the well, tugging at the lid, leaning over, looking down.

"Be careful, sweetheart," Claire said.

"There's water down here."

"Sure there is," he said. "And it's been tested and it's all right to drink. The roof doesn't leak. The fire-place is good. There's a big old iron cooking stove in the kitchen. We could live here all year and never miss a thing. You like it?" he said to Claire. "You really like it?"

She swung round to look down the slope of grass to the trees and the road and the rangeland stretching off. She held out her arms and looked up at the bright blue sky and turned back smiling to the house and said, "It's fine. It's going to be just fine." And for the first time since Ethan had died, she held him.

Then she was breaking away, hurrying down the grass-grown stone path toward the house.

"The only thing I don't like is those trees in back," he called after her "The slope here is perfect. It lets us see anybody coming up. But those trees. They give too much cover."

But she wasn't listening. She was already at the door, turning the knob, straining to get in. "I can't get it open. It's stuck."

"Try this," he said, coming up, showing her the key.

The door swung open and the smell of must was overpowering as she slipped in, pausing a moment to look at the gray dusty sheets over the furniture and the leaves in the fireplace and the cobwebs in the corners, and then she was sliding back the curtains, opening the windows, letting the light in. She was heading for the room in back on the left when he remembered. "Sarah. Where is she?"

She wasn't by the well anymore.

He stepped off the porch and went to the side, and she had the door to the shed open, peering in.

"Daddy, there's a funny kind of seat in here. With a hole in it."

"Of course," he said. "That's the outhouse."

"The what?"

"That's where you sit and go to the bathroom."

"I do?"

"Sure," he said. "That's the way they used to do it in the old days."

"But what about when it's snowy and cold?"

"You don't sit there very long."

He smiled, and once she started giggling it was all she could do to stop.

"Come on," he said. "Let's go see what Mommy's up to."

She was finished with the room on the left and was already checking out the kitchen when they came in. The floor was smooth stone. There was a big stout wooden table in the middle, cupboards all along one wall, a window over the dry-sink, a massive eight-lidded cooking stove against another wall. She was rolling up her sleeves as she came back into the living room and started folding up the sheets, dust rising up in thick musty clouds.

"Well?" he said.

"Well," she answered. "I don't know what you've got planned, but while I'm cleaning up this mess, you're going to bring in some water to fill the heater and light it and then I'm going to have the world's longest hottest bath. And one more thing."

"What is it? Anything."

"As soon as you're done with the heater, why don't you pour yourself a drink from the bottle you bought in that pack, sit down, and figure out what you want for supper."

"Spaghetti," Sarah said.

"Then that's what it'll be," he told her.

It was in a can. It had to be because when he'd been there with the real-estate man he'd seen there was no refrigerator. How could there be? There wasn't any

electricity. There was an icebox for when the snow came
and ice formed in the streams and they could store
meat, but in the meantime he'd been careful to buy
only cans, and he brought in wood that was stacked
against the back of the house for the water heater and
the stove, and they sat at the big wooden table that
night, light from a coal-oil lantern in the middle, eating
spaghetti and Spam with ketchup poured over everything and bread to sop up the sauce, and even Claire
who didn't like spaghetti from a can ate hungrily, and
he was so hungry himself that looking at the steaming
plateful, knowing it was still too hot, he couldn't wait,
tasting a big forkful, burning the roof of his mouth.

"Christ," he said happily. "Jesus Christ."

He finished it all before he remembered the bread,
mopping the plate shiny.

Then they heated some water and washed the dishes
and went into the living room slumping onto two chairs
and the sofa, him pouring another drink from the bottle, liking the good wood smell from the stove in the
kitchen.

"Daddy, how long will we stay here?" Sarah said
stretched out on the sofa.

"Oh, I don't know. Through the winter I guess. Unless it gets too cold. I haven't thought that far ahead.
Why? Don't you think you're going to like it here?"

"No, I was just wondering when the snow comes if
we'll be able to go sledding down that hill out there."

"You bet we will," he said. "Don't you worry. We'll
be able to do a lot of things."

She was struggling not to yawn.

"Right now I think you'd better go to bed."

"I don't want to. I want to stay out here with you."

"We'd only keep you awake. Come on. You've got a big day ahead of you tomorrow. You're going to help me cut down that long grass in front of the house."

"I don't want to. Go to bed I mean."

"You'll just be in the next room over there. We won't be far from you. And you don't need to worry about spending the night alone either. We'll be coming in shortly to stay with you."

He got up and walked over.

"Come on," he said.

And she didn't move but she didn't resist either when he picked her up and carried her into the room. The bed was long and wide with a curved metal headstand and a thick quilt over it, and she didn't have any pajamas but he told her to take her socks off at least and then he tucked her in, kissing her, walking over to the window to close it. He looked out, but he couldn't see anything in the darkness.

"Daddy?"

He turned.

"Can I have a light in here?"

She was in under the covers, sunk down in the soft bed, peering over at him.

"Of course you can," he said. "The place is strange to us all. There's nothing wrong at all with wanting a light in here."

He raised the top of the kerosene lamp on the table by the bed, striking a match, touching it to the wick, then lowering the top as the flame began to grow, adjusting the knob at the side until the light was yellow and dim.

"In the night, if you have to go out to the bathroom, wake me and I'll go with you," he said and leaned down to kiss her again. She nodded, and he went out, leaving the door slightly ajar behind him.

Claire was up and looking out the left front window toward the northeast.

"You can just see the lights from town," she said.

It was more like one light, a kind of vague gentle glow far off out there he saw as he came up beside her. They stood there a moment in silence, and without thinking, he put his arm around her.

"It's going to be all right," he told himself.

"Sure it is," she said.

But he couldn't tell if she believed it or not.

She leaned close to him, the side of her breast against his chest, and he brushed aside her hair, kissing her on the back of the neck.

"What about Sarah? She'll hear."

"We'll be quiet," he said.

Later as he sat in the dark in the living room staring out the window toward the far off glow from the town in the night, he thought how if someone wanted to catch them off guard the best thing was to wait outside in the dark until they had to go out to the bathroom or how if someone had come bursting in while they were making love on the floor they wouldn't have had a chance.

"HAVE YOU GOT any horses for sale?"

"I might have. It depends," the old man said.

"On what?"

"Oh, on a lot of things I suppose. Like what you need them for and how much you know about horses in the first place and how much you want to spend."

He was standing on the hard sun-baked ground at the back of the ranch house, looking through the dirty screen door at the old man studying him. He'd been a long time deciding which ranch to go to, this one to the north near town or the other two to the south away from it. Just to be safe he had chosen the two to the south and they had sent him to this place near town anyway. The house was warped and listing, windows dusty, dead weeds lying in the flower beds.

The old man opened the screen door and stepped outside, and for the first time Bourne saw that the old man was chewing something.

"I'm sorry. I didn't mean to catch you at your lunch."

"It's all right. I was almost finished anyhow."

He had on cowboy boots and faded jeans and a sweat-stained denim work shirt free from his belt. His shoulders were stooped and his skin was hanging slack under his chin, but his sleeves were rolled up and the muscles of his arms were hard and stark. "About these horses," the old man said.

"I need them to pack gear into the mountains. I want to do some hunting."

"How many?"

"Three. One to ride, the other two for packing."

"You're going up by yourself?"

"I've done it before."

"Suit yourself. These horses aren't like pigeons, you know. You get in trouble up there, they don't come back with messages."

He started walking off, and Bourne turned to follow, the sun full in his eyes now, toward the barn, its boards as parched and weathered as the house. The corral was in back of the barn, six horses, a water trough, a feed bin. He squinted at the horses as long as he could stand it, and then resting his eyes from the sun, glanced down at the scum on the water in the trough.

"This is it," the old man said, and he must still have had a bit of food at the side of his mouth because he started chewing again. "That's all there is. I don't work the cattle much now, just rent the land to the fellow down the road and hang on to these few horses to keep my hand in."

"That's what he told me. He said you might not mind parting with some of them."

"Maybe. You know much about horses?" He was leaning against the fence now, looking at them.

"A bit."

"Which three are the best?"

So that was it, he thought. The old man didn't mind selling, or at least if he did mind he was willing to sell anyhow, but not to just anyone. You had to qualify. You had to have credentials.

The horses had looked up from nosing the ground when the two of them approached, and now they were still staring, three bays, a sorrel, a buckskin, and a pinto. They were all mares, all short, compact, and trim, with the big solid haunches of a quarter horse. Except for the pinto, which was even shorter and thin in the legs and small-headed, like the runt in a litter.

He climbed up over the boards of the fence and dropped down into the corral, letting them size him up once more before he walked on over, his hand out to the buckskin's nose. The buckskin didn't respond for a moment, then dipped its nose down sniffing, nuzzling the hand, looking for sugar likely or maybe an apple. He glanced at the others. Two of them, one bay and the sorrel, were circling slowly to his left. The rest were standing nearby, curious. He brushed his hand across the buckskin's face, patting its neck. Then stepping to the back, drawing his hand along the buckskin's side, he swatted it firmly on the haunch, getting it in motion. The other two just stood there, and then swatting the pinto as well, he had them moving too, the one bay and the sorrel joining in. As they circled the corral, he walked back over to the old man and then leaning against the inside of the fence, he studied them.

He hadn't been lying to the old man when he said that he knew a bit about horses, but then he hadn't exactly been telling the truth either. He should have said more than a little but less than a lot. His only experience with them was from when he had taken riding lessons as research for a book that he had once been writing and from the manuals he had read to learn about the different breeds and how they behaved and what you had to feed them. But if it had all worked out right in his book, it had been mostly from theory and little practice, and now, he told himself, now we're going to see just how well you learned it.

"The buckskin is blind in one eye," he said. "I can't tell from just looking at her, though, whether it's from an accident or whether it's something like cataracts that'll turn up in the other eye."

"She was born that way, but I couldn't bring myself to shoot her. I used to have grandchildren coming here anyhow, and they got some use from her."

"The one bay has a broken shoe on the right front hoof, but that's no problem if you see to it soon enough. The other two bays look pretty good, although they're getting old and I don't think there's more than a year or two of heavy work left in them. The sorrel's another matter. She's got a swelling on the upper part of the cannon bone that I don't like at all."

"Calcium build-up."

"I don't think so. What did the vet say?"

"Calcium build-up."

"Sure. It looks to me like that's where she's been kicking herself when she runs, though, and if she keeps doing it, she's going to cripple herself. The only one I can't decide on is the pinto. I can't tell if she's sickly or just naturally that slight. I'd have to be suspicious though."

"So what's your judgment?"

"No question, your three bays are the best. The other three are workable if you handle them right, but that sorrel, I doubt you'll see her this time next year, and the pinto, you'd have to go awful easy on her. I take it that if you decide to sell the last three are the ones."

"If I decide to sell. Two horses for packing. You must be taking up a lot of gear."

He shook his head no. "One horse for packing gear, the other for grain and oats."

"Yeah, that's the way I'd do it too. Why not just rent them? As soon as the season's over or the snow's too deep, they won't be any use to you then anyhow. Why not just rent them and save yourself the extra money?"

He shook his head no again. "If I get up there and something happens to one of them, I want to be sure it's my own horse I'm shooting, not somebody else's. I don't want to have to feel that you're looking over my shoulder at your property. When the time comes that I'm done with them, I'll sell them back to you. For a lower price I assume. But the difference will be the same as the rent, and this way they'll still be my horses."

The old man thought about it. "Not bad," he said and started chewing again. "That's as neat as I've ever heard it put. Not bad at all."

"Then it's a deal?"

"Not quite. There's still that other matter we've got to talk about."

"What's that?"

"How much cash you've got to spend. Do you like pure grain liquor?"

"I've never tried it."

"Oh you'll like it fine. Just fine. Why don't we go on in the house and sit a spell and have a glass or two?"

━━━━━━━━━━━━━━━━━━━━━━━━━━ *3*

HE SPOTTED THEM about the same time they spotted him, just as he was coming out of the hardware store, shouldering his knapsack. He'd been in there buying a gun belt for the magnum he had taken from the guy in the backyard, which was a western-style revolver anyhow and seemed to go naturally with a gun belt, a three-inch-wide strap of smooth flat-brown leather with loops for bullets and a small buckled strap around the middle of the holster and a leather thong for tying the holster to his leg. He had no use for tying the holster down. It would be awkward and restrictive but just hanging there the thong was ornate all the same, and this way he wouldn't have to tuck the gun in under the belt of his pants whenever he went walking in the woods with Sarah and he wouldn't have to carry a reserve supply of bullets in his pocket. He bought an extra box of bullets, tucking the gun and the belt and the bullets into his knapsack just before he opened the door and went outside, and he was never quite sure what made him look across the street just then.

They were walking along the sidewalk directly opposite him, two of them, wearing jeans the same as everybody else, but their shirts were different, red-checked wool hunting shirts with khaki army field jackets unbuttoned over them, and one nudged the other, looking over at him. He didn't let on, just stood there long enough to hitch the straps of his knapsack up over one shoulder, and then letting his eyes slip past them toward the post-office truck going by, he started walking slowly down the sidewalk.

It was a warm bright Friday. 3:01 the big clock hanging up over the corner a half a block away said. There were cars and trucks parked all along the street, people from all around came to town to cash their pay-checks and buy supplies and have some fun to start the weekend. A woman was coming toward him, pushing a little boy in a stroller as a man carrying two sacks from a feed and grain store toward a truck at the curb nearly bumped into her.

Take it easy, he told himself.

But he started speeding anyhow and had to force himself to slow.

Just take it easy. This might be nothing. Maybe it's just some girl over here that caught their eye. Maybe they think you're somebody else they used to know.

Maybe nothing.

He wanted to turn around and see if they were still watching him, but he couldn't let himself, and he finally stopped in front of a drugstore, pretending to look at the razors and shaving soaps displayed in the window, glancing at the reflection in the window of them farther along the street, directly opposite him now, standing, staring at him.

He was going into the drugstore before he knew it.

How had they found him this soon?

Never mind this soon. How had they found him at all?

"I need the largest first aid kit you've got," he told

the girl in white behind the counter. "And some heavy grain aspirin and some multiple vitamin tablets." And what else? he thought. What else were they going to need that he had not thought of? And the strain must have showed in his voice because the girl behind the counter looked strangely at him a moment before she went and got what she was told.

The place smelled of disinfectant.

A knife, he thought. When I was in the hardware store I should have bought a knife.

He stood half-hidden behind a counter of hair sprays and bath salts, looking out the window, and they were coming across the street now, waiting for a motorcycle to pass before they kept on coming and stopped between two cars parked at the curb.

"Here you are, sir," the girl said behind him and he turned and she was standing there at the counter putting everything in a large brown paper bag. "That'll be eight dollars and seventy-six cents."

He gave her a ten and took the bag.

"Your change, sir," she said.

But he was already going out the front door.

They were standing there between the two cars, watching him. Twins, he saw, as he turned to the left toward the hardware store. Tall, thin-faced, thin-lipped. Short blond hair, sideburns trimmed even with the middle of their ears. As soon as his back was to them he looked at the reflection in a window that was angled their way and they were following him.

"Hello again," the guy in the hardware store said as he came in.

"I need a skinning knife."

"What kind?"

"I don't care."

The door opened, bell tinkling, and one of them was coming in, pausing to look at him, then walking over to a rack of fish poles, touching them.

"I don't mean what brand," the guy from the hardware store said. "I mean what kind. Short blade, long blade."

"I want a straight blade, five inches long with a double cutting edge, I want a thick metal guard between the handle and the blade."

"Just the thing," the guy said, reaching under the counter.

There were specks of sawdust on the wooden floor. The twin over by the fish poles wasn't touching them anymore, just standing, watching him.

"How about this one?" the guy from the hardware store said, setting a tray of knives on the counter, picking one up and showing it. A dark wood handle with a smooth shiny blade and a thick rounded tip that wouldn't break.

"I need a case for it."

"They come as a package. I'll be with you in a moment, sir."

"I'm just looking," the twin over by the fish poles said.

The twin followed him when he paid and left. This time there wasn't just his double out there but another guy, dressed the same, hair cut the same, but taller, heavier, square-faced with a mustache and a high-powered rifle complete with scope. They were following him so close now that he turned into the next place he came to, a restaurant, drab metal coffee maker behind the horseshoe counter, meringue-topped slabs of pie behind the glass doors of a cooler, hamburgers sizzling greasy on the grill. There were men in cowboy hats sitting at the counter and in some of the booths. There was an old lady in a hairnet working at the grill.

"One of those hamburgers," he said and sat in a booth.

"Three coffees," he heard in the booth behind him.

He almost turned to look.

His agent, he realized. His agent was the only way they could have traced him. On a guess they must have phoned New York and some of their men had gone to see him. God knows what they'd done to make him talk. He should never have phoned him.

But he had to.

Then he should have had the money sent to another town.

But they'd still have traced him. They'd just have gone around to every town nearby until they did.

The hamburger tasted like sawdust.

"Listen, you've got to stop," he stood and turned and said.

"I don't know what you mean," the guy with the mustache looked up and told him. He had his rifle propped barrel up against his leg inside the booth.

"Sure you do. You know damn well what I mean, and you've got to stop."

The guy was frowning at him now. He looked over at the twins across from him in the booth. "You know what he's talking about?"

"No, I don't know what he's talking about," the one twin said.

"No, I don't know either," the other twin said.

"You've been following me. You've been hard on

my back ever since I came out of the hardware store
the first time."

"The hardware store?" the guy with the mustache
said.

"Hey, that's right," the one twin said. "Now that I
think of it, he was in that hardware store while I was
checking out their fishing poles."

"Jesus, stop it!"

Everybody was looking at him now. The old lady
was stopped in mid-motion reaching to flip over a hamburger on the grill. Except for the sizzling of the hamburgers there wasn't a sound.

"Hey listen, buddy, you just better take it easy," the
guy with the mustache said. "I mean I know it's been
hot lately and I can guess what kind of trouble you
maybe have at home, but you've got to take things
more easy. I mean this kind of commotion isn't good
for anybody. I tell you what. If you're so sure that
we've been following you, why don't we go outside and
leave these people to their food and talk about it?"

"No!" he said. He was stumbling back, holding his
stomach, clutching the side of a table. "No!" and he
hoped it looked good because this was the only chance
he was going to get and if he didn't convince them, he
was through. He leaned over, retching dryly, looked up
at a sign pointing through a swinging door toward the
men's room, and lurched toward it as if he needed to
get there fast, shouldering through the door, knapsack
clunking, and his fear now was that this hall would be
a dead end, that there'd only be the men's room, but
there it was, the exit at the far end, and he was straightening, the door flapping behind him as he hurried down
the hallway, praying the exit wouldn't be locked,

twisting the knob and the door opened and he was racing down the narrow garbage can littered alley toward the sidewalk.

_____ *4*

"CLAIRE!" HE SHOUTED, stumbling out of breath up the slope toward the cabin. He tripped and fell, hands out, palms scraping on the hard sun-baked dirt of the wagon road. His face struck the mound of grass between the ruts, sweat smearing across his chin, lips tasting of dust as he staggered to his feet and swayed there a moment before he lurched on up the hill.

He didn't have much time. He was sure they hadn't seen him as he crisscrossed through town and then out through the fields on the other side. They obviously didn't know where he lived. Otherwise they would have come straight here instead of checking out the town. So they only had two choices: either get in their car and drive around until they maybe spotted him, or ask around town, the hardware store guy or the real-estate man, for anybody who might have a line on him. The first was too slow and chancy, the second more sure. Fifteen minutes, a half hour at the most and they'd be here.

He shouted for Claire again, lunging on toward the top, and he had the taste of salt mixed in with the dust in his mouth now, and he knew it was from where his lips must have cracked open when he hit the ground back there.

Sarah was waiting for him at the top.

"Where's your mother?" He was breathing so hard he could hardly get the words out.

"In the house."

"I don't have time to explain. Lie down here and watch the road." His chest was on fire. He could hear his heart pounding. "Yell the second you spot anyone."

She started to say something and he cut her off. "Don't ask questions. Just do what you're told." He was pressing her down, running on toward the cabin, and Claire was standing stark-faced in the open door-way.

"Christ, don't tell me."

"Three of them in town. They can't be far behind. We've got to pack and get out."

"You're sure? There isn't any doubt."

"None at all." And he was slipping off his knapsack, taking out the gun belt and buckling it on. He checked the magnum to make sure it was loaded and holstered it. He hooked the knife in its case onto the gun belt.

"Here," he said to Claire. "Fill my knapsack the same as yours and take them and the saddlebags out back. Grab the blankets off the bed."

"Daddy, someone's coming."

They looked at each other.

"I'll meet you where the trail starts," he said to Claire.

He turned, racing back toward Sarah, and she was standing out there, pointing toward the road.

"Someone's coming! Someone's coming!"

"Get down," he told her, diving, knocking her down

into the grass, crawling to the edge of the slope, and they were coming all right, the same three in their red-checked hunting shirts and jeans and field jackets, small down there, hiking up the road through the trees toward the open slope. Except that they all had rifles now, not just the one with the mustache, and now that he looked harder, none of them had a mustache, and neither of them were twins, and one of them was round-faced instead of thin or square and another was stocky and Christ these weren't the same three at all. They were coming in shifts. And they were so sure of themselves that they were just coming casually up like that in open sight.

Or maybe the other three were in the woods behind the cabin.

"Get moving," he told Sarah. "Your mother's waiting at the trail."

But she didn't move, and when he looked, she was holding her stomach, gasping from when he had knocked her down, and he had to grab her, dragging her back with him, saying, "Hurry, sweetheart. You've got to go."

He managed to get her on her feet, running, holding herself, around toward the back of the house, and he was rushing into the house again, up the stairs to the tower on top, the only spot in the house where he could see to them. He had to create a diversion, slow them, force them to think he was making a stand from the house, and the moment he came dodging to the side of the open window up there, he was drawing his gun, firing three times blindly, recoil kicking, down toward them, watching them scatter as he fired yet once more and ducked out of the tower toward the stairs, hearing the ca-rack of a high-powered rifle, the window shattering loudly behind him.

He nearly fell rushing down the stairs. He swerved around into the kitchen and out the back door and Claire and Sarah were up there where the trees started, waiting on the trail.

"Those shots," Claire said.

"Me. Don't worry about it." And then they were moving again, him hoisting the knapsacks up one over each shoulder, Claire lifting the saddlebags, running awkwardly, Sarah racing short-legged ahead of them. It was cool in under the trees, the branches bare, leaves spread crisply yellow all around them. There were fall birds singing and then the birds stopped and they ran harder, thrashing through the leaves, working up through the trail between the trees toward the upper level.

They'll hear where we've gone, he thought.

But there wasn't anything he could do about it and he was too out of breath to worry about it anyhow, and then the trail turned to the right, grew steeper, turned to the left, even steeper, and they came bursting out of the trees into the sunlit level clearing up there.

They came so loudly, so abruptly, that the three horses skittered nervously in the corral, backing off, neighing, into one corner. He had found this place the second day after they'd come here. A log-fenced corral with water and feed troughs and one tumbled-down equipment shed from where the cabin's owner must have kept his horses during hunting season. That was what had given him the idea of the horses in the first place, and he had brought Claire and Sarah up here to show them what to do if trouble ever came, going over with them what they'd learned when he had taken riding lessons, and each day he'd come up here to feed and exercise the animals. In the end he'd even persuaded the old man to let him have one of the bays instead of the lame sorrel, and he'd pretended to be unhappy about the pinto even though he was secretly glad because a horse that small was perfect for Sarah, and if the buckskin was blind in one eye, at least it could run and he thought he knew enough to be able to handle it.

"Help me with the saddles," he told Claire, dropping the knapsacks, shouldering open the door to the shed. Claire was dropping the saddlebags, helping him heave the saddles up onto the fence, and Sarah was doing exactly what she'd been told, running around the corral to where the horses were, climbing onto the fence and shooing them over toward the shed. He paused just a second to make sure she wasn't getting into trouble with them, and then he was grabbing the bridles from the shed, vaulting the fence, waiting till a horse came near, the pinto, slipping a bit into its mouth, hitching a halter up over its ears, buckling it. He slid a saddle blanket down over the pinto's back, easing a saddle onto it, cinching it, going on to the next horse, the bay this time, while Claire tied a pair of saddlebags onto the pinto behind him.

It was taking too long, he told himself. They'll be up here any minute.

He tried to hurry, but that only made him clumsy, and he had to slow and do it right, finishing with the bay, turning to the buckskin, and the buckskin shied away and he had to waste time calming it.

"I hear them. They're coming," Claire said.

And she was right. The trees down there were echoing with the sound of someone rushing up through the leaves.

"Open the gate," he told Sarah, helping Claire buckle on her knapsack, easing her onto the horse.

"Get going," he said, slapping the bay, and it bolted through the open gate, breaking into a sudden gallop, almost dropping her. He picked up Sarah and set her on the pinto, slapping it as well, telling her "Hang on" as the pinto bolted through the gate after Claire across the clearing, and then he was finished with the buckskin, buckling on his own knapsack, swinging up into the saddle. The thrashing in the leaves was so close now that the sound wasn't even echoing anymore. He kicked the buckskin sharply in the ribs, and digging its back hooves into the ground, the horse charged forward, lurching so close past one side of the open gate that he had to lift his leg to keep from crushing it.

Ca-rack and something whunked into the trees ahead to one side of him. He kicked the buckskin harder, forcing it faster across the clearing, his holster thumping against his leg. He saw Claire and Sarah galloping up throught the trees and the trees were looming closer as he heard another ca-rack, a simultaneous whunk, and this time something was punching against his back nearly jerking him off his horse as he leaned close to the horse's neck, frantically kicking, thinking your knapsack, it's all right, you're not hit, they only hit your knapsack, and then he was into the trees, galloping up after Claire and Sarah, and there was another ca-rack, another whunk, this one just past him into a tree, bark flying, but it didn't matter because the trees were too dense now for them to get a shot at him anymore and he was riding hard up toward the sound of hooves thudding and for now he was safe.

The light changed almost immediately. He glanced up through the dark bare branches of the trees, expecting clouds, and saw instead that the sun was already half down behind the western crest of the mountains far off to the right up there, swollen, flooding the forest with red. A half hour till dusk, and then an hour till dark. They had to get as far off by then as they could. He could hear where the two horses were thudding up ahead of him to his left now, and he reached to where the trail turned up that way, easing off on the half-blind horse, letting it pick its own way carefully. The trail straightened, angling higher, and he had to lean forward, clutching the saddle horn as the horse surged up over the top, jostling him, picking up speed across another open level toward Claire and Sarah galloping. He saw Claire kicking her horse, hooves pounding into the sparse brown grass, clods flying, Sarah's pinto following, and he was kicking his own horse faster toward them, gaining, coming up behind, and then they were all three together, angling to the left across the level toward another trail up through the trees. They took it one at a time, Claire leading, Sarah in the middle, and then they were up on yet another level, angling left again, always left. It was the way he had practiced with them, the way he had shown them on the terrain maps he had bought in town. If somebody came they needed to get as far up into the mountains as fast as they could, and the route they were taking was the only way.

Two levels up they finally saw it, a sheer wall of rock that showed clearly on the terrain map and the narrow wash of boulders and shale and rotting timber that was the only way up through it. The map hadn't shown whether they could climb it though, and this was the farthest he had come to scout, clearing some of the timber, charting a route, and he knew it was a chance but it was their only chance and they had to take it. The next route up over this cliff was twenty miles to the right.

They came galloping up to the base of it, reining hard, dismounting. The horses couldn't have kept up this pace anyhow. The sun was almost down behind the mountains, the air suddenly cold and gray, and his eyes were watering from the rush of the ride as he rubbed his sleeve across them, staring up past the cliff walls on both sides toward the gray-white tangle of rocks and timber that stretched up the quarter-mile wash in front of them.

"My jacket," he told Claire. "In my knapsack. You and Sarah put yours on too." It was a solid brown woolen jacket with a hood. He had chosen it to blend with the autumn color of the mountains, Claire's and Sarah's the same, and the moment he was finished buttoning it, feeling the sudden heavy warmth against him, he grabbed his horse's reins and started up through the fallen timber, crisscrossing, working as hard and as fast as he could, first this way and then that, the horse struggling to hold back on him as he stopped to let it find a better footing before he urged it farther on. He slipped, scraping his face against a boulder, righting himself, tugging steadily on the horse's reins, glancing back to make sure that Claire and Sarah were keeping up, that they weren't in any trouble. Claire was doing fine but she wasn't getting much speed, held back by Sarah in the middle who was having problems scrambling up herself, let alone leading a horse behind her.

"Daddy, I can't make it!"

"You've got to. Take your time. Take it one step at a time."

And then she was angling nearer, and he started up again, working this way and that, past boulders, in and around mazes of timber, shouldering logs painfully to one side. He glanced back toward where they'd come from through the trees. Nobody. He looked up ahead, and the top of the wash seemed as far away as ever.

Keep moving.

"Daddy!"

He looked back, and she was leaning exhausted against a rock.

"Don't stop," he told her. "You've got to keep moving. We're almost there," he lied.

And little by little she pushed herself off from the rock, struggling with the horse, and then the horse reared up, almost kicking her as she fell out of the way between two boulders, and the horse struggled to turn in the narrow space and lunge back down the slope.

"Don't move," he yelled to her, tying his horse to a log, scrambling down toward her. "Don't move. Tuck your legs in."

He was coming down fast, jarring his shoulder against a stout branch on a log, holding himself, wincing, as he made it down, one hand out now to quiet the horse, saying, "There now, there now," settling it, for the first time noticing the echo of his words.

"It's all right now. Come on out," he told her, and

she was crying, frightened, exhausted, and he should never have tried to make her lead the horse up in the first place, a miracle that she had got it up even this far.

"We'll leave one horse here for now. You're coming up with me," he told her, holding her, and then to Claire, "Tie yours. Bring the pinto. I'll come back for yours as soon as we make it up there."

And he didn't have time to quiet Sarah much, just to dry her tears and kiss her once, holding her, and then he was helping her up to where he'd tied his own horse, sending her on ahead, Claire working up with the pinto behind her, the bay standing tied farther back down there, looking blankly around, confused, alone.

Maybe it was because she was frightened or maybe in a kind of hysterical shock from when the horse had nearly kicked her, but Sarah made it to the top well ahead of him and at least she was safe, and wanting to have someone up there with her he worked even harder up through the rocks and timber, reaching a barren open stretch near the top, hooves clattering on the smooth weathered stone slope, up over the top into wind and scrub grass and a seemingly endless sweep of trees. Sarah was slumped down against a stump, face white, breathing hard, wind blowing through her hair. He touched her going past, tying his horse to a nearby tree, slipping off his knapsack, rushing back to the edge, and Claire was just then coming up over the top. He pointed warningly toward Sarah behind him, rushing on past, down the slope toward the horse they'd left behind, slipping. A jumble of rocks spilled out from under him, bouncing down the slope toward the horse, nearly hitting it, flying past as the horse tried to rear up and avoid them, and he had to take things slower, glancing now at the horse, now at the tree line down there, expecting any moment to see the red of hunting shirts as they ran up onto the level.

No, he thought. Night coming, they'll go for horses first. They won't try to come for us on foot.

But he kept glancing toward the tree line anyhow and then he was even with the horse, gentling it, untying it, working as fast as he could with it up the slope. They were eating when he finally came up over the edge, and it was all he could make himself do to tie the horse with the others before he slumped down beside them. Chocolate bars. And they should have been too sticky and sickly sweet, but he was so tired, so in need of quick energy, that he hardly tasted the sugar of the caramel and chocolate at all, just chewing, swallowing one, biting into another.

"We made it. I can't believe we made it."

But they really hadn't, he knew that. This was only the first step, and if they were ever going to get away, they were going to have to keep moving longer, faster, farther up into the mountains.

He reached over to stop Sarah from taking another candy bar.

"Better save them, sweetheart. We're going to need them all before this is done."

He looked down at the blood on his hands from where he'd cut them on the boulders, wiped them on the grass, stood and walked over to the edge of the cliff, looking down past the clearing toward the trees.

No one.

"Let's get moving," he turned and told them.

"Already?" Claire said. "But we only just sat down."

He pointed up to where the sun had disappeared entirely behind the mountains. The light around them was pale, turning into darkness. "We've still got maybe a half hour before we'll have to stop anyhow because of the dark. We have to use all the time we've got." He reached into his knapsack and took out a terrain map, studying it, barely able to make out the contour lines in the dusk. "There's a stream up through these trees. About a mile. Let's see if we can make it." Then the wind gusted harder, blowing dust and leaves, and he looked out toward the east where black clouds were hulking in the last light on the horizon.

"Storm coming maybe," he said.

But it never did, and the horses were still so tired that they had to be walked, the three of them leading their horses up through the shadows of the trees into the stillness just before night.

5

AT FIRST he thought that he'd misread the map. They'd come at least a mile now he was sure, and still no sign of the stream, and the trees were closing in on them in the fast-fading light. He led them into a small clearing that would have been perfect for camp with another small clearing closeby joined to the first by a small game trail like the narrow part of an hourglass, and the second clearing was partly free of leaves, patches of mountain grass showing through where the horses could eat, and if they wouldn't get much nutrition from it, at least they would get some, and he wouldn't have to use the small sack of oats he'd tied to the saddle horn on the buckskin when he was saddling it.

The light was so bad now that he decided they'd have to do without water for the night and use this place anyhow when he heard it. Hardly anything at all, just a faint trickle, but it was enough, and tying his horse to the limb of a tree, he pushed through some bare branches to where the mound of the clearing sloped down, and there it was, a stream just wide enough that he couldn't step across. It rounded this edge of the clearing, running smoothly and freely down to a different section of the lowland they'd just come from, and he knelt in the cool stillness, stooping to rinse his hands and cup cold water to his mouth.

"Is it all right to drink?" he heard Claire say behind him.

He was just then tasting it, knowing the answer even before he did, cold and sweet and pure, cupping more to his mouth, rubbing his wet hands all over his face, turning to her. "This far up it almost always is. You just have to make sure it's running and there isn't any scum on it. Mostly the trouble comes in the spring when you get snow melted with red algae on it. That stuff will hurt you, give you cramps so bad you'd swear you were going to die."

From one of his books, he remembered.

He almost smiled.

"Come on and try some. You too, sweetheart," he said to Sarah beside her.

They didn't move.

"I know it seems strange, but this isn't like the streams near town. I wouldn't drink that water myself. But this. This is all right. Believe me."

They still didn't move, so he turned again to the stream, easing down onto his stomach, dipping his face in, nostrils aching with cold water as he drank. When he sat up, shaking his head, wet hair dripping, he saw them drinking uncertainly beside him.

"It tastes funny," Sarah said.

"Of course," he said. "This doesn't have fluoride and a lot of other chemicals in it. This is the real thing."

"But it's dirty. I can feel something gritty against my teeth," she said and spat.

"That's just a little silt. It'll give you roughage."

"Give me what?"

"Nothing," he said and smiled. "Just drink some more. Get used to it. This is the only kind of water you're going to have for a while, so whether you like it or not, you're going to *have* to get used to it."

"But where does it come from?"

"Up on top some place. Snow melting, lakes draining." And then thinking of the lakes, "You're going to see things you've never even dreamed of before."

"It tastes kind of sweet."

"There, you see, now you're getting the idea. Come on. We've got a lot of work to do. It'll soon be so dark that we won't be able to move without bumping into each other."

He was leading them back up the rise through the trees into the clearing, and the dark was upon them enough now that it was distorting everything, making the campsite seem wider, larger.

"Here," he told Sarah, handing her the three canteens from the saddles on the horses. "Take these down to the stream and fill them."

"You forgot to fill them when you stored them with the saddles in the shed?" Claire said.

"No, I didn't forget. I deliberately didn't do it. I figured the horses would have enough weight to carry at the start and I knew there'd be plenty of water up here anyhow. Besides, the water would just have gotten stale from sitting in them so long. What are you waiting for?" he said to Sarah.

"I'm scared."

"To go back there alone?"

She nodded.

"There's nothing to be afraid of. If anybody comes, you'll be able to hear them in plenty of time to get to me."

"But what about animals?"

"You'll hear them too. Anyway it would only be deer or elk. This time of year the bears have all settled in for the winter. Go on. There's a lot of work to do and we've each got to do our share."

He waited until she started off, and then turned to the buckskin, uncinching it, slipping off the saddle. "Better uncinch the other horses," he said to Claire. "Arrange the saddles for pillows where there's a place that looks comfortable for us to sleep."

"What about a fire? Shouldn't we see to that before anything?"

"No," he said and turned to her. "No fire. Not until we absolutely have to."

"But how will we cook?"

"We won't. Not tonight. In the morning if we've got

time and we can build a small fire that won't make much smoke, then maybe. But not tonight. There's too good a chance they got their hands on some horses faster than we expected, and if they're anywhere around up here, they're liable to see the light from a fire and come over."

They looked at each other, and then the pinto began tugging at where its reins were tied to the branch of a tree and Claire went over to it.

"What do you want for supper?" she asked quietly.

"We don't have much choice, do we?"

"That's right," she said, uncinching the pinto's saddle, slipping it off and carrying it awkwardly past him toward the base of a tree, and she didn't look like she was going to say anything more after that, so he just said "Help your mother" to Sarah coming up through the trees with the canteens drooping heavily from her arms, and taking the coil of rope from the buckskin's saddle on the ground, he led the horse out of the clearing, down the narrow game trail into the second clearing.

There were three ways to do this, he knew. He could tie the horse by a long rope to a tree, but horses got curious the same as people and if there were some smell on the other side of the clearing that the buckskin wanted to investigate, it would only get frustrated from not being able to go over. As well he could hobble its hooves together, tying the front ones to the back, in which case the horse could move just a little with each step, eventually getting over to what interested it but just as likely to get frightened, try to move too fast, fall and break a leg. Which left the third way, and he had to search the edge of the clearing for quite a while before he found a fallen log that was big enough that the horse wouldn't get into the forest with it but small enough that the horse could still drag it around, and tying a makeshift halter around the horse's head, he tied the other end of the rope securely to the log. Then he slipped off the horse's bridle, easing out the bit, and let the horse sniff the grass, smell the air, before it finally settled down to eating.

Water, he thought. Christ, I forgot to let it get at the water.

So he led the other horses to the stream next time and let them drink their fill before he took them over to the next clearing and anchored them each to a log the same as he had done with the first. Then he came back with a canteen and his hat, filling the hat, letting the buckskin drink repeatedly until he had to come back with yet another canteen, and finally the horse had drunk enough. He looked around at the little he could see of the clearing, the horses in separate parts of it, eating, occasionally lifting their heads to sense the air. The pinto made a low flat rumbling noise in its throat, but it didn't seem nervous, and he guessed that they were going to be all right. The only thing that could go wrong was for them to get tangled in each other's rope, but he didn't see how he could prevent that. All the same he waited with them. There was a moon coming up. He couldn't see it yet, but he could make out the change in the night, a kind of chill white glow that was spreading over the horizon. Somewhere close by a few crickets had started. He didn't understand how they could still be alive up here with the cold coming on, but they were, and their sound was unmistakable. He took a deep breath, certain without seeing that it was coming out in frost, and then at last turning, the dew on the grass soaking through his pant legs, he started back to camp.

"You're not eating," he said when he came down the game trail across the clearing toward them. They were sitting on the ground, propped up huddled against their saddles. In the dark he could only make out the vague white of their faces.

"We're waiting for you," Claire said.

"Just a minute longer."

He went down to the stream again, filling the two canteens, and then looking around down there as well, satisfied that everything was all right, he came back to them.

"There's just the one last thing to do," he said.

"And what else after that?" Claire said.

"No, really, there's just the one last thing to do. I know this is tedious and seems to go on forever, but it all has to be done, and as soon as we get used to this, it'll all get done much faster."

"Well, what is it?" Claire said.

"This business of going to the bathroom."

"Oh, Daddy," Sarah said.

He couldn't tell if she was embarrassed or just thinking he was funny.

"No, listen. Come on over here. It's important."

He was walking over to the far edge of the clearing, standing just inside the trees, waiting for them.

"Peeing isn't any problem," he said when they came over.

"Maybe not for you it isn't. All you have to do is stand behind a tree and let it go, but with us it's a little more complicated," Claire said.

"I know. I'm getting to that. Just wait a little." He turned his head abruptly toward where something skittered through the leaves out there. A raccoon maybe or a badger. Nothing to worry about. Just take it easy, he told himself. All the same he kept his head turned that way a moment longer before he looked back at them. "Peeing isn't any problem. The only thing you've got to remember is not to do it anywhere near the stream. We're drinking from it after all, and if anything seeps down into it, we're not going to like the taste very much, not to mention the hell it'll play on our insides. Pick a slope that drains away from it. I know you've got to dry yourselves, and the only thing I can suggest is some leaves that aren't too brittle. If you don't want to use leaves, you're just going to have to wash yourselves carefully after you go. You'll probably want to do that anyhow—dried urine will leave a rash.

"OK, that's fairly simple. It doesn't give us much problem. But the other business, the solid waste, does. We don't want to leave it spread all around the trees around our camp. We find a big rock like this. We turn it over and dig out some of the dirt underneath like this, and when we're done, we fill in the dirt and then we set the rock back on top and then we wash ourselves, and we have to make sure we go every day. It doesn't matter if we feel we have to or not. We've got to go. There's only one rule up here. You don't do anything you don't think through first. You wash yourselves every day. You go to the bathroom every day. You rinse your clothes out whenever you can. You eat even if you don't want to. I'm making an issue of all this because there'll be times when you're so tired and dirty that you won't feel like doing anything but lying there, and the next thing you know you'll have body sores and you'll be sick and you might just as well give up then because you won't even have the sense of an animal."

He started to say something more, but he realized that he'd only be repeating himself and he didn't like the idea of making a speech at them anyhow, so he just stood there, feeling strangely empty and embarrassed while they looked at him, and then rousing himself, fighting to break the mood and sound cheerful, "Anybody hungry?"

"Yes." Sarah's voice was so quiet that it seemed she hardly opened her mouth or even breathed.

"Let's go eat then. I know what. Why don't we try a vitamin pill for dessert?"

But it wasn't much of a joke, and nobody even smiled.

————————————— 6

THEY ATE BEEF JERKY and a can of peaches, slipping the peaches into their mouths and chewing hungrily, sharing the thick syrup, drinking plenty of water. There was only one blanket for each of them, and they slept rolled up in the blankets, crowding close to each other, Sarah in the middle. Once Sarah woke, saying "I'm cold," and he soothed her back to sleep. Later he himself woke from the explosion, and he sat upright before he registered the muffled roar and saw the faint red and green flickering of the underwing lights far off up there and understood that what he'd heard was a sonic boom.

The early songs of the morning birds roused them just before dawn, and when he went to check on the horses, he found that one of them had got tangled in the rope of another after all, but they didn't hurt themselves, and he led them all back to camp, letting them drink from the stream, feeding them each a handful of oats, then saddling them. There wasn't time for a fire to cook, he finally decided, and after tending to themselves, washing, urinating, they ate as they rode, more beef jerky, some crackers, a little chocolate.

"We'll stop somewhere later on and cook up a complete meal," he told them, but it was a lie, he just wanted to get them moving and keep them moving. He needed to get them as far off as he could. Whenever they came into a broad open space, they broke into a canter, never urging the horses very much, saving their strength, letting them move at what seemed their most comfortable pace, slowing as they worked through more trees. By eight the sun was well up over the horizon to the east, warming them, drying the dampness out of their clothes. By nine they were walking the horses, by nine-fifteen riding again, and that became the pattern, ride forty-five minutes, walk fifteen. He stopped and gave the horses a rest at noon.

"This is where we'll be going for tonight," he told Claire and Sarah, showing them on the map where there was a lake and then pointing directly up from them toward a far-off fir slope between two low-slung peaks. "We'll have to go some to make it but I think we can, and there's a half dozen lakes on either side so it won't be obvious that this one is where we've gone."

He heard the far-off constant rumble of a motor as he mounted, and looking back the way they'd come made out the flash of a helicopter a long way off down there above the trees.

"For us?" Claire said. "Them looking for us?"

"Maybe. I don't know. It could be just the forest service checking out what looks like the start of a fire. It could be anyone. If it is them, they won't be anywhere near us today. There's a lot of square miles up here for them to cover, and their best bet is still to come tracking us on horseback."

"You're sure they'll be coming?"

"They didn't try very hard for us back at the cabin. In some ways the point isn't even to catch us, just to keep after us."

"You mean if they catch up to us again they might just give us a start?"

"They might. It's hard to say. But the snow will be here soon. It's held off too long already. And when it comes, this won't be like any camping trip anymore. They'll want to end it as fast as they can so they can get out."

The helicopter was rumbling closer to them.

"We'd better go," he said, nudging his horse, Claire and Sarah coming behind. There were fir trees mixed in with the bare aspen and dogwood now, giving them better cover, and he knew that in a few hours they would be up where there were only the fir trees, so tall and thick that they wouldn't be spotted even if a helicopter did fly over.

They came to where a stream angled down from left to right ahead of them, stopping briefly, letting the horses drink.

"Can't we ride up through the stream and try to hide our tracks?" Claire said.

"It wouldn't work. The bed's too soft, the water too slow. Three horses riding up would leave tracks that maybe wouldn't wash away for another day or two. What you want is swift water and a gravel bottom, and even then the trick would only slow them down, it wouldn't stop them. They'd just split up and follow either bank until they saw where we came out and then they'd be following again."

He had a strange kind of doubling. *The stream twisted and turned, and he followed it. Soon there would be dogs after him he knew, but he did not bother wading in the stream to try to throw them off his scent. That would only slow them down, and since he would have to come out of the water sometime on one bank or the other, the man working the dogs would merely split the pack along both banks until they picked up the scent again, and he himself would just have wasted time.* He'd been here before, said this before.

No, he'd written it. And there had been a helicopter then too, and he was suddenly certain that the helicopter was definitely not the forest service at all, shaking his head to clear it, not just nudging his horse now but kicking it, urging it farther up into the trees, shouting for Claire and Sarah to follow. He surged up to a fir bow, leaning low to clear it, straightening, galloping farther up the slope, getting control of himself, slowing as he neared the top.

"What was that about?" Claire called, riding up behind him.

"Nothing," he said. "I thought I saw something. It was nothing."

The next level was entirely fir trees, close and cool and shadowed, no longer the thrashing of the horses' hooves through crisp fallen leaves, just the slow steady muffled plodding over the thick carpet of dead brown lodgepole needles.

"We won't be going to that lake after all," he told them, certain he had said this before too. "If that *is* them in a helicopter down there, it would be too easy for them to land in some clearing nearby and check those lakes up there to find us. There aren't that many lakes anyhow and they aren't very big, just a small cluster of them."

"Then where will we go?"

"Up around to the left. The map says there's another stream up there."

"But I want to see the lake," Sarah said.

"I know it. So do I. But this is how we'll be doing things for a while. We'll pick a spot where we want to go, but we'll figure the spot is so obvious they can guess we'll be going there, and then we'll pick another less attractive place. It's a matter of guessing and second-guessing. Don't worry. You'll see lakes in time. A lot of them. But not just yet."

The level became another rise, and they angled up across it.

7

THE STREAM WAS BETTER than he'd hoped, not like a brook but a real stream, wide and swift and deep, surging loudly down a trough of rock into a big smooth stone basin and then swirling over the lip of the basin down the slope again. They reached it an hour before dusk, hearing the roar before they came plodding slowly up through a thick patch of trees and saw it strangely magnified.

Sarah was already off her horse and running toward it when he stopped her.

"Hey!"

She turned and looked at him.

"First we work. These horses are a lot more tired than you are, only they can't take care of themselves. You just pitch in and help, and then maybe we can all have some time in the water."

She looked once more at the water and came slowly back.

"Another thing. The way you threw those reins around that branch, your horse could have broken loose in a second. If she got deep into those trees and something spooked her, we could have spent all night trying to find her. I told you last night. You've got to be careful."

She was knotting the reins securely now, not looking at him.

"Fill the canteens the same as you did before and then help your mother."

She nodded, still not looking at him, and she didn't look at him all the time he was uncinching the saddles, watering the horses, feeding them the last of the oats, at last tethering them.

"OK," he said, coming up behind her and touching her shoulders. "Now we can take care of ourselves."

But she didn't make a move to come with him and he had to tug at her.

"Hey now, listen," he said, turning her around, lifting her chin to look at him. "When somebody corrects you, take it. No moods. No pouting. I'll forget this if you will. But next time do it right. Is that a deal?"

She nodded her head slowly.

"All right then. Come on. Let's get in the water."

He was already sitting on the rim of the basin, taking off his boots and socks before she made a move to join him.

_____ 8

"THESE MAPS. You might as well learn about them. In case something happens to me."

There were three of them, wrapped in a plastic folder in his jacket pocket. He took them out, opening one of the area around them. It was two-feet square, an apparent jumble of blue curving lines and occasional random numbers.

"The lines are slopes and ridges. The numbers are altitude. There are only two things you need to know to read one of these. First, the contour lines don't always represent the same height. You need to look at this code down here at the bottom of the map. Vertical scale fifty feet, it says. So all right, every blue line means a change of fifty feet. If the line curves like this ⁀, you'll be going up. If it curves like this ⁔, you'll be going down. Horizontal scale one inch to one thousand feet, it says. So you know that if you get only a few contour lines every inch you'll be going into country that isn't very steep. But if you get the contour lines so close together that you can hardly tell them apart, then you know you're going to have a cliff in front of you. Like this:

Where the lines curve and spread up is the draw we came up last night. The close straight lines on either side are the cliffs. Of course the draw could still have been so cluttered with rocks that we couldn't manage it. The map isn't detailed enough to give that kind of information, and from now on we'll just have to take our chances. We'll chart a route before we start, and if we come to a place that isn't passable, we'll have to chart another route. The trouble is, the people against us can read a map as well. They know which places look easy, and they'll be waiting for us there. We'll have to pick routes that aren't as likely as others."

"You said two things," Claire told him. "What's the second?"

"This," he said, reaching into his pocket.

Sarah's eyes widened with interest.

"So far I haven't needed to use it. Our direction has been fairly simple and mostly we've been able to see the spot we're going to. But once we get over the next ridge, we'll be going down to a level that's almost as low as where we started and then we'll be going up again, only the country on the other side is full of box canyons and intersecting ridges, and in a while we'll be so turned around that we won't know which way is north and south anymore. We'll have to start lining up our map and using the compass."

"What about the sun?" Claire said. "Or that business about moss on trees?"

"Moss grows every direction on trees, and the sun doesn't move directly east to west. The only way to be sure is to use a compass. There's an awful lot of hunters who tried it the other way, using the sun, and all they managed to do was get themselves lost and die up here."

"Isn't that what we are anyhow? We know where we are and everything, but we're lost just the same, aren't we? Where are we going? What are we going to do?"

"I don't know," he waited and said, "I suppose we'll try making it over the top of these mountains and down the other side—unless the snow gets here first. If it does. . . ."

He didn't know what else to say, so he just let his words trail off and sat back against a tree, watching Sarah play with the compass, turning it, smiling as the needle always swung round to the same direction.

9

"DADDY, I'M SICK."

He was back at the house just after Ethan had died and the doctor had given them the pills, him rushing up the stairs to her, saying "How bad?" her answering "I have to throw up." Only he wasn't back at the house at all. He was huddled cold and damp in his blanket in the clearing near the stream, and someone was shaking him, saying "Daddy, I'm sick," as he came awake enough to see her lurching away from him hand over her mouth to behind a tree and retching. He was instantly up and around to her, holding her. Claire was beside him.

"What is it?"

"I don't know yet."

Sarah retched again, nothing coming up, face ashen, stomach heaving violently. With his hand over her stomach, it felt like something in there punching at him.

"Daddy," she moaned, gasping, and the spasms were convulsive now, abrupt hollow sounds coming up her throat from her stomach as she heaved once totally and a thin stream of dull yellow bile shot out of her mouth, collapsing her. She lay on her side in the grass by the tree, holding herself, knees tucked up, moaning.

"Sssshh," he said. "Take it easy. There's nothing to worry about."

And he'd said that before too and he didn't know what was happening to his mind as he knelt beside her, touching her cold clammy forehead, feeling her frantic heartbeat, standing, trying to think.

"Is it something she ate?" Claire said. "Some of our food that went bad?"

"No, we all ate the same thing, and anyway you can see that she digested it. She's not bringing up anything but bile."

"What is it then?"

"I think it's altitude sickness."

"It's what? I don't understand."

"She's smaller than us and she's reacting faster and that run up through the draw the other night must have taken more out of her than I thought."

"I still don't understand."

"Salt. She's used up all her salt, and there hasn't been enough in the food we're eating."

She was on her knees again, saying "Daddy" just as she shot up more bile and he was kneeling beside her once more, holding her, saying, "It's going to be all right. Don't worry. It's going to be all right," looking up at Claire. "The air's too thin up here. You have to work harder and you sweat more. But you need the salt to keep water in your blood, and if you don't get it, you just keep on sweating, losing more water. It doesn't matter how much water you drink. You'll just keep on losing it."

"My God, you mean she's going to die?"

He looked sharply up at her, gesturing with his head that he didn't want Sarah to hear as Sarah said "No more" and vomited again, hardly anything coming up.

"Not if I can help it. We've got to get her down out of here. Quick, hold her while I saddle the horses."

He was running across the clearing to where he'd tethered the horses, this time to trees because there wasn't room enough for them to move around anyhow, close enough for them to reach the stream and drink, pale mist rising off it in the cold morning air, thinking, salt, I've got to get her some salt, why didn't I think to bring salt?

10

THE SHACK was padlocked. He could see that from where he lay on top of a slope that angled down through the pine trees toward the front door. The window next to it was shuttered as he assumed the others would be. There was a corral to the left and a feed shed, it padlocked as well, and the place looked like nobody had been around for a while, but he couldn't take the chance.

He crawled back from the top of the slope, not standing until he was sure that he could not be seen by anybody from below, and began circling through the trees, stopping from time to time to study the shack from a different direction. Still no sign of anybody. He kept checking the ground ahead of him for any tracks where somebody might have gone down to the shack, but there weren't any although that didn't mean much. Anybody after him would know enough to hide their tracks. All the same he checked the ground.

He came carefully down through the pine trees well

off to one side, glancing at the shack, glancing around him, continuing to circle. If he had finally noticed the dot on the map that was this shack, they could have too, and since this was the only one nearby, they could easily have guessed that this was where he might come for more equipment and food.

And salt. Up above where he had first been studying the shack, Claire and Sarah were waiting, and if he had to take his time and check this shack out thoroughly, he also had to hurry. If Sarah kept on retching, she might start showing blood.

There was a wooded hollow on the other side of the corral, and when he had completed his circle, certain there were no tracks, he came up through it, stopping to listen for any sound of someone waiting, going on up, reaching the corral and circling it as well, keeping the feed shed between him and the shuttered window on this side. There were no windows in the shed and the door was securely locked he saw, so he didn't have to worry about someone in there. No one would be able to break out in time to get at him.

He bolted over to the side of the shack, listening next to the shuttered window for any sound from in there, finally made his choice, picked up a broken piece of crowbar, ducked around to the front door of the cabin, and worked the metal between the lock and the door. One quick jerk and the lock cracked away, wood splintering. The next thing he was dropping the crowbar, angling in through the door, gun ready, and there was no one.

At least he thought there was no one. But it was dark in there, especially after the bright sunlight he had come through, and he ran crouched to the corner on his right, stopping motionless, waiting for his eyes to adjust before he was sure. There were wooden bunks one on top of the other against the left wall, mattresses gone, no springs, just wooden slats. There was a black potbelly stove to the right, metal ducts going up through the ceiling. The place smelled of damp rotting wood, equipment packed high on shelves against the back wall, heavy bulging burlap sacks hanging from the rafters.

He was a moment before he relaxed enough to move, breathing slowly. At the door he waved for Claire and Sarah to come down, waiting, not seeing them, fearing someone had come upon them, and then through the trees up there he saw them emerge, Claire riding double with Sarah, holding her, leading the buckskin and the pinto. They grew larger as they came down, and just where the rocky trail that led down to the shack turned into soft ground he motioned for them to stop, going over, helping Sarah off. She slumped down onto the ground.

"Feeling any better?"

She nodded weakly.

"Sure." And then to Claire dismounting, "Wait here with the horses. I'll bring you what I find and you can load it."

He found two sleeping bags wrapped in plastic on the second shelf. They weren't what he was looking for but they were the first things that caught his eyes and he took them out to Claire anyhow, going back in, looking for the salt. The rancher who stocked this place surely must have left some. The guy would need it for his horses in the spring, and for any of his men who might get caught in a blizzard up here or for anybody else who might get into trouble.

But there wasn't any on the shelves, just cans of beef

and salmon and sardines, flour and Bisquick and pan-
cake mix wrapped in plastic bags, navy beans, raisins,
everything but salt, and there wasn't any salt in the
first sack he took down from the rafters, nor from the
second, and he was beginning to get worried now, rushing toward the third and final sack when he suddenly
realized and went back to the second, and there it was,
only he had thought that the plastic bag mixed in with
the coiled ropes and leather straps and cinches was
nuggets of sugar candy and now he was tasting it bit-
terly and it was rock salt, tiny solid chunks of it, clouded
white and sometimes specked with black. He took a big
piece, sucking on it as he hurried out the door and over
to Sarah.

"Put this on your tongue," he said. "Don't try to
swallow. You'll only bring it up. Here," he said to
Claire, giving her some, and then back to Sarah, "Suck
on it. Take a sip of water. Just a sip."

And then he heard it again, the drone of the motor.
At first it was so far off and low that he couldn't be
certain, and then it was unmistakable. He looked at
Claire, and she had heard it too. They didn't need to
say anything. Claire was already hoisting Sarah up
onto the horse and he was already putting his boot
into the stirrup of the buckskin when he realized.
The shack. He couldn't leave the shack looking like
someone had been here.

He ran back through the open door, starting to hook
the sacks up onto the rafters when he thought better,
dumping the second sack, stuffing its ropes and straps
into the first, hooking that one onto the rafters, taking
the empty sack and filling it with cans and boxes from
the shelves, careful not to take so many from one place

that the gap would be obvious. He ran to the door again, closing it behind him, setting down the awkward bulging sack and fumbling to replace the padlock as best he could, shoving its screws back into the wood, cramming a big chunk of wood back into the door. The repairs wouldn't fool anyone up close, but from far back it would look like no one had been there, and anyway it was better than leaving the door broken open to advertise, and he'd spent as much time fixing it as he could afford, picking up the sack and racing with it to Claire and Sarah with the horses, hooking it onto the saddle horn of the buckskin and swinging up into the saddle. The motor was louder now, its muffled roar approaching as they reined around, Claire holding Sarah on the bay, him leading the pinto, and galloped up the rocky trail, stones flying, hooves clattering, up over the rise and into the shelter of the woods.

11

HE DIDN'T HAVE A CHANCE to check the map for the best route away. He just had to get them out of there as fast as he could, over ridges, down through draws and hollows, up more slopes and down again, cornering themselves once and riding hard out of the box canyon, angling around and up from it, deeper into the forest, higher into the mountains. He stopped just once to listen for the motor, but it had either set down

or swung deep behind a ridge or swept away. At any
rate he couldn't hear it anymore, although that didn't
matter, they would hear it soon enough again or hear
riders eventually behind them, and he kicked his horse
into motion again, skirting a meadow, angling deep
into a twisted maze of ravines and draws and hollows.

He stopped just long enough to give Sarah another
sip of water and some salt, and then looking at the
heavy soapy lather on the horses, seeing the way they
heaved to breathe, he knew that he couldn't make them
work this hard any farther without killing them. Dismounting, he led the buckskin and the pinto, letting
Claire and Sarah ride slowly behind him on the bay.
They were angling down a dry creek bed now, pebbles
crunching, fir trees crowding closely on both sides,
their branches meshed so thickly overhead that there
was no sun. He took out the map, studying it as he
walked, but shut in by the trees he couldn't line up the
map with any landmarks, and they had come this way
so randomly that he couldn't tell where he was. The
creek bed angled down more steeply now, and he followed it, catching glimpses of sunlit rock down through
the trees. Then the trees were thinning and the rock
was more open down there and they came out onto a
slope of shale that led down to an enormous open canyon, cliffs to the right and left of him, circling around
to meet about a mile away. The cliffs were high, and
the shale slope he was on slanted down to a smooth
rock floor that finally merged with brown scrub grass
that took up most of the middle. He had never seen
anything like it before. The reflection of the sunlight
off the cliffs and rocks was almost blinding. There
was a strong breeze whistling over the cliffs across
the canyon.

He found the place on the map almost immediately. At least the edge of it was on his map. He had to pull out a second map to get the main part of it. SHEEP DESERT the map said clearly, and he could see why, explaining it. When the sheepmen had moved into this part of the country, the cattlemen had driven them high into the mountains, grudgingly allowing them only the worst part of the country up there. "In the end the cattlemen didn't like them to use up even this kind of land, and you got the range wars. A group of ranchers would come up here with rifles and kill the shepherds and drive the flocks up onto these cliffs and over the edge. The people who owned the sheep then hired Basques from Spain to come over here and mind the flocks, and these Basques had been shepherds for as far back in their families as anyone could remember and they didn't like anyone even looking at the sheep. So the next time the ranchers came up to places like this, the Basques lay in wait and ambushed them. Back and forth. More ranchers coming up. More Basques protecting the sheep. In the end the ranchers won of course, but that kind of war was going on in this country right up into the nineteen-twenties. If we went right across, we'd still find shacks and fences and rock walls left over from when the Basques were here."

But they weren't going across. This kind of rocky floor around the bottom of the cliffs was exactly what he'd been hoping for. The graveled stream bed they'd been following would help hide their tracks, and the shale slope they were on would help even more, and the rock floor down there would finish the job. He could see where breaks in the cliff walls slanted up to the country on top, so they wouldn't be trapping themselves by going into the canyon, and he could tell by how far the trees were back from the tops of the cliffs that there was mostly rock around the rim, so they wouldn't be leaving tracks up there either. They'd be long gone by the time the people after them figured out which break in the cliff they had used to get out of there.

The only problem was scratches that the horses' hooves might leave on the rock, and when Claire had dismounted, carrying Sarah to the bottom of the shale, he himself leading the three horses down, he ripped up one of the blankets, wrapping thick wadded pieces around the horses' hooves, tying them around their ankles. It took the horses a while to get used to the wads of cloth under their hooves, pawing them flat so they could walk more easily, but then they seemed to be all right, and the three of them mounted, Claire still holding Sarah, him leading the pinto, riding slowly around the rock floor at the base of the cliff to their right. With the pieces of blanket tied to their hooves, the horses made a faint muffled clopping sound as they walked. Except for that and the shriek of the wind over the cliff tops, the place was still and quiet.

He passed up all the breaks in the cliff for the first third of the way around the canyon. It would be too obvious going up right away, and besides that would only be taking them back in the general direction that they'd come. He wanted to get as far off in the opposite direction as he could, heading into brand-new territory. The sun was past its zenith, slanting down toward them, and even with his wide-brimmed hat on he could feel the heat soaking through onto his head. He unbuttoned his jacket, pulling his wet shirt away from his chest. He looked up at the stark blue sky, and there was a bird up there. A hawk, he guessed. Or maybe a falcon.

"Take another piece of salt," he told Sarah behind him, and then they were halfway around and he began looking seriously for a good break in the cliff that would take them up out of here. The first was too steep. The next one, fifty yards on, was just right, smooth and easy all the way up, and for that reason, because it was too obvious, he passed it by. The next didn't go up. It went straight in, about three horses wide, turning before he could see where it led, and for a reason he did not understand, he took it.

Where the passage turned, it grew wider, and once they were out of sight of the entrance behind them, the clomping of the horses echoed. He looked up at the strip of sky far up above them. He looked ahead where the passage forked, and he took the one on the right, beginning to worry now that they weren't going anywhere, that they'd soon reach a dead end and have to turn and go back. He decided that as soon as they came to a spot where they wouldn't be able to turn the horses they would stop and go back, but whenever the passage narrowed, he could see ahead to where it opened out again, and he rode through, legs crossed over the saddle horn, rock scraping the leather of the saddle. The passage forked again, and again he took the one on the right, not wanting to make things complicated and confuse himself in case they would have to find their way back. Once his horse felt so closed in that it tried to rear up and turn and he had to stop and calm it, patting it gently on the neck, whispering softly. Then he reached where the walls came together so close to his head that he himself began to feel constricted, dismounting as soon as the passage opened out, leading the horse by its reins. He looked back at Claire holding Sarah as she rode and knew that close places bothered her even more than him and wished there were a way for her to get off as well. The rock walls were cold and damp as in a cave. The passage angled down a little, forking again, and to break the pattern he went to the left, certain now that they would soon have to turn back, deciding to go on anyhow since they'd come this far and might as well finish what was left, imagining what all these forks in the passage must look like from above. He looked at his watch. They'd been at this quite a while. He looked ahead. The passage turned. And as he came around the bend, sunlight struck him hard in the eyes, forcing him to shield his eyes and squint.

Perhaps it was the effect of the heat haze from the sun, or perhaps the contrast with what they'd just come through, but as he led his horse out into the open from the passage, he couldn't believe what he was seeing.

"What is it?" Claire said.

"I don't know. It shouldn't be here," he said, fumbling with his map. "Look. Here's the sheep desert. Here's the country on this side of the wall. If the surveyors thought to mark something as small as that line shack back there, they'd sure as hell have thought to mark something as big as this."

They were standing at the upper end of a long low river valley that stretched away for as far as they could see, steep cliffs on either side, then gentle wooded slopes, then the river far below them glinting in the sun, and the whole scene was like pictures he had seen of deep narrow mountain valleys in the Andes, the trees and meadows a bright rich green that shimmered in the heat haze as if in a mirage. But the valley was clearly marked on the map. That wasn't what was bothering him. What was, so large and obvious in a large open meadow by the river that his eyes were drawn unavoidably to it, was the long narrow rectangle of a town down there, one main street dividing it, side streets dividing it again, this time into squares, a town big enough for two or three thousand people but no sign of movement anywhere.

"Something's wrong. You must be looking at the wrong map," Claire said.

"No," he said, taking out his compass, lining up the map with it. "No, there's no mistake. The valley's clearly marked all right. It's just that there isn't any town on it."

"But that's impossible. How could anybody survey all this and not make a note of the town?"

"I don't know. Sometimes they map this country by plane. Sometimes they just climb up on some high point and map everything around from there. It could be they just didn't notice it or maybe they were in such a hurry that they didn't remember to mention it."

But he didn't believe either one, and the only explanation that finally even half-satisfied him was that they had left it off the map deliberately, letting historians and state officials know but keeping the news from everyone else, not wanting souvenir hunters to come up here and destroy the place the way the Indian pueblo ruins had been destroyed in Arizona.

Maybe. But he still didn't really believe it, and he was already leading his horse down the steep stone slope to the trees below before he realized how much the place was drawing him. He tied his horse to a fir tree, climbing back up to help Claire dismount and carry Sarah down to the trees, then coming back up once more to lead the two horses down. It was dark and cool in under there after the brightness of the sheep desert, and he gave Sarah another sip of water, told her to take another piece of salt. Then they all remounted, Claire still holding Sarah, and started down. It was like being in a park, no undergrowth, just tall thick ever-greens rising up evenly spaced all around them, branches not beginning until well up over their heads, the forest floor a smooth cushioned mat of dead brown pine needles. In a while the air grew chill enough that he had to button his jacket again.

The river made hardly any sound when they came to it, and he registered then what he'd been sensing all along, that aside from the hooves of the horses there hadn't been any sound in the forest either, no autumn birds singing, no animals scuttering over the pine needles or across the branches of the trees. And the chill he'd been feeling wasn't just from the air. It was the place itself, the sense that something was wrong.

But while the river was almost soundless, more like a whisper than anything else, it was wide and swift and deep, and they had to ride down along it, looking for a ford. To the left there were tumbled cabins in among the trees. Farther down there were logs set out to form the foundations of cabins that had never been built. Then they came to a pale cracked listing wagon, the spokes of its crumbled wheels splayed out beneath it. They circled it, reaching a place in the river where rocks and silt and gravel had gathered enough to form a ford, crossing it, the water knee-high on the horses, spotting a huge rusted metal pan down there under the water.

For a moment he was afraid that the wide motion of the water would spook the horses, make them rear up and try to dump them, maybe Sarah, but then before he expected they were across and he was feeling easier out in the bright open of the meadow away from the trees, stopping to let the horses drink, something he knew he should have done earlier but that his feeling in the woods had not let him. The horses drank until he had to force them back, fearing they'd get sick. Then look-ing at the tall green grass of the meadow, so unlike the scrub grass of the sheep desert or for that matter any other grass that they had come through, he imagined how obvious the path that the horses would make through it would be from the air and decided to stay along the riverbank, following down it, spotting the rusty head of a shovel in the shallows now, its handle long since rotted away, reaching a kind of road that angled off slightly to the right through the grass toward the town, the grass barely ankle-high on the horses, mixed in with patches of dust and the vague outlines of wheel ruts, and if the town was as old as the cabins he had seen in the trees behind him, the road shouldn't still have been here, let alone the town itself.

It was about a hundred yards ahead of them, the buildings all low and slant-roofed and uniform except for the flat-roofed two-story buildings down both sides of the main street. There were occasional shacks now, and then they were reaching the outskirts, and the buildings were listing, their doors rotted off their hinges, windows broken, but they weren't made of logs like the cabins back on the other side of the river. Their wood was flat and even-planed, and there were wooden side-walks propped up over the dirt of the street, and there was the tall spire of a church down at the far end, and if the planks now were warped and cracked and the sidewalk partially collapsed and the crucifix on the spire snapped dangling, it was obvious that once there had been a good deal of pride in their making. MARERRO a sign said, blown down into the middle of the street. The word was etched deeply into the wood. And below it, POPULATION 4000, the number almost indiscernible, slashed out, 350 awkwardly under it. They passed a candy store, a tobacco shop, a drugstore, two laundries, one directly across from the other, a barber shop, a dry goods store, their signs fallen down in front of their doors or still painted neatly on a few surviving windows. They were halfway through town before he stopped them and looked around and finally dismounted.

MARERRO HOUSE the sign said in front of the biggest building. It was wider than the rest and taller with a false front of wood on top of its two stories. There were big dusty windows on both sides of the double door, a row of smaller ones on the second story, a balcony jutting out, and hitching his horse to the rail in front, he stepped onto the sidewalk toward the entrance. There wasn't any sound at all now, not the creaking of signs in the wind or the whistling of a breeze through broken windows, nothing, so that when his foot cracked through the sidewalk, the noise was startling. He thought irrationally of snakes and yanked his foot out, ripping his pant cuff.

"Christ," he said, and the word was like dust in his mouth.

He tested the boards this time before he put any weight on them, walking carefully across, the wood bending under him, opening one of the double doors, then an inner door, looking in. The bar took up the whole left wall, a dusty cobwebbed mirror behind it, a dull copper rail along the bottom for a foot rest, cuspidors in the middle and at each end. There were tables and chairs in the middle, some with bottles and glasses still on them, the chairs pushed back as if people had only a moment ago got up and left them. A dance hall stage against the back, a piano in one corner of it, dusty ragged red velvet curtains bunched together on both sides, a stairway along the right wall that disappeared up through a break in the ceiling to the second floor.

Marerro, he thought to himself, turning to Claire and Sarah in the street, saying, "It's all right. We can go on in," his words like dust again, and then he entered, looking around, glancing up at the candle-studded wagon-wheel chandelier hanging from the ceiling. He followed the path of light until it ended in the middle of the room. "Open the other door," he told Claire as they came in behind him, and the extra light showed the thick dust on the tables and the bottles and the glasses. And on the floor he noticed, seeing behind him where he had made tracks through the dust to where he was standing.

He went over to the stage, floorboards creaking under him, examining the burned-down candles that had been set along the rim with metal reflectors behind them for footlights. Marerro, he thought again, Claire and Sarah coming behind him. "Who the hell or what was Marerro?"

"He was a Mexican," the voice said behind him.

The voice paralyzed him. For a moment he couldn't move or breathe or anything, and then something snapped and he was swinging around, gun drawn, but

Claire and Sarah were in the way, and as he lunged to the right, crouching, aiming, he saw the tall grizzled white-haired old man standing in the open doorway pointing the shotgun at him, and the big dog beside the old man was braced, teeth bared to leap, and the old man was saying, "Hey now, sonny. Point that gun the other way. I've no doubt you could hit me, but my fingers are solid on these triggers and before I dropped I'd hit you too and if that didn't finish you the dog surely would, so just point that gun the other way."

But he didn't. He just kept crouching, aiming, his finger tensing on the trigger, and the old man was saying, "I could sic the dog on the little girl. Then you wouldn't know where to shoot first and I could drop you for sure. Come on, it's a standoff. Point the gun the other way."

But he still didn't move, tensed, hand shaking, and the old man was staring at him nervously, suddenly shrugging, lowering the shotgun, uncocking the hammers, setting it against the wall inside the door. "All right, if it's up to me to make the first move, there I've done it. Now it's your turn."

He relaxed a little. "What about the dog?" It was still braced to leap, and all the old man had to do was say "Hush" once and the dog was immediately down.

He relaxed even more, straightening, breathing.

"I'm not asking you to put the gun away or anything," the old man said. "Just point it the other way."

And he finally did, uncocking it, lowering it by his side.

The old man grinned, showing jagged yellow teeth. "That's the stuff, sonny. The way your hand was shaking there, I was sure we were both dead where we stood." And then he started laughing, his mouth a gaping hole in his face. His skin had passed beyond the wrinkle stage, the flesh under it eaten up, so that it had smoothed out and conformed now to his jawbones and cheekbones and forehead, gaunt and sallow like the perfectly preserved face of a mummy, and his ragged pants and shirt and jacket hung loose on him around the shoulders, hips, and waist as if the flesh underneath them were gone as well, all bones and skin, and his laugh was high-pitched and crackling. "Yes sir, both dead where we stood," he abruptly finished. "He was a Mexican. He came up here and found a twenty-three pound gold nugget, and when the rest of them came up here to strike it rich just like he did, he told them he knew where there was country around with nuggets just as big as the first, so when they built this town they named it after him. Then they caught him messing with some white woman and they lynched him and afterward they felt so bad about losing all that gold that they kept the town named after him anyhow. It got to be a kind of joke."

"You make it sound like you were here."

"Almost, sonny. But the town was built in eighteen seventy-nine and I might be old but not that old, not quite. I read all about it in the records at the courthouse. That's just down the street. Your little girl not feeling well, is she?"

She was slumped in a chair at one of the tables, a dusty bottle and glass incongruously before her, face puffy and pale, eyes drooping, dull.

"The altitude made her sick."

"It'll do that all right. But not down here. In a while down here she'll be as good as can be. How you feeling, sweetheart?" he said, starting over, and the dog moved to follow, and he said "Hush," the dog sitting back where it was. "That's just so you don't get anymore nervous," the old man told him, continuing over. "I don't want you to start shaking again like you got the palsy." Then he laughed again, and Sarah drew back from him when he reached the chair. "That's all right, sweetheart. You've got nothing to fear from me. It's been so long that I just want to look close at a little girl. What's your name?"

She looked away from the old man toward him, and he nodded, and she answered, "Sarah."

"Sarah, eh? That's a nice name. I knew another little girl named that once, and her mother was named that too, but it's been so long now that I can't remember either face. Except they were pretty. I remember that much at least. Just like you. How old are you, Sarah?"

"Eight."

"That's the best age to be. Don't ever be anything else. I remember once when I was eight. That was with my father on his farm in California. I had a dog a bit like that one over there but not so big. Did you ever have a dog?"

She shook her head no.

"Would you like to see this one?"

She thought a moment and shook her head yes.

"Would it be all right?" the old man turned and said to him.

He didn't know.

The old man waited.

"All right. Yes."

"You're sure now? You're sure now even with that gun in your hand that you can trust me?"

"No, but you can show the dog anyhow."

The old man grinned and whistled. The dog came immediately over. It was dark and square-faced and massive, face taller than the table, and Sarah shrank back from it.

"You've got nothing to worry about. Just hold out your hand and let him sniff you."

She hesitated. Then slowly, uncertainly, she held out her hand. The dog sniffed her fingers once and licked them, then stood at attention beside the old man.

"There now, you see," the old man said, patting it. "There was nothing to worry about."

She was sitting up straighter now, looking curiously at it. "What's his name?"

"He doesn't have a name. I never got around to it. I just call him dog."

The animal's ears perked up.

"I found his mother up here wandering in the woods. A German shepherd. Likely separated from a hunter or maybe just gone wild. Anyhow I mated her with a wolf and this was the only pup but dog enough for a whole litter. His mother froze to death two years ago. You been vomiting, Sarah?"

She nodded.

"Got pains in your stomach and lower?"

She nodded again, flinching as he raised his hand.

"Take it easy, Sarah. I just want to feel your forehead." And then to him, "You're sure now you won't mind?" He was grinning those yellow teeth again. "You're sure now you won't shoot me or anything?"

He didn't answer, and the old man cupped his hand over her forehead. "Her temperature's too low. You been giving her salt?"

"As soon as I could."

"Well, that'll help some, but you need something more. You've got to get more liquid in her and make it stay."

"She'll only bring it up."

"Not if she drinks what I give her. She'll keep that down all right."

"And what would that be?"

"Come on down to my place at the end of the street and I'll show you."

"We like it here."

"Oh, do you now? I never liked this much myself. The guy who ran it. Couldn't stand him. Always liked the hotel at the other end. Got a nice place there. Room to myself and everything."

"You just said you weren't old enough to be here when the town was alive."

"Did I? Well, there's not two ways about it, is there? This way or that, I must be mistaken." And then he grinned again and looked around at the place and said, "Maybe you're right. A person shouldn't be set in his ways. It's a sign of age. Just this once I'll make an exception."

He started for the door.

"Wait a minute. Where are you going?"

"Where do you think? Down to my room to get my stuff. Why? Don't tell me you want to come along."

"I think I'd better."

"Well I wish you'd make up your mind. One second you don't want to come, the next you do. You'd better watch it or you'll get all mixed up." He reached to pick up his shotgun.

"No," Bourne told him.

"How's that, sonny?"

"The shotgun stays here." Keeping a distance between the old man and himself, he went over to the shotgun and picked it up.

The dog stiffened and growled.

"Hush now," the old man told it, grinning. "Sonny here's just being careful. No need to get excited." And he kept on grinning all the while Bourne took the shotgun over to Claire.

"Forget the twenty-two. If anybody comes in, use this. Don't let the kick worry you. The other guy will feel it a lot harder than you do."

"Somebody else?" the old man said. "Is that what's got you bothered? You think I've got somebody else here with me and while we're gone he'll come in here—"

"That's right," Bourne told him flatly.

"Well, your instincts are good. I'll say that for you. But like I keep telling you, there's nothing to worry about. The whole reason for living up here in the first place is to stay away from people. You don't think if I wanted company I'd be living up here, do you? With you three here, the place is too crowded for me already. If I thought you were going to be here for any length of time, I'd have to make plans for moving on."

"Just the same."

"Oh sure," the old man said. "No hard feelings. I'd do the same myself." And with that he was walking out the door, the dog following, him stopping just once more to turn and tell him, "But your daughter isn't getting any better while we stand around and talk about it. Let's get moving. You've got horses to stable. It'll be dark soon." And with that he was gone.

Bourne followed him out onto the sidewalk.

"The stable's just down here a ways," the old man told him, walking down the street, the dog beside him.

Unhitching the horses from the rail, Bourne walked behind him.

"What are you doing up here anyhow?" the old man said.

"Camping."

"Sure. With no tent and no pack horses."

"We only planned to stay up here a few days. We got lost."

"Sure. With the outline of those maps and compass bulging in your jacket pocket."

"I didn't know how to use them as well as I thought."

"In which case you would have wept for joy at seeing me instead of pulling your gun. No, those pads tied to your horses' hooves and everything, you're on the run all right. Hell, the way you came in here, a person lost would never have gone in through those breaks in the cliff. You went in there deliberately. To throw somebody off."

"I told you we're lost. The little girl got sick and I took a chance on a shortcut to get down out of here. The town's not on the map anyhow. What would have been the point of deliberately trying to make it through those breaks in the cliff if I didn't think they were going to take me anywhere?"

"I must be having hearing troubles. A minute ago I was sure I heard you say you didn't know how to read a map."

That stopped him. He stood motionless where the main street was cut across by a narrow side street, a restaurant on one corner, dust and scrub grass all around, and the old man went on a few more feet before he realized he wasn't being followed. "Anyway, of course the town's not on the map," the old man stopped and said. "It's never been on a map. They put it up so fast and left it so fast that nobody ever really knew that it was up here. The stable's just down here a ways." He was pointing halfway down the block to the left. "Those pads are all ripped to hell anyhow. The horses will be just as glad to get them off."

And then they were angling over toward the stable, big doors pinned open against the walls on both sides, the stalls slanted with sunlight in there. A thick smell of sawdust and rotted grain and must hung in front of the doorway, and feeling the same uneasiness he had felt in the forest, Bourne stopped again.

"What is it?" the old man said.

"You first."

"No matter." And snapping his fingers for the dog to follow, he went on in.

Bourne hesitated, shaking once, and went in after him.

12

THE MUST FILLED HIS NOSE, choking him. There were ten stalls on each side, half of them tumbled over, the worn board floor littered with dust and straw so dry it turned to powder as he walked. He tied the horses to the first rail he came to, and ready with his gun, ducked into the second stall on the right, staring up at the hayloft across from him.

As much as he could tell, there wasn't anyone.

He dodged across to the left, checking out the loft on the right as well, and partly satisfied, hurried down past all the stalls, looking in at them, going over to a ladder that was built onto one thick post, testing its rungs as he climbed up to check the far corners of the loft. Still no one.

"You're really something, you know that?" the old man chuckled, looking up at him.

He didn't answer. Halfway down, one rung snapped, and he barely caught himself. The old man snickered. "Yeah, you're really something. Oh I don't say you're wrong for being careful. All the same you're really something. Who you running from anyhow? Surely you don't think I'm one of them."

"I told you," he said, stepping down angrily. "We're not on the run from anybody."

The old man sucked at the corners of his mouth. "Suit yourself, sonny."

"And stop calling me sonny."

"Whatever you say. No need to get worked up about it."

He sucked the corners of his mouth once more, and then snapping his fingers for the dog to follow, he started toward the back door.

"Now just hold it right there," Bourne said, aiming.

The old man turned and eyed him patiently. "Listen, sonny, I'm doing my best to be as friendly as I can, but if every time I move to break wind or something you start aiming that gun at me, we're just not going to get along at all. There's a well outside and unless you want your horses to drop from thirst, I'm going to pick up that pail over there and go on out and get them water. If you'll let me."

Bourne didn't say anything, and picking up the pail in a moment, the old man went on out.

13

HE TOOK TOO LONG coming back. Thinking of Claire and Sarah alone at the hotel, Bourne hurried toward the back door, and just as he reached it, the old man banged it open, coming in stooped over, holding the handle on the overflowing pail of water. He was breathing hard. "Get nervous, did you?" He was grinning. "This is good for me. It keeps my arm from atrophy. That's a good word, atrophy. You know what it means?"

"I think so."

"Shrink up and shrivel away." He was over by the horses, setting the pail down, breathing hard. "You know, like what your thing does after sex. I read it once in a book. We'll have to gather up some long grass to feed them and bring them in more water but in the meantime I guess we'd better get their saddles off." He was starting in on the buckskin, uncinching it, leading it into one stall. "The way I figure it, you're either on the run from the police or somebody against the police, and that nice-looking family you got, you don't look too bad to me, it must be the other guys. Right?"

"I told you—"

"Yeah, I know, you're not on the run at all, but am I right or am I?"

He didn't have the strength to deny it anymore. He just shrugged.

"Of course I'm right. Now don't you feel better?"

But Bourne couldn't tell if the old man was talking to him or the buckskin he was patting in the stall, removing its bridle, setting in the pail of water, and backing out, closing the gate on the stall. "What have they got after you?" the old man said and turned.

"Three horsemen. A helicopter. I don't know."

"What did you do to them?"

"Made them mad."

The old man laughed. "I bet you did. Well I don't want to know what you did to them anyhow. I've got my own sad stories. Just tell me this. Do they know what they're doing?"

He nodded.

"Well, we'll see. The helicopter isn't any problem. We can hear it long before they're anywhere near and get a chance to make preparations for it. The horsemen are another matter. We don't have time before sundown now, but tomorrow morning we'll go on up to the cliff and pry down a couple of boulders to block the passage you came through. If they get down here in the meantime, there are plenty of places to give them a fight from. Who knows, with luck you might even get a few days' rest before you have to move on."

The tone was unmistakable. "You mean in a few days you want us to move on regardless."

The old man thought about it. "Yeah I guess that's what I mean all right. Even as it is I'm going to have to move on too. This place is going to be damn crowded for a while. Of course you can't ever tell. This town down here is funny. Sometimes you see it from on top, and sometimes you don't. The last person found his way down here was twenty years ago, and that was me."

"Then you couldn't have known the guy who ran the hotel."

"You must be right."

He was going to work on the pinto now, unbuckling its saddle.

"Say you wouldn't mind giving me a hand, would you? These aren't *my* horses, you know."

And then in a moment, "Yeah I'll move on anyway. Just to be safe. Once the snow starts I'll come back." It was like he was talking to himself. Then he turned. "In the meantime you just stick with me. The things I know, I'll show you how to keep away from them. Yes sir, it'll be just like in the old days."

14

"A MEAL LIKE THIS," the old man said, wiping his mouth and leaning back, "a meal like this, just beans and biscuits and dried beef, would have cost you close to twenty dollars back then and wouldn't have been half as good." He was smiling across the table toward Claire as he said that, and in the lamplight his smile was easier to take and Claire thanked him.

She had found a kitchen in the back room of the hotel while they were gone, building a fire in the big black stove, and she made sure to get dried wood from boards outside that wouldn't smoke, but birds had built nests in the stovepipe vents, so that when the old man and himself came back, there was smoke anyhow, not outside but all through the kitchen, and the old man had to show him how to dismantle the pipes and help him clean them before Claire could start to cook.

The old man left the dog at the front door in case anybody came, and bringing an unopened bottle from the shelves behind the bar, he came back to the table in the middle of the saloon where they were sitting.

"It's good stuff," the old man said. "You've got to pour off the oil on top, but after that it's fine."

"But all those bottles. They must have left in an awful hurry not to take them."

"Smallpox."

Sipping, Bourne gagged, shoving the glass away from him. "Smallpox?"

"Oh, it's all right now. If there were any germs still around, I would have been dead from drinking this stuff long ago. Besides you're inoculated against it, aren't you? Go on. Take another sip. It's not going to hurt you."

The old man drained his own glass in two quick mouthfuls and poured himself another. "Go on," he said again, and raising his glass, Bourne swallowed.

It was sharp and gagging and even with the top drained off, still faintly oily, burning all the way down. He shook his head.

The old man cackled. "See, I told you. It's not too bad at all. Just takes a little getting used to." And while Bourne reached for his canteen to chase the taste, the old man drained his glass again, and poured himself another.

"Yeah the first case hit them just about the middle of the summer. A lot of people saw what was coming and left right away, but a lot of others couldn't bear the thought of leaving all that gold and stayed. They built a cabin far back up in the woods away from the river and quarantined the family whose son had it and the son died of course and then the mother and father got it and died and so did their two other sons. But there wasn't any other sign of it showed up in town, and when the stench from the bodies started drifting down from the cabin, the town council got drunk one night, went up and set torches to it.

"They picked a good night for it, I'll say that for them, storm on its way, thunder booming, lightning already flashing down at the far end of the valley, but the flames from the cabin spread to the trees anyhow and before the storm finally came and put it out the fire had burned off nearly thirty acres of good timber. People were already packing up, afraid the flames were going to reach the meadow grass and spread to town, before they saw the storm was doing its job. Then they figured that a fire that big had maybe been a good thing after all. If there had still been any germs in the trees around the cabin, they were gone now for sure, and people started breathing easier.

"At least a little easier. Because there was always the chance that the smallpox would show up again anyhow, and it wasn't until the first of September that they finally decided the danger was over. They mined a big haul that month, mostly from the river, although some of them had started digging high up in the hills, running sluices down from streams to help separate the gold, almost a thousand pounds of it that month alone, and they were just waiting for the packers to bring in supplies for the winter when the second case showed up.

"That was just about this time that year and the snow hadn't come then either, 1881, and I shouldn't say case, it was cases, four of them, and they built more quarantine cabins for them, but the next week there were four more cases and eight the week after that, and what with people leaving or dying and then the snow finally coming they lost fifteen hundred before Christmas. Of course once the snow started piling up they couldn't build cabins anymore, so they had to section off the town, one half for people with the sickness, the other half for people without, a kind of no man's land in between.

"But by February the part of town for sickness was two-thirds. Then there were suicides and people trying to walk out of here, freezing to death, and well, when the thaw finally started, of the original four thousand there were just three hundred and fifty left and they got out of here just as quick as their legs could take them. Word must have got around how bad it had been because people didn't pay attention to the talk of gold up here, they just remembered the smallpox, and nobody ever came up here after that. The valley is fairly humid, so the town didn't bake to powder and crumble or catch fire or anything, and it was far enough from the slopes to keep from being caught in snowslides, so it just stayed pretty much the same as it was, and that rich meadow out there holds more graves than a person would care to think of. The whole story's in the town records. If you get a chance, read them." He drained his glass and poured another. "You're not drinking."

"Which part of town was set aside for the small-pox?"

"This part of course. That's why I live at the other end of the street, why I don't like to come over here much. Not that there's anything wrong. It's just association. This hotel here would have been a kind of hospital. You can imagine them lying all over the floor, blistered and fevered and moaning, the cold outside, them dying." He shook his head and took another drink. "It must have been quite a sight, coming in here." Then his eyes went blank and he didn't say anything, and finally rousing himself, pushing back his chair, legs screeching, he wiped his mouth again, said "Well," and stood. "I guess we'd better have a look how your little girl's medicine is doing."

He walked over to the bar where they'd set a pot from the stove, bending close, sniffing. "Yeah, I guess it's cooled enough now. Let's give it a try."

"You still haven't said what's in it."

"A little of this and that. I'd rather not say. You might not let her drink it."

"Then you drink it."

The old man turned and looked at him. "Still being careful, huh? Think I might want to poison her, huh? All this trouble I'm going to. I've half a mind to walk off and leave you."

But he didn't. He just picked up the wooden spoon by the pot on the bar, dipped it in, and sipped from it, pale green liquid dribbling thickly from it like pea soup.

"There now, you satisfied?" he said, making a face.

"She won't just be taking one spoonful. Try another."

"This stuff doesn't taste very good you know."

"Try another."

He dipped the spoon in and sipped from it again, sucking the liquid loudly past his lips and teeth.

"That's it."

"Not quite. Once more."

He didn't even bother saying anything. This time he jammed the spoon down into the pot, jerked it up to his mouth and shoved all of it in, sucking it clean. "Now that's the last," he said, gesturing with the spoon. "If that doesn't satisfy you, take care of her yourself."

"I'm satisfied." He stood up from the table, went over and got the pot, and took it to where Sarah was huddled, eyes closed, in a sleeping bag in the corner.

"Hey, sweetheart," he said, kneeling, shaking her gently. "Wake up. I've got something that'll make you better."

She sighed but her eyes didn't open and otherwise she didn't move either.

"Come on," he said, shaking her a little harder. "Wake up."

She peered up at him, her face in shadow this far from the yellow lamplight. "Is it morning?"

"No, a long way from it. I want you to take some of this. It'll make you better."

"I don't want to."

"It'll keep you from throwing up anymore. That's right, isn't it?" he said, turning toward the old man by the bar. "It'll keep her from throwing up?"

"Sure, if anything will," the old man said. "And get some nourishment in her. And some salt. Just let her have a few spoonfuls to start, then a few more in an hour. By morning she can try something solid. But she's not going to like the taste. You're going to have to force her."

There was something about the way he said the last that made Bourne look at him a moment longer before he turned back to her. "Did you hear?"

She nodded.

"Well, come on then. Sit up and try some."

He raised her gently, propping her against the wall, the other sleeping bag for a pillow.

But when he brought the spoon toward her mouth, she turned her face. "I don't want to."

She was holding her stomach.

"You have to," he said, and catching her off guard he slipped some of it between her lips.

"Ugh," she said, screwing up her face, and he had to put his hand over her mouth to keep her from spitting it out.

She tried to push the spoon away as he raised it once more toward her mouth. "It tastes awful."

"Of course," he said, and it shouldn't have sounded funny but it was. "Of course it tastes awful. It's medicine, isn't it?"

And she relaxed enough to open her mouth and grin, and before she realized, he had slipped in another mouthful.

15

"THEY DID IT like this," the old man said, propped up against the wall beside her, taking another drink and setting the glass by the bottle on the floor beside him. "They took a big pan like this and squatted down by the riverbank and scooped it full of water and sand and gravel. Then they swirled the water around in the pan so that some of it spilled over the edge, taking some of the sand and gravel with it. They kept swirling it around like that until in a little while all they had left in the pan was a bit of water and fine sand and if they were lucky maybe even a big chunk or two.

"But that didn't happen very often and mostly they were happy to get just the sand because of course it wasn't sand at all but gold. Placer gold. Little bits of it washed down out of the hills to here and because the gold was heavy it finally sank to the bottom where the water wasn't strong enough to wash it along anymore or where there was a kind of natural dam in the water to catch the gold and let it sink. That's why the old prospectors used a pan like this. Because the gold was heavy enough that it would stay in the bottom after the water had taken most of the gravel over the side. Of course they had to be quick about this. It didn't pay them to spend a half hour on just one pan of gravel, and most of the old timers could rinse out a panful in less than a couple of minutes.

"Then they got tired of bending over scooping up gravel all the time and decided to let nature do some of the work for them. So they found a spot in the side of a hill where it looked like there might be a lot of gold and then they dug the gravel up and put it in a wheelbarrow and dumped it in a big wooden box at the bottom of a water trough. When the box was full, they channeled a stream down the trough into the box, controlling the speed of the water so it was just strong enough to take away the gravel but leave the gold and at the end of a day all they needed to do was look at the bottom of the box and there the gold was.

"Most people, though, when they went looking for it never found the gold at all, and when the few of them did they almost always spent the money from it right away or invested in more equipment to find an even better spot to dig, and towns like this didn't help much either. As soon as the gold started coming in, prices went up and before long what had been a beefsteak for five dollars was beans and salt pork for twenty dollars.

"There just wasn't any way to win, except maybe for the shopkeepers and saloon owners and anybody else who fed off those who worked the gold. Not to mention frostbite and mud slides and God knows what else that might catch up to you. No, there were easier ways to make a living, that was for sure, but it was like the gold wasn't really what they were after anyhow, it was the idea of being out on their own, moving on when they felt like it, staying when they found a spot they liked, coming into town to have a few drinks with the rest of the guys once the day's digging was done. There was a lot of claim-jumping and back-shooting and all, but there was a lot of comradeship too."

He had been looking up at the shadows on the ceiling as he talked, off somewhere, slowing toward the last, and now as he finished, he looked toward Sarah to see how she was taking it and she was asleep. He smiled to himself, looked toward the left front window and the pale moonlight out there on the buildings across the street, and then pouring another drink, draining it, he braced himself and stood. Or almost stood. The effort caught him off-balance and he fell back against the wall and had to brace himself again before he managed to get up, the bottle in one hand, groaning. The bottle was three-quarters empty.

Bourne had been watching him for the past half hour, standing at the bar, staring over into that corner. Three-quarters of a bottle and maybe the old man was having trouble standing but his speech wasn't slurred and he was walking over to him just fine. He glanced from the old man toward Claire at the bar beside him and her face was stark and except for the moment when the old man had thanked her for the supper she still did not feel confident enough to relax around him.

"It's cold," the old man said, reaching them, rubbing his elbows. "You can feel it coming. Can't be more than two or three days away."

"What's that?"

"The snow." He rubbed himself again. "Never seen an autumn like this, warm so late the way it's been. It's going to be a hard winter."

Off somewhere, even with the doors closed, Bourne heard the long growing howl of a wolf. Two yips. Then another howl. Under a middle table the dog perked its ears and stood.

"Hush," the old man said.

One more howl and then another on top of it coming from a little to the left of the first. Ears still perked, the dog went over to the door.

"Hush," the old man said again, flat out and hoarse. "They don't want you up there no matter if your dad was one of them or not. Big as you are, they'd finish you in a minute."

"I would have thought he'd do well up there," Bourne said.

"My smell on him, they'd never accept him, and on his own, he's been around me so long, the edge for hunting is off, he'd never last the winter." He leaned against the bar, staring at his reflection in the mirror back there. "Time to sleep," he said. "We've got to be up there by first light tomorrow. God, is that what I look like? I think it's time to sleep." He took the bottle and a patched-up blanket he'd brought with him off the counter, shuffling around behind the bar, wrapping the blanket around him, taking a sip from the bottle, corking it, and lying down.

"Go on," he said.

"I think I'll stand watch for a while."

"No need. The dog'll wake us if anything goes wrong."

"I think I'll stand watch anyhow."

"Whatever."

And then he and Claire stood silently, looking at each other, and in a while he could hear the old man snoring.

"I'd better wake Sarah to feed her more medicine," Claire said.

He leaned over and kissed her on the cheek, paused and nodded. Then taking his own blanket and a chair from one of the tables, he went over to the corner by the right front window, sitting back in the shadows, looking out at the barren moonlit street. There was a chill wind come up, blowing dust down along it. He could feel a draft coming up through the boards of the floor, and wrapping the blanket snugly around him, he settled back. In a while Claire was done talking with Sarah, feeding her, and then she was blowing out the light, and he could hear her unzipping the second sleeping bag, crawling in, snuggling beside Sarah.

"Good night," she said quietly over to him.

"Good night," he waited and said.

The wind picked up, blowing dust against the windows, shrieking thinly through the floorboards. Then it died and he heard the old man snoring and the sounds of quiet even breathing over by Claire and Sarah. Then the wind picked up again, and he sat in the darkness looking out at the cold dust-blown street, imagining how it must have looked, wagons stopped, people walking or leaning against doorjambs talking, or riders going past, a piano playing somewhere maybe in the old days.

16

THE FIRST BOULDER was easy. In the cold gray light just before dawn, they dismounted, roping the horses to trees in a clearing on the fir slope, giving them room enough to move around and crop the stiff night-frosted grass that crunched under their boots as they set off up through the trees to the shale and the cliff wall. The old man led the way, working along the base of the cliff until he reached a narrow ledge that angled up and followed it. Then he reached another ledge that angled up the opposite way and followed it as well, moving low and loose-limbed and naturally, never needing to stop to breathe or look around for a new place to climb, just crisscrossing the cliff face, reaching, climbing, and from below, looking up, Bourne couldn't believe the places the old man was finding, certain that the next time the old man came to the end of a ledge he'd be cut off and have to turn around and come back and find another way, but always there was another ledge or an outcrop of rock or a fissure for a handhold, and he guessed that the old man had come up this way several times before or else that he'd been living in the mountains so long that he could plot a course up a cliff from just one glance at it. Soon they were above the tips of the pine trees, the air turning lighter all the while, and once, glancing down, the rocks below strangely magnifying, Bourne slipped and dangled and almost lost his handhold before he scraped his boots back into the fissure he'd been standing on. "Don't hug the rock. Lean out from it. Let it help you," the old man told him, and the old man was quite a ways up, and his voice should have been a shout, echoing, but it was low and flat, reaching him all the same, and Bourne couldn't understand how the old man did that. He looked at his hands, the skin scraped bloody off the tips of his fingers, flesh swollen numb from the cold, and he didn't look down anymore after that, just kept looking up to where his hands would go next, his feet, edging along a narrow sloping lip on the cliff face, reaching up to find a place to put his hand, and there wasn't anything, just open air and sky above his head. One more foothold, another after that, and he was groping up onto the level, running stooped to where the old man was crouched waiting for him by a mound of leafless scrub brush.

"Your hands," the old man told him, and Bourne didn't need to look at them to know what he meant. They were shaking. He couldn't stop them from shaking, and he didn't know if it was from the cold or the blood or the fear of nearly falling, but he didn't let himself think about it, just followed the old man running bent over to the other edge of the level, diving low, crawling flat to the rimrock that looked down on the sheep desert. From this high angle, the circle of the canyon was even more apparent, the rock floor around the base of the cliff down there, the scrub grass in the middle, and directly in the middle the specks of a shack and some sheds and a corral left over from when the sheepmen had been up here, and they hadn't been on the map either he recalled. The old man pointed, and at first Bourne thought he meant there were people down there by the sheds, and he stiffened, straining to see, before he realized that the old man was pointing past the sheds toward the opposite cliff wall and the low black clouds scudding thickly over the horizon toward them. Snow, he thought, remembering what the old man had said the night before, and he shivered, rubbing himself, watching the clouds blot out the sun, turning the air gray once more as they scudded toward them. Not yet, he thought, but soon, and then turning, he saw that the old man was already squirming back from the edge of the cliff top, rising only when he was far back enough not to make an outline against the horizon, stooping all the same as he turned and glanced around and started running low to the right toward the tops of the fissures that led through the cliff wall into the adjoining river valley.

The old man was already testing one big boulder when Bourne caught up to him. From up here it was obvious which passages in the maze down there led only to dead ends and which one connected all the way through, and they were both heaving against the rock when it gave unexpectedly, tumbling once before it rolled over the edge, crashing back and forth against the passage walls until it cracked solidly in place down there. The rumble echoed loudly up to them like thunder down out of the mountains.

"That's good," the old man said. "They'll think it's from the storm."

"You saw them?"

The old man didn't answer. The boulder hadn't blocked off the passage. It had just made the passage more difficult to get through, and he was already running farther along the top, pointing toward another boulder, larger, farther off.

"You didn't answer," Bourne said, catching up to him. "Did you see them?"

"No, but you've got to assume they're around."

The boulder wouldn't move. They heaved against it, shoulders straining, gasping, but it wouldn't move. They picked up a thick limb from a dead tree, wedging it under the boulder and lifting. The tip of the tree limb broke. The second time it didn't. The boulder moved once and settled back, and they heaved again, and the boulder rolled once, stopping. It took them three tries like that, the boulder rolling each time once and stopping, before they reached a slight incline that led down to the passage, and even if the incline wasn't much, it was enough to keep the boulder rolling, not even stopping as it reached the edge and tumbled over, the rumble of its fall reaching them before they even got to the edge, looking down at it wedged between the passage walls, and there wasn't any way a man could get a horse to climb over.

"Of course they might leave the horses and go through on foot," the old man said, running on to yet another boulder, but it was the biggest yet and they never did get it over, slumping down exhausted, deciding that a man on foot could climb over no matter how big the boulders were, that the point was to make it look as if nobody on horseback had gone through.

The edge of the cloud bank was directly over them now, looming past them toward the river valley and the town, bringing with it a sudden chill that made Bourne reach into his big jacket pocket for the thick wool gloves he'd brought up with him, slipping them over his bloody swollen hands. Then the wind started, piercing, biting, bringing tears to his eyes, and he turned his back, flipping up the hood on his coat, looking across the remainder of the bluff toward the town. It was in light, and then the shadow of the clouds was over it, and a few white specks of snow swept past him.

"We'd better get down before the horses spook," the old man told him, and it was as if the wind and the cold didn't bother him at all. Sure, he had his hat down close to his head and his jacket buttoned tightly, but his face was half turned to the wind and his hands weren't in his pockets, just directly on his knees, and he was hunkered down looking around at the way the wind was blowing up dust and bending the scrub brush and scraping tree limbs together more as a matter of interest than concern.

"One second," Bourne said, the town down there reminding him, and groping with his glove he reached into his coat pocket, coming out with the photograph. It had been tacked to the wall behind the bar in the hotel, where he'd noticed it as he wandered around checking out the place the night before after supper.

"That's the way the town looked just before the smallpox," the old man had said, and Bourne had been drawn to it, yellow from the lamplight and yellow on its own anyhow, cracked and wrinkled and brittle with age, five to six inches wide and high, the kind that came from big box cameras with tripods supporting them and bulky plate-supported negatives you slipped in and long black cloths hanging down the back where the photographer had to crouch in under to study the viewfinder. It was a long high far-away shot of the town down in the valley with smoke haze hanging over it and people and movement down there, the spot of what looked like a wagon heading out of town toward the river.

"That's from up where we'll be going tomorrow," the old man had said, and on impulse Bourne had taken out the tacks, slipping it gently into his jacket pocket. Now as he looked from it to the town and back to the photograph, he saw how right the old man had been. The photograph had been taken from up here for sure. His angle and the photographer's were almost the same. The town was just a little more to his right than it was in the photograph, and he crawled that way to compensate, trying to line them up exactly.

"What are you doing?" the old man said. "We've got to move."

"In a second," he repeated, crawling farther to the right, comparing them again, then crawling forward a bit. He stood hunched forward the way the photographer would have, looking now at the picture as if it were the viewfinder in a camera, shifting it slightly back and forth to line it up with the town. He almost managed, although he knew he could never line them up exactly. The picture had been taken in summer for one thing, and where it showed bushes in the foreground, there weren't any, and where there were bushes now, there weren't any in the picture, and there had been leaves then on the bushes, but now the bushes were bare, and there was a similar problem with the town. Although the town was the same as then, it had nevertheless somehow changed, gotten smaller, shrunk, settled with age, and the absence of motion down there made it seem smaller yet. Then and now, the photograph now as old as the town, he had a strange sense of doubling, and as the wind gusted, sweeping more specks of snow past him, he was afraid that the force of it would rip the photograph out of his hands, leaving him only the brittle corners.

"Come on, we've got to go," the old man said next to him, and even he seemed to be feeling the cold now, bunching his hands into his jacket pockets, hunching his shoulders in the wind. "It's only a photograph."

But it wasn't just a photograph, or at least there was something about the photograph that made it seem more than what it was, and he didn't understand. He had it and the town lined up as exactly as he could now, compensating for the hundred-year change in terrain and the difference in the town, but there was still something wrong and he couldn't place it, something unaccountably different, some unregistering detail that made him realize his fear wasn't from the chance that the wind might rip the picture out of his hand but from the picture itself, and then he saw it. Down there in the left-hand corner in among some thick-leaved bushes at the cliff edge. A man hunched almost invisible, his mottled jacket blending almost perfectly with the brush, his face barely distinguishable from the intersecting leaves.

Or was it a man or just a shadow pattern, he couldn't tell, and was that a rifle projecting through the bushes or just a barren branch pointing toward the picture. No, that was wrong, it would have been toward the camera, toward the photographer. Toward *him*. He glanced toward where the bushes would have been, and the old man was over there now, scampering toward the edge of the cliff, his mottled jacket the same as in the photograph, and as the wind gusted through his jacket, chilling him to the bone, his eyes widened and he couldn't move.

"We've got to go," the old man was calling over to him. "If this wind gets any stronger, when we climb down it'll blow us off the cliff."

But he still couldn't move, just stood there, eyes wide, watching the old man hurry along staring down studying the face of the cliff, and then abruptly the photograph was gone, ripped out of his hands, corners crumbling, jerked by the wind out over the cliff into the valley. Running, reaching for it, he was almost over the edge before he realized, stopping, glancing furtively toward the old man easing himself down over the edge. He glanced back at the photograph, just a speck now, hardly different from the sporadic snow-flakes, flipping, tumbling down out of the high ground into the sheltered valley. The next thing he was pulling off his gloves, easing himself over the edge the same as the old man, touching a narrow ledge down there, gripping a lower handhold, setting down, inching along, feeling for a lower handhold, thinking I've got to get the photograph, but he never would, and he knew that even as he gripped an outcrop of rock and let himself down, bracing his boots in a crack in the rock, grabbing another handhold, stepping farther down, dangling, groping, dangling again, feeling an urgency even greater than when he had been saddling the horses back at the corral the first day of the chase, taking chances now that he would never have thought to manage climbing up, just a few feet to the left of the old man by the time he reached the bottom.

The horses were whinnying down there through the trees, and the old man and himself just needed to look at each other once before they were sliding down through the shale, running into the trees, Bourne knowing without the old man even having to tell him that they had to split up, coming on the horses from opposite directions in case anyone was down there with them, and it was only after he had circled widely, spotting the horses skittering nervously in the clearing that he realized that it didn't matter if he and the old man had split up or not, the old man didn't have a gun, cursing himself for not letting the old man have the

.22 at least, suddenly realizing why the old man hadn't asked for it in the first place. The old man had been hiding a gun on himself all along.

He kept circling through the trees, stopping, listening, circling again, hearing the wind in the trees, the snow now like pellets clicking down through the fir needles, seeing the old man in the clearing, walking toward the horses, hand out, calming them, and it was only later that he knew he should have checked the woods more thoroughly, fearful the old man was going to take the horses, hurrying toward the clearing.

"It's just the wind, the snow," the old man was telling the buckskin, patting it.

"Where is it?"

The old man turned and looked at him. "I don't know what you mean."

"Your gun. Where is it, tucked in under your belt? In your boots? Where is it?"

The old man thought a moment.

"It's in a shoulder holster under my jacket."

"What kind? Let's see it."

"Why? Don't tell me you're going to take that too. You might as well know I won't let you."

And that stopped him. It was the same kind of standoff they'd been in the day before, only now he knew he couldn't shoot him. Because he would have done the same thing in the old man's place and he realized he was angry because he'd been fooled.

"No," he said. "If you'd been planning to use it on us, you would have done that long before now. You've had enough chances. I'm just spooked from the weather. Like the horses."

"Sure you are," the old man said, staring at him.

"It's an old Army Colt revolver. A forty-five." And he was unbuttoning his jacket, reaching in, showing it, a long barrel western-style like the magnum but the metal was dull and gray and there was a crack in the crude wooden handle.

"It still shoots good," the old man said. "Don't worry. I can use it."

"I'll bet you can." And then without either of them moving or changing expression or needing to say anything he knew that everything was going to be all right again. "Hold the buckskin," he told the old man, and then he was untying the rope he had used to hitch the horse to the tree, coiling the rope and walking toward him.

_____ 17

THE SNOW WAS AN INCH DEEP by the time they got back to town, drifting against the buildings, gusting against their backs as they hunched down stiff-legged in their saddles, the manes of their horses matted thickly. Riding by the hotel he saw Claire coming out holding herself in the cold, watching him, and by then he was so frozen through and tired that it was all he could do to nod at her and shake his head as if commenting on the snow. They rode into the stable, unsaddling the horses, feeding, watering them, making sure they were secure in their stalls before the two of them came out closing the stable doors behind them, turning into the wind to walk up the street through the blowing snow toward the hotel. He felt his eyebrows caked with snow, started running, squinting ahead of him, realizing the old man wasn't with him anymore. He stopped and turned. The old man was back there in the middle of the street, standing motionless, holding himself.

"Are you all right?" he said, coming back to him.

"I don't know." He was holding himself rigidly as if any motion at all, a breath even, would break something in him, his face gray against the driving snow. "It's a cramp or something," he was saying. "From climbing that cliff or heaving those boulders or something. I'll be all right in a second."

But he wasn't. The second stretched on, snow gusting past them, and Bourne had his hand out as if to help him but he didn't know what to do so he just continued standing there like that. The old man's face went suddenly rigid as well and his eyes closed, grimacing, and then like a shadow that was there and gone he was breathing easily again, face loose, eyes opening. "There. You see. I told you I'd be fine."

"Well, let's get you out of here."

"I told you I'm all right."

"OK," Bourne said.

They stared at each other, and then the old man was brushing past him, walking heavily up the street into the wind toward the hotel, and Bourne stood there looking after him a moment before he followed.

Claire was waiting for them at the door.

"I want to see you," Claire told him.

"Why? What's happened?"

"You heard me. Now."

She was walking away from him along the bar toward the kitchen.

"Family troubles?" the old man said.

"I don't know," he answered, puzzled.

"Well, you'd better see to it. I'll pass some time with your little girl."

He nodded, walking slowly toward the kitchen, hearing the old man brushing snow off his jacket, patting the dog. "What is it? What's the matter?" he asked Claire in the kitchen.

She was standing with her back turned by the stove. "Close the door."

He did.

She turned on him. "I went down to the town hall this morning after you left. Sarah was strong enough to walk and she went with me. We found those records he's always talking about. A couple of ledgers with about an inch of dust on them on a shelf in back, and they aren't as full as he lets on, but they're full enough. There wasn't any Mexican who was lynched, and there wasn't any smallpox. The town wasn't built in 1879, it was built in 1890, and the people weren't forced to leave. The gold just gave out and they moved on to better pickings."

He didn't know what to say. "You must have missed another set of records that tell a different story."

She shook her head. "We went through that place from front to back. We even checked out the basement and the attic. Believe me, there aren't any."

"The difference in dates. He's an old man. It could be just a faulty memory."

"That doesn't explain the business about the lynching and the smallpox."

"Well, a lynching's not the kind of thing you want to put in your records. The smallpox might have been on them so fast they never had a chance to mention it."

She shook her head again. "The ledgers go right up to when there were only a handful of people. The last entry is just a formality, a note by one of the last people here to say he's closing the books off. If there'd been smallpox, he surely would have mentioned it."

"If he took the time to close the books, why didn't he take them with him? Are you sure they're even for this town?"

"The name's right on the covers. For all we know he was planning to come back and get them and he never did. That's not the point. That old man's crazy, and I don't feel safe around him. As soon as it stops snowing, I want us out of here."

"But where else is there to go?"

"I don't care. I don't feel safe with him around me and Sarah."

Sarah, he thought suddenly and turned opening the door.

She was directly across from him huddled in her sleeping bag in the corner, the old man sitting on the floor beside her. "Just about this time of year," he was telling her. "And it was snowing then too, just like now, not enough to make it very hard to get around but bad enough to let you know there was more coming and you had to get your work done and get out." He was sitting with his back turned so he couldn't see Bourne, his words droning on and on in an even low-voiced monotone, like he was working a spell or telling a story he'd told so often that he knew it by rote, and the voice was so hypnotic that it drew Bourne quietly out of the kitchen over to the bar.

"A river valley like this too," the old man was saying quietly, "only there wasn't a town like this but a village and the people weren't white but Indians. You could see their horses and teepees and wood fires small down there from up on a bluff like your father and I went to this morning, and the fires were smoking from the snow, and you could see the women walking around clutching blankets. That was when I was sixteen, why I went away and came up here."

Bourne looked and Claire was standing at the bar beside him, staring over, and he didn't know why but he was afraid of what was coming.

"They'd been stealing horses, you see," the old man was saying, "and not content with that they'd started stealing cattle, and two of them had been caught breaking into the general store down on the rangeland. Then the townspeople down there caught one of them messing with a white woman and they lynched him. That's what finally started it."

Like the Mexican, Bourne thought, uncertain.

Sarah was wide-eyed, totally absorbed, unable to speak.

"They sat around getting liquored up all night, and in the morning they'd decided to teach those Indians a lesson. So about forty of them rode up here drinking and talking and laughing, flashing their rifles, and when they got close enough that they didn't want to be spotted, they left their horses and spread out along the bluff to see how best they could do this. That's when it started snowing, and they knew that whatever they were going to do they had to be quick about it.

"But not too quick. Because they'd already figured out that if this was going to work they were going to have to do it just like the Indians would have. Which meant no horses, no wild shouting ride down there into the camp, giving them time to mount up and get out or grab their rifles and start defending. No, they were going to climb down off the bluff and spread out in a circle, coming in on foot from every side, using the long grass for cover. And now that they thought about it the snow was a good thing after all, giving them extra cover. So they had a few more drinks, passing the last bottles around until they finished them, and then they started down. It was late afternoon when they finally started moving in through the grass, and it was another hour before they were close enough.

"I was one of them. Like I said I was only sixteen and I didn't know any better. I wanted to see what was going to happen. So they let me come along, leaving two other boys to watch the horses. They put me with a man named Arondale. He was a man who used to be good friends with my father, but my father was dead then, and this man had become like a second father and he used to drop around all the time to see my mother. I think he would have married her. And I admired him so much you can't imagine. He used to take me up hunting a lot and he showed me just about everything I know. A big man. Huge shoulders. Face like a rock. Kind of gentle, though, like your father."

And for the first time Bourne realized that the old man was aware that he'd been listening all along. Claire moved closer to him at the bar.

"I was with him moving through the grass. I had a shotgun like the double-barrel I use now, and I never forgot how that grass was so stiff and bent over in the snow and wind as we crawled through it. Wore the knees out of my pants that day. And when we were so close that we could see the grease on the women's faces as we peered out at them through the grass, he held up his hand for me to be quiet and we waited. There was a time when we had all agreed to start you see. When we knew we would all have had a chance to get in position. Two minutes after five. I remember the pocket watch he used to check that. The glass was cracked. Somewhere coming up he'd knocked against a rock and cracked it. Then somebody started shooting on the other edge of the village and we couldn't tell if it was one of us or whether one of the Indians had spotted us, but there was a whole lot of shooting then and we were jumping up out of the grass, running and firing. I remember the squaws nearest us dropping, and all around our side of the camp I could see men standing, firing, and we were running, Arondale ahead of me, shooting the first big Indian buck that came lurching out of the teepee ahead of us to find out what was happening.

"No, I'm wrong. When I said we all jumped up firing, I was wrong. I didn't fire at all. I just kept running and I must have thought I was firing but I wasn't and there was a kind of rhythm to the attack that just drew me into it. Arondale shot three more bucks coming out of that teepee and when he ran on to the next one, he didn't bother waiting, he just emptied his rifle into the deerskin, bullet holes all across it, and then he turned and clubbed an Indian that was running past him and then there was so much commotion, so many people running and screaming and shooting that I don't remember clearly after that.

"Except that I was standing in the center of it all,

that much comes through to me, and I was never quite sure how I made it through that day without getting shot. The real fighting only took five minutes, mostly all the Indians were dead by then, and there were some of the townspeople running around finishing the wounded, and there were some others that started in on the horses and the cattle. I never understood that, how if the stolen horses and cattle were a lot of the reason they'd come up here in the first place why they'd set to killing them, but they did, and the next thing I remember is an Indian girl, sixteen, fifteen, looked as young as I was anyhow, she'd been pretending to be hit, lying on the ground by her dead mother, hoping nobody would come around, but Arondale did, nudging her foot, and she bolted up like some kind of rabbit.

"She'd lost one moccasin, her blanket was off her, showing a kind of deerskin dress with those red beads on it, only now that I think they could just as easily have been blood, and she was running, long black hair streaming after her, into the wind and the grass. I don't know why but I was running too and Arondale was ahead of me running, and he'd been in the cavalry you see. He had this long saber dangling by his side that he'd saved from the war and had put on as a joke, running after her, not bothering to tackle her or anything, just drawing his saber and slashing at her. It must have been freshly sharpened. He slashed at her sideways, and he was a big man remember, the force of it cut her right in half."

Over by the bar, Bourne felt Claire clutch his arm.

"And she didn't die right away, you see," the old man was saying. "Don't ask me how, but I came running up to where Arondale was standing looking down at her, she was still alive, breathing, opening her mouth to say something but she couldn't, blood coming thickly out of her mouth and her body. There wasn't any white to her eyes, just big and dark and wide, and you could still see how pretty she'd been as I looked and Arondale was doing something with his pants, un-buttoning them, pulling himself out."

Claire was clutching him harder, fingers digging into his skin as he pulled away from her, walking over, standing behind the old man, and the old man didn't let on he'd noticed, just kept droning on. "He was cutting the skirt off the bottom, lifting her torso, joining with her, lunging into her—"

And Bourne had his hands around the old man's throat, choking him, strangling him, digging his fingers in under the old man's voice box, crushing, ready to tear his head off to make him stop, and the old man already had his hands up, prying at the fingers, grip-ping the little finger on each hand and working them back to snap them.

"He was jerking her torso back and forth against him while she watched," the old man screamed, and he shouldn't have been able to talk let alone scream but he was, working at Bourne's fingers to snap them, screaming, "and that's when I shot him. Put both bar-rels to his head and blew his head off. Blew it apart. They never found enough pieces to put it back to-gether, and that's why he never married my mother, and that's why—"

He suddenly had Bourne's hands free, spinning around as Bourne raised his fist to hit him, and the old man had Bourne's knife out, pressing it hard into his belly. "You want to know what she felt like?" the old man was screaming at him, red-faced, eyes bulging. "You want to find out? You touch me once more, sonny, you lay a hand on me again, and I'll slit you open and let your guts drop out."

18

HE WAS NEVER QUITE SURE what came first after that, Claire's scream or the explosion that blew apart the left front window. It could have been Claire's scream first, from the way the old man had the knife against him. Or she could have been screaming from the explosion. He never knew. And his first thought was that somebody had thrown something through the glass or that the wind had broken it, but then it registered on him that two bullets had whacked close together into the wall beside him and he dove to the floor.

"Christ, they're here. Get down," he was telling Claire. "Down."

She was running across, diving beside Sarah, and the old man was still so worked up that it was all he could do to stand there, the knife in his hand, looking around.

The wind was shrieking in through the shattered window, snow gusting in, and then the right front window was crashing in as well, bullets whacking, wind doubly shrieking.

"Get down," he told the old man, tugging at his leg,

and he finally had to yank the old man's feet from under him, toppling him, face cracking to the floor. He grabbed the knife from the old man's hand, drawing his magnum, aiming it toward the windows and the door.

"They'll come, they'll be coming."

The old man was shaking his head, blood trickling from his mouth.

"Draw your gun," Bourne was telling him, and then the old man had cleared his head enough to do what he was told.

"You damned old fool," Bourne told him. "Those boulders didn't fool them. The noise only told them where we were."

"Maybe," the old man said, or at least it sounded like that, the word was hard to tell, obscured by the crack of a rifle outside, the simultaneous whack of a bullet into the piano up there on the stage behind them, wires snapping, jangling, mallets striking in grotesque imitation of a chord.

"Out the back," Claire said.

"No," Bourne said. "If they're out front, they'll be out back waiting for us too."

"He's right," the old man said. "Our only chance is to go upstairs."

"What kind of chance is that? They'd only have us trapped even worse."

And thinking of the back door, he suddenly noticed how Claire had closed the kitchen door when she followed him out, how somebody could get in there from the back without his noticing. He thought he heard somebody out there and fired through the door, Sarah screaming, the close-in report of his handgun ringing in his ears. But the dog must have heard somebody out there too. It was standing, teeth bared, going over.

"Hush," the old man said.

It stayed where it was.

"Hush," the old man said again, and the dog returned. Because the old man must have smelled it even before Bourne did, and now Bourne was seeing it as well, the thick acrid black smoke that was spewing out under the bottom of the kitchen door, rising, spreading out all around the cracks at the side and the top of the door. And glancing toward the front, Bourne saw two bright lanterns arcing in with the snow through the broken windows, glass shattering as they hit the floor, the sickly sweet smell of kerosene gusting toward him just a second before the flames caught, whooshing toward the ceiling in one great solid wall of flame between them and the windows and the door.

The smoke from the kitchen was billowing thicker, wafting toward the ceiling. He heard Sarah coughing. He saw bright orange flames licking thinly through the dense black smoke at the bottom of the door.

"Hold your shirt over your mouth. Breathe through it," he was telling Sarah.

"Upstairs," the old man said. "I told you."

But the old man wasn't moving that way. He was crawling low across the floor toward the bar, grabbing the shotgun where Claire had leant it, disappearing into the smoke around the bar.

"What is it? What's the matter?"

"This," the old man told him, crawling back in sight, coughing, clutching a rifle along with the shotgun.

"Where did that come from?"

"I went and put it there last night while you were sleeping."

"Christ."

"That's right. Upstairs I said."

And this time he wasn't waiting for a reply. He was already crawling past them, standing, charging up the stairs. The wall of flames spread toward them, crackling, eating at the floor and the ceiling. The door to the kitchen was almost burned through, flames dancing through the walls on either side. He could feel the heat singeing his face.

"Let's go," he said, standing, dragging Claire to her feet, stooping to lift Sarah.

"I can walk now."

"Do it then. Let's go."

And as they ran to the stairs, swinging around, charging up, on impulse he grabbed Sarah's sleeping bag and his knapsack, running after them, his footsteps pounding hollowly on the stairs. The heat was scorching through his jacket. The room down there was totally in flames.

"This way," the old man told them, waiting at the top.

"But the fire. It'll catch us up here too," Bourne said.

Smoke was coming up through the floor. Flames started showing through the cracks.

"I don't have time to explain," the old man said. He was running down a hallway parallel to the street, half-shadowed, half-flickering from the flames, reaching a doorway at the end, heaving against it.

"Help me."

The fire was roaring in the room below them, heat swelling, the hallway choking them with smoke, and they heaved but it wouldn't give. They heaved again. It still wouldn't give.

"The shotgun," Bourne said, reaching.

"No, they'll hear." And the old man heaved again, and then in one last desperate lunge they both cracked against the door, snapping it free like kindling, stumbling through into the next room.

"We're in another building," the old man said. "The guy who ran the hotel owned this too. This was his office."

And the four of them were hurrying across past the big desk and the long since rotted, mouse-eaten leather padded chair toward the opposite wall, the dog running with them, Bourne stooping to squeeze sideways through a rough shoulder-high hole that had been chopped through the wall. The roar was behind him. The air was pure and cool.

"I did this all through town," the old man told him. "So I could get around unseen if anybody came."

They squeezed through into a room stacked with wooden boxes, one big box pushed near the wall to hide the hole, squirming around it, rushing down a corridor of boxes, past a stairway, through another hole, into a jail cell.

Bourne recoiled from the inch-thick bars, the metal bunk stacked against the wall, thinking Christ we're trapped again, before the old man leaned against the bars, and it wasn't locked, the door was squeaking open.

"We're almost there," the old man said.

They ran out past a desk and slots built into the wall for rifles and pegs driven into the wall for keys and gun belts, and this time there wasn't any hole in the wall, just a hatch that closed off the way downstairs.

"I'll lift. You aim," the old man said, prying his finger through the ring in the hatch, lifting abruptly, and

Bourne was ready, aiming down the stairs, but there wasn't anybody.

"Good," the old man said. "That's all I was worried about. Now we've got them."

"What are you talking about?"

But the old man was going down, stopping halfway to check the room, continuing down, and the rest of them were coming after. The sheriff's office. Another row of cells, a desk, an empty rifle case, a wooden file cabinet in the front corner, a map nailed to the wall, wanted posters all around it, no pictures, just names and charges and reward money, murder, arson, rape, and he just had time to glance at everything once before the old man was over to a back door under the stairs by the cells, opening it, peering out. Even in the middle of the room, the wind chilled him. The snow was blowing over to him.

He glanced toward the small windows on each side of the front door, straining to see through the gusting snow out there. He glanced back at the old man, and the old man was gone. Then the old man was back.

"There's nobody out there. Now's our chance."

And for a second Bourne felt his excitement rising, thinking they might get away after all, before he stopped himself. "They might have somebody watching the stable."

"Stable? What are you talking about stable? I'm talking about going after them."

He couldn't believe it. "What?"

"Two in front, one for each lantern they heaved in through the windows. One in back to start the fire in the kitchen. We'll take the one in back first."

"But that's crazy. There might not be three. There might be a dozen."

"It doesn't matter. In this snowstorm there might as well be three. We'll be onto them before they know it."

"Maybe you will. I'm getting us out of here."

"Are you? Listen. You run now and they'll just keep after you. There'll never be another chance like this. You know where they are. You've got the storm for cover, and they don't know where you are."

"But there's something else, isn't there? You're not doing this for me. It's for you, and I'm not going to risk my family to help you do it."

"You're damn right it's for me. This is my town they're burning. No, not just my town, my home. And I'm not going to let them get away with it."

"For what? The town is finished. When they're done with this side, they'll start on the other. There won't be a wall standing by the time they're through. It'd be different if there was a chance of saving anything. But just to get even? No way. We're leaving."

"I'll shoot you where you stand."

And they had come full circle, the old man holding the shotgun on him again, him aiming the magnum at the old man, and this time it was going to be himself that would have to back down. The old man would shoot. He was sure of it. And he himself wouldn't, too afraid of the others out there hearing the shot and coming for them. It wasn't a standoff. It was suicide.

He smelled smoke.

The old man cocked both hammers on the shotgun.

"All right," Bourne said. "Tell me how you want to do it."

The old man smiled. "You just watch me."

He moved the barrel away, and Bourne breathed again.

"The fire," Claire said.

He heard it. The flames were roaring, crackling, very close. Smoke was creeping through the wall.

"We'll have to hide them in the grass outside," the old man said, pointing toward Claire and Sarah, and there was a moment as the old man turned to lead them out and find a place when Bourne knew he could crack the old man's skull in with his gun and get to the horses. But he didn't. It was as if a choice had been made for him and he was going with it, grateful to be at last doing something, telling himself that maybe the old man was right—there might never be a better chance. In a half hour or so, one way or another, all of this might be finished. They might never have to run again.

19

THE SNOW WHIPPED at him. Even with the light from the block-long string of fires it was hard to see, smoke mingling with the blizzard, four o'clock more like night, and they had to keep walking into it, their arms up shielding their faces from the sharp lashing sting. They came around a shed, angling toward the burning almost gutted hotel, almost onto a man huddled against the side of the shed watching the back of the hotel before they spotted him. Or at least the old man spotted him, stopping abruptly, shouldering Bourne back around the corner of the shed. The old man didn't even take a chance that Bourne might not understand. He put his hand cold and hard and bony directly over Bourne's mouth to keep him from saying anything. Then he stooped, drawing a long bowie-type knife from his boot, disappearing around the corner of the shed.

Bourne didn't understand. If the old man had been hiding the knife all along, then why when they had been fighting at the hotel had the old man pulled Bourne's knife instead? Because he couldn't get at his own? Because he wanted to show Bourne how easy it was to get a knife or a gun away from him?

He never knew. In the roar from the storm and the fires, he never heard the guy watching the hotel scream when the old man knifed him either. If the guy made a sound at all. The way the old man handled himself in this kind of situation the guy probably didn't. The old man was just suddenly coming through the snow around the corner of the shed again, wiping his knife on his pants, saying "Come and help me," and as if in a trance Bourne followed.

The guy was lying face down in the snow. Even with the drifts piling up quickly against the shed there was still a lot of blood, turning from crimson to red to the faintest shade of pink in the snow, and the way the top of the guy's head looked from where the old man had gripped his hair, cutting, yanking, blood caked through the rest of his hair and down his neck onto his clothes, broke the trance. He looked from the guy's head to the mass of hair and flesh and gore hanging from the old man's belt, stumbling back, saying "Jesus Christ, you scalped him," and the old man waved the knife at him, saying, "Shut up and help. I'll give you the same if you don't help. I can't afford to have you out here getting in my way."

The old man was pulling the guy's legs, turning him

around and dragging him face down toward the fire, leaving a swath of blood in the snow.

"God damn it, help I said."

And once again Bourne obeyed, stumbling forward, grabbing the guy's hands, lifting him half off the ground, dragging him sideways now toward the fire, the swath of blood wider, thicker. The snow was melting on Bourne's jacket. The hair on his hands was crinkling gray. They couldn't get any closer, lifting the guy totally off the ground, swinging him back and forth, letting him fly toward the fire. He flopped down just this side of the fire, one arm twisted under him, the flames licking at him, and Bourne smelled the sharp stomach-turning stench of hair burning, not sure if it was his own or the guy's as he turned quickly to protect his face from the flames, staggering away, stopped by a roll of bloody insides that had slipped out of the guy when they had been dragging him. He held himself, watching the old man stoop and gather them and, arm back, heave them into the fire, watching them flip through the air dangling as they fell into the fire, dropping his eyes to the guy's body, clothes on fire from head to toe, turning, sinking to his knees, holding himself and gagging.

"Get up," the old man told him.

But he couldn't. He was far enough away from the fire now that his hands were numb again and his face, but he was breaking out in a cold pale sweat, and he was holding himself, heaving dryly.

"Get up I said," the old man told him, pulling at him, dragging him up. "We don't have time for this. I'm going this way." He was pointing toward the back of the sheriff's office. "I'm going to work around across the main street to the buildings on the other side. You go this way and do the same." He was pointing in the opposite direction, toward the entrance to the town. "We'll catch them between us."

He wanted to say something but he didn't know what and it wasn't any use. The old man was suddenly gone, running off into the storm, and he was standing there, sweating, staring at the fast-drifting swath of blood in the snow, smelling burned hair and clothing and flesh, racing abruptly in the direction he'd been told, hurrying along the line of burning buildings, reaching a side street that led toward the main road, almost taking it.

But the flames had spread to the buildings on the next block, filling the side street so that there was only a narrow corridor to run down and he knew he couldn't do it without getting burned, running farther along the backs of the buildings, reaching where the fire had not yet spread, rushing on, reaching the next side street before he knew it.

He stopped without thinking, pressing himself against the back of the last building, peering around the corner, gun ready, staring up between the buildings toward the main road.

Nobody.

He raced up, pressing himself against the wall again, staring around the corner again, this time down the main road and the sidewalks and the fronts of stores, grateful that the snow wasn't driving into his eyes now but against the back of his head, squinting all the same as he strained to see through the snow and the smoke down there and the gloom if there was anybody.

No one that he could see, and holding his breath he bolted across the street to the corner on the other side.

Still no one, and he started working his way down along the edge of the sidewalk, checking the windows of stores that he was passing, checking the snow-shrouded sidewalk opposite him, hurrying on.

He didn't expect anyone on this block. Chances were they were waiting across from the hotel on the next block down, taking their time, making sure nobody left the burning building before the place collapsed and they could be sure that none of them had survived. All the same, if there were more than three of them, they might have stationed themselves all along the main street just in case, and he had to make certain of himself, checking all the storefronts as he moved along. He reached where the fire had spread along the stores opposite him. Squinting, he made out the intersection ahead of him and up across from him on his right the whole block of burning buildings with the hotel in the middle of them. He slowed as he neared the intersection, stopped as he heard the gunshots. Three of them. Down at the next intersection. So muffled by the roar of the fires and the storm that he couldn't tell if they were from a rifle or a handgun. The old man, he thought without reason and in spite of everything he wanted to hurry down and help him but he was stopped motionless and that second's hesitation was what saved him. Because the white figure that rose up ahead of him out of the snow in the middle of the intersection seemed to grow larger and larger and the guy shouldn't have been that big, but he was, and he kept looming larger and larger until Bourne realized that the sound of the shots had made him crouch and that the hugeness of the figure ahead of him was a trick of perspective made double by the white camouflage suit the guy was wearing.

He dropped from crouching to kneeling and then dove face forward into the snow. It clogged his mouth and filled his nostrils coldly. He fought to breathe and couldn't, held his breath, heart thumping, chest constricting, glancing up toward the figure abruptly running away down the street toward the sound of the shots. Two more. Closer now. From a handgun he was sure, and Christ, the old man was using up all his ammunition. He wouldn't have time to reload the handgun and he didn't have the shotgun anymore, he'd given it to Claire, which left the rifle, but in the storm he wouldn't be able to see to shoot until somebody was almost onto him and in those close quarters aiming with the rifle wouldn't be any good.

Another shot, this time louder, fuller, unmistakably from a rifle, but he couldn't tell from where and he couldn't take the chance of stumbling across another white-suited figure huddling hidden in the snow. He had to stay low, started crawling through the snow the rest of the way across the intersection toward the buildings opposite the fire, glancing continually ahead of him for any sign of anybody, stopping, listening, crawling forward.

He reached the sidewalk, crawling along the edge of it, using it for cover against anybody who might see him from inside one of the stores. That was the only place they could be. The storm was too bad for them to want to stay out in it. They would have judged by now that nobody could have survived the fire, waiting in the stores until the storm lifted and the fires died and they could go over to make sure.

No, that was wrong. If one guy had been waiting at the intersection, there'd be more outside as well. But there might be some in the stores all the same, and he found himself glancing everywhere as he crawled, wiping the snow from his eyes, groping, slowing.

Another shot. Another after that. Rifles again. And now someone screamed. It wasn't the old man, he was sure of that. The old man had got one of them. Or had he? Maybe the old man had been the one screaming after all.

And he finally couldn't take it anymore, had to get on his feet, out of the snow, away from them, his hand freezing to the metal of his gun as he lunged up, charging across the sidewalk, shoulder heaving against a door, crashing through into shelter. He swung low, checking the place. A dry goods store, or what had once been a dry goods store, a counter down each side, empty shelves behind them, cobwebs and dust and dirt all over the snow on his clothes as he dodged behind one counter, checking it, across to the other counter, checking it, whirling toward the door in case someone had heard him crashing in.

No one, and he backed off from the front, working into the shadows in one corner, stumbling over a box as the back door flew open and out of the wind and the snow a figure burst in, gun ready, and they almost shot each other before he realized it was the old man.

The old man barely stopped to notice him. He was lurching white-faced over to the opposite counter, setting something on it, and at first Bourne thought the old man had been shot, he was moving so awkwardly. Then he realized this was the way the old man had looked when he'd stopped before in the middle of the street holding himself. Cramp nothing. The old man had broken something inside him. He couldn't hide it anymore. And then Bourne saw what he was fumbling with on the counter. A lantern. And the old man was shaking it to hear that it was full, lifting the glass top, lighting the wick, snapping down the glass top, and reaching back to throw it.

"What are you doing?"

"Shut up," the old man said. "Leave me be." He twisted to one side, jerking free from where Bourne was grabbing at him, whipping the lantern against the row of shelves, glass cracking, the fire catching almost immediately, spreading, rushing up the whole wall of shelves.

"They've nested in the stores all along here. I'm giving them the same chance they gave me." He was heading awkwardly toward the front door. "They'll be coming out and I'll be ready for them."

And it didn't make any sense. The old man had come after them because they were burning his town, and now he was burning the town himself and he wasn't out to get them for what they'd done, he just wanted somebody to get no matter what the reason, worked up into such a frenzy that he couldn't keep himself from laughing as he stumbled out the door. And this was why the old man had stopped them from running, and this was why Claire and Sarah were huddled freezing in the drifts in the long grass, hiding, and Bourne couldn't hold it in anymore, shouting at him, screaming at him, "You crazy bastard! You dumb fucking—"

But it didn't matter. Because the sidewalk was only as far as the old man got. He was dropping his rifle, clutching both arms around his stomach as he sank to his knees, laugh broken into a groan, and the shot that followed from out there lifted him to his feet, slammed him back through the door and flattened him. He made a liquid noise just before he jerked and died.

And Bourne couldn't move. He knew he ought to dive for cover and shoot back at whoever was out there. He knew he ought to try to make it out the back before they came. But all he could do was stand there, staring at the old man spread out, chest blown open, ahead of him by the door, screaming, "You bastard! You dumb fucking bastard!" firing three times into the old man's jerking body as the flames from the shelves spread across the floor and touched the tips of the old man's fingers. A bullet whacked crashing through the window, slamming into the counter beside him. He fired once more into the old man's body, shattering his head, fired once more out the open doorway, and was gone.

$$\rule{3in}{2pt}\quad 20$$

HE WAS NEVER SURE how he made it back to Claire and Sarah. The storm was worse as he lunged out the back door, the snow driving hard against him, and he didn't look around to see if any of them were out there waiting for him, didn't try to crouch and make himself a smaller target or dive for cover or hide in one of the sheds or in a drift beside a barrel by the corner of a building, he just ran. He knew without thinking that with the storm as bad as it was they wouldn't be able to see him if he cut directly across the main road and down a side street toward the field where he'd hidden Claire and Sarah, but running became an uncontrollable impulse, and he just kept on stumbling, lurching to his feet, running again, thinking, "You crazy bastard! You dumb fucking crazy bastard!" Or maybe he shouted it. He never knew. He just kept running blindly, past the stores and the sheds that he sensed were all around him, across side streets, down alleys, stumbling, falling, and he was never sure either when he realized that he wasn't in the town anymore but out in the fields and that he was going to freeze to death, die out there. It was only later that he reconstructed what had happened and understood that the slash of the grass across his face when he fell must have told him, but at the time he was too far out of himself to register that, and all he could think was that without the town for bearings he was going to wander out there, freeze to death and die, and that finally was what brought him to himself, that Claire and Sarah were going to wait and freeze and die the same.

The town on fire became a beacon, leading him back, guiding him. He stumbled around the edge of the buildings, across the main road where they had first come in, around the edge of more buildings, letting the fire guide him along, staggering through the grass, coming upon Claire and Sarah before he knew it, them huddling under the sleeping bag he had taken with him from the hotel, crouching in a hollow in the grass, the snow drifted up around them, and he had told Claire to use the shotgun for anybody who came and didn't use his name, so she almost shot him before she realized.

"My God, I didn't know what was happening," she

said. "I heard all those shots and the fire was spreading and I didn't think I'd ever see—"

"I know," he said. "It's fine. Don't worry. It's going
to be all right now," hoping she believed him.

They were half frozen and there wasn't time to rub
their hands and feet or work out the stiffness from the
cold, they had to get moving again, and his first
thought was to try making it through the snow across
the fields into the trees but he knew they'd get lost and
their feet would freeze and they'd never make it, they
had to try for the horses. He knew the chances were
that some of the others would be watching the stable,
but he had to try for the horses anyhow, at least try,
and if when they came close they saw that some of the
others were watching the stable after all, well they'd
have done their best. They would be able to head off
walking through the storm toward the trees, knowing
that there'd been no other choice.

They swung around, approaching the stable from the
far end of town. Sarah was so cold that he had to carry
her now, stumbling through the drifts, and then as he
felt her settling against him, nodding, he realized that
he was going to have to make her walk anyhow, that
she was going to fall asleep if he didn't and her metab-
olism would slow and she would freeze. He set her
down, forcing her to walk, urging her through the snow,
bracing her as she faltered, hands on her shoulders,
working her ahead of him, and then they came to a
corner on the main road where the stable was in the
middle of the block to the left across from them, and
even with the snow lacing against his face, he could
make out where the fire had spread to the first buildings on both sides of the street down there.

"We've got to go in front and back at the same time," he told Claire. "If there's anybody in there, we've got to distract them from both directions."

"But we won't know to go in at the same time," Claire said.

And she was right. It wasn't any good. They were all going to have to go in together, him first. Once they split they might never find each other. This was either going to work or it wasn't. There just wasn't any way to take the risk from it. Pushing Sarah, running with her, he crossed the street, Claire beside him, ran down the side street and around to the alley on the left, stopping just far enough away from the back door of the stable to give him a chance to check it. He motioned for them to stay behind him while he worked forward, crouching, studying the drifts in front of the door to see if there were signs of footprints. There weren't. And the drifts were deep enough that they looked as if the door hadn't been opened since the storm began. He glanced down the alley, blinking in the snow, toward the fire. He glanced behind him at Claire and Sarah coming carefully, and taking a long breath, grabbing the wood handle on the door to the stable, he kicked away the drifts and yanked it open, running in, diving toward the stall on his right. He came up rolling, aiming the gun along the stalls, the horses scudding back and forth from the smell of the smoke and the sudden noise of his entrance. He glanced up at the loft, began working his way along the stalls, glancing up at the opposite loft, and if there'd been anybody, he would have been dead by now.

"Come on," he said, hurrying to saddle the pinto. "We don't have much time."

They rushed across to the other horses, Claire saddling the bay, Sarah rubbing her hands by the ladder to the loft, stamping her feet to get them warm. His own hands were numb and swollen from the cold, and it was taking him too long to cinch the pinto's saddle, slapping his hands against his thigh, slapping them again before he went back to working the straps through the buckles, tightening them, securing them. He was just swinging around to the next stall where the buckskin was when Claire screamed, and looking up he saw the guy standing up there in the opposite loft. He had a rifle pointed at them, and he must have been waiting for the noise of them working with the horses to hide the sound of him walking over. He was young and dressed in white the same as the other guy, hood thrown back, grinning, aiming, as Bourne dove over the side of the stall, fumbling to draw his gun, but his hand was so numb that he dropped it, and looking helplessly up he saw the guy grinning even more as he snuggled the stock of his rifle in close to his shoulder and lowered his cheek to get the sights lined up quite perfectly, and the roar of the twin explosions was deafening as the guy disintegrated up there, face going one way, arm flying another, chest caving in, the rifle dropping as the guy rose up toward the ceiling almost as if he had been hoisted and then slammed down out of sight up there in the corner where he must have been hiding.

He didn't know what had happened. He didn't think Sarah would ever stop screaming. He looked, and Claire still had the shotgun in her arms aiming it up toward the loft where the guy had been. She wasn't moving or blinking or breathing, just standing there aiming, and it was all he could do to pry her hands away before she started crying. He didn't have time to comfort her, didn't even know himself how he could be moving so efficiently, leading the bay and the pinto out of their stalls, forcing Claire and Sarah to take the horses out the back door, cursing, anything to get them moving as he rushed back to the buckskin, no time to saddle it properly, just cinch it and slip on a bridle and hope he wouldn't fall off as he led it out the door and swung on, kicking it, flailing at the other horses as he rode past, yelling at Claire and Sarah to get moving. They galloped out of the alley, swinging to head down the side street across the main road toward the fields of grass and snow on the other side of town. There was a shot behind them from the main road, but he didn't hear the bullet anywhere near them, kicking at his horse, clutching the reins and the saddle horn to keep from falling, Claire now on one side of him, Sarah on the other as the storm cleared enough for him to see the fields ahead and then they were into the long grass, crossing, when he heard the second shot behind him and heard it hit and it was a good thing Sarah was on one side of him because she never had a chance to turn and see as he did, already knowing what he would see but looking all the same, the last look he would ever have of her as Claire toppled forward, her bloody gaping face leading her body down off the horse, the hole in the back of her head obscured by the several flopping tumbles her body took as it landed.

21

HE WAS A LONG TIME getting control of himself. The shock of what had happened to her so stunned him that he just kept kicking his horse, urging it farther and farther on, faster and faster, Sarah beside him. He was well up into the trees before he knew it, riding higher, harder, yanking at his horse's reins to twist around a wall of brush that was suddenly before him, yanking the other way to get around a blockade of fallen timber, kicking up through a break in the trees toward a clearing above him. But the clearing frightened him, and at the last moment he swerved to the left around it, skirting the edge, charging up another slope of trees, angling toward another, then another, kicking, flailing, and he might have kept on like that until his horse dropped out from under him if he hadn't realized that Sarah wasn't with him any longer. He reined his horse back, head bent, yanking to turn, and she was down there at the bottom of the slope, her horse foundered in the snow. He galloped down, nearly falling, stopping, slipping off, tying the horse to a tree and running to her, afraid from the way her leg was pinned under the horse that she had broken it, realizing that the snow was so deep that her leg was only cushioned out of sight down there, wading in, easing her off, grabbing the pinto's reins and tugging to get it out. It came very slowly, and he stumbled tugging, and when at last he had it free, tying it to a fir branch, the struggle with it plus the shock of what had happened to Claire finally caught up to him, legs shaking, barely able to slump down against a fir trunk underneath its branches before he would have collapsed. The storm was easing, snowflakes sparse again, made even sparser by the shelter of the forest, boughs still shifting in the falling wind.

Then the wind was gone as well, and in the dusk and gloom from the storm clouds passing over, there was a kind of muffled silence, occasional far-off clumps of snow rustling off branches and thudding down onto drifts.

"Where's Mommy?" Sarah asked. She was crawling toward him, voice flat and muffled in the sound-absorbing snow.

He couldn't stop his arms and legs from shaking.

"Where's Mommy?" she asked again.

"Back down there."

"Why isn't she coming?"

He didn't answer.

"Will she be coming?"

"I don't think so."

The look of her face when the bullet had blown through, ripping it away. He couldn't get it out of his mind. He peered up at the cloud-scudded sky, peered down at his hands, couldn't stop them from shaking, looked at Sarah and reached out for her.

"Your mother's dead, sweetheart," he said and drew her to him. She didn't move all the time she was against him. When he held her away from him to see her face, it hadn't changed, cold, gray, expressionless, the way it had been for too many days before.

"What happened to her?"

"She was shot."

"Are you sure?"

"When we were crossing the field outside of town down there. I saw her just after she was hit."

"Are you sure she's dead?"

"I'm sure."

And he held her to him again. But the questions had started something, and that night was the beginning of the doubt that would never leave him. The snow that had been blowing across the field down there, the frenzy of trying to get away, he had only seen her face for a moment as she fell. It had seemed much longer, but it could only have been a moment, and maybe she wasn't dead after all. Maybe she'd only been grazed and the blood on her face wasn't from a bullet plowing through, but from a nick at the side of her face, and if he'd turned and gone back and picked her up, maybe he could have nursed her through.

Maybe nothing. That hadn't been just blood on her face, it had been open flesh, and the hole in the back of her head had been like someone had knocked her skull in with a pickax. She'd been dead before she hit the ground, and no amount of second-guessing was ever going to bring her back.

But the sight of her face, of the gaping hole in her head, he couldn't get them out of his mind, and clutching Sarah, holding her to him, he fought to clear it, scrunching his eyes shut, biting his lip, fists clenched, trembling, realizing how much his shock was really fear, how that blown-out face could have been his, how that could have been him toppling from the horse, flopping across the ground, the pain ripping through his head, and his guilt became double, Claire dead, him worrying about himself. And with that, thinking how that body down there could have been his, imagining what they might do to it, remembering the old man's story about the Indian girl, his guilt doubled again and he couldn't stand it anymore. He shouldn't have left her down there. No matter what, he shouldn't have left her.

He drew Sarah away from him again. "Listen to me. I have to go back. With the snow stopped and the wind gone, it's not so cold now. You'll be safe to sleep. I'm going to fix the sleeping bag here so you'll have some kind of shelter and the horses will be here so you won't be alone. We'll have something quick to eat and I'll tuck you in. But I have to go back."

She didn't question him, just looked at him with the same blank gray emotionless face while he dug into his pockets to see what he had. Since the line shack, he had made it a rule to carry food on him, chocolate, some jerky, salt, and they ate in silence, the horses nickering, pawing at the snow to get at any grass.

"We don't have our canteens," he said. "But the snow isn't safe to eat. It'll only make you cold, so if you get thirsty, you're just going to have to wait. Now I don't want to leave you here, but I've got to go down and I can't take you with me. I promise I'll be back. You'll be lonely and in a while you'll be afraid but try to sleep and the next thing you know I'll be waking you. I promise I'll be back."

She was holding a chocolate bar, looking at him, nodding blankly, and he nestled the sleeping bag into the snow under the branches of the tree the way he'd said he would, snuggling her into it, zipping the bag shut, kissing her, looking at her once more, and then he was gone.

22

AT FIRST HE THOUGHT he'd try making it on foot. He didn't want the horse to maybe whinny and draw attention to him going back, and working through the trees at night would be easier on foot than with a horse. But then he realized how numb his feet were in the snow, and he understood that he'd likely ridden several miles in blind panic before Sarah's horse had foundered and he'd stopped, and he knew he'd never make it down there and back without the horse. So he took the horse, and as it was, night was well onto him before he reached the edge of the trees, the start of the grass, and the horse wound up following its earlier tracks down through the trees anyhow, so it turned out he had done the best.

He slipped off, boots crunching in the snow as he tied the horse to a tree and looked off across the far field of snow and grass toward the town. The clouds still hadn't lifted, but the town was in clear sight over there just the same, embers a bright orange glow, here and there flames shooting up to show that except for a few walls still on fire and a few unburned shacks the town had almost totally been leveled.

He started across, following the tracks of the horses. Sometimes they were faint from where the wind had half obliterated them or the snow had continued falling into them, but always they were recognizable, a different gray from the gray of the snow in the dark on either side of them and the closer he got to the glow from the town the easier they were to see.

He walked straight up at the start, unafraid of showing himself, knowing that from the viewpoint of the town he would just blend into the black of the woods behind him. Coming closer, he began to crouch, depending now on the glow from the fires ruining the night sight of anybody who might be looking out toward him.

But they might have someone out here hidden in the snow although he doubted it. They wouldn't expect him to come back. That wouldn't make any sense. Unless they counted on Claire's body drawing him, and suddenly afraid again, he bent even lower, eventually crawling. He was wearing a pair of thick wool gloves, his hands warm and feeling again, and now he had to take one off, stuffing it into his jacket pocket, drawing his gun, his hand cold and sticking to the metal.

As he crawled, he was trying to remember where Claire had fallen. They had been out of town already, heading toward the middle. No, he could be wrong about that. He might have just thought they were near the middle, projecting himself that far in anticipation of getting farther away, and she had fallen to his left, what was now his right, so that she would be some distance away from the tracks and he would have to crawl away from the tracks soon, heading that way.

The glow was closer. He heard something, he didn't know what, some kind of scratching sound to his left, and he stopped, listening. He crawled a little farther on, and stopped again. Nothing. An animal maybe, a rabbit or ground hog coming out of its hole. Maybe he had only imagined it. He crawled farther on.

The glow was tinting the snow. He could see a figure over there in the town, or what was left of the town, walking outlined against the glow. He put his hand in his pocket, clenching it, warming it, bringing it out and clutching the gun. He looked around, listening, started crawling to his right toward where Claire might have fallen. He imagined reaching out, crawling, touching her without knowing, coming face up against her own. He shook his head.

She wasn't where he had thought she would be. That didn't surprise him. He had expected to make several mistakes in direction before he found her. He heard the scratching noise to his left again and stopped. He stayed motionless for what seemed a half hour before he started again, the cold of the snow against him turning from pain to numbness, putting his hand back in his pocket again and working it.

She wasn't the next place either, and by now he was so close to town that he was certain that the figure walking around the embers over there would see him. He'd come too far. She was somewhere in back of him. He turned, crawling back, thinking of Sarah alone up in the woods, wanting to hurry and find Claire and get her body up where he could find a way to bury it, stack wood over it or stones, anything to keep them from finding her in the morning. But he couldn't let himself hurry. To find her he had to do this right, check every possibility, cover every piece of ground where she might be, crossing back and forth over this stretch of ground on this side of the tracks, peering up, staring, crawling. Keep moving. Have to keep moving.

He'd gone too far the other way. He was sure of it. He was sure they had not gone this far into the field before she was hit. She had to be back where he'd just come from, closer to town, likely very near where he'd stopped and if only he'd gone on a few more feet he would have found her. So he turned around again, checking farther away from the tracks, crawling closer to town again, going past where he'd earlier stopped, moving so close to town that he knew she couldn't be around there. Back the other way again, stopping, listening, crawling, and he didn't know when he started crying, he just felt the trickle of tears going down both sides of his face, warm just for a moment, then cold in the night, freezing on him, and he did his best to wipe them away, to clear his eyes, but they just kept coming, trickling, freezing, and in the end he simply let them come, there wasn't anything he could do to stop them. They'd found her. There wasn't any question that they'd found her. He thought of Kess wanting some kind of proof. He thought of the old man's story about the guy assaulting the Indian girl. He groped to his feet, stumbling, running all along the stretch of ground where she might have been, running across the field toward the trees, anything to get it out of him, crying, sobbing, the crack of the tree against his face slamming him back flat.

He didn't know if he lost consciousness. He might have. He wasn't sure. All he did know was that he was suddenly lying there in the snow, fighting to clear his nose and breathe, touching himself, feeling the warm-cold, sticky blood coming from his nose, and in the dark he stumbled to find his horse, checked himself, realizing that he had gone in the wrong direction, going the other way, remembering to untie it, slipping on, clutching the mane, nudging the horse gently as it started off up through the trees.

They'd found her.

There was nothing more he could do.

It was only when the air began turning gray that he understood the clouds had lifted, that he'd been down there most of the night searching for her, and his only blessing was that Sarah was fast asleep in her sleeping bag in the snow when he got back to her. Mechanically he tied his horse to a tree, registered that another horse, the bay that Claire had fallen from, had somehow found its way up here and stayed, tied it to a tree as well, and slumping down beside Sarah to give her extra warmth, careful not to wake her, rubbing snow on his face to clean the blood, he dozed, waiting for the dawn.

Part

THREE

TIME LOST all significance for him. At the start, when the three men had come looking for them at the cabin and they had been forced to ride up into the hills, he had kept a careful mental record of the days. Friday the twenty-fourth of October, that was when they had started up, that much he was sure of. Saturday they had camped near the long deep pool at the base of the wide rushing stream. Sunday Sarah had got sick and they had found the line shack. Monday they had found the town. No, that was wrong. They had found the town late Sunday afternoon. Or had they? So much had happened in so little time that he had the feeling he had maybe added a day or even taken one away, and he was never able to tell for sure the day or date when Claire had died, Monday or Tuesday, even Wednesday, and as the days drew on, one after the other, almost imperceptibly, turning into weeks, he finally gave up trying. Tuesday the twenty-eighth, he decided without reason, and he measured all the days from that until at last those too confused on him and he didn't even know the month.

IT WASN'T MUCH. The slope under the snow turned from ground to rock, the horses stumbling, and as they left the trees behind them, the incline grew steeper, and about the only good thing was that the higher they went, the more the wind seemed to lessen, as if the walls of the draw were coming close together, providing cover. Then the slope leveled off, and they were into some kind of narrow pass, the wind easing enough that with the snow no longer gusting he could see rock walls and patches of boulders and bare stretches of rock where the snow had drifted off, the wind keening across the clifftops up there but down here mostly still, and directly ahead a little to the left was a corrugated metal shed, dark against the snow. But that wasn't what he was immediately looking for, and assuming it would be on the wall closer to the shed, he glanced that way, looking all along, and there it was, the entrance to the tunnel, a half-hidden hole in the side of the cliff.

He nudged his horse slowly over to it. What helped to hide it were the mounds of snow-covered rock that spread out on either side of it, too obvious to be camouflage, more likely just the stone that the miners had blasted out of the tunnel and dumped outside to form a windbreak, the corrugated metal of the shack sug-

gesting that this was a later enterprise than the town,
its claim more likely fully registered as protection
against jumpers. He saw the loading car tumbled on its
side against a mound of rock before he realized there'd
be ties and tracks in under the snow, and dismounting
he gave the bay's reins to Sarah—he had taken it
instead of the half-blind buckskin—telling her to wait
a moment, walking toward the entrance, stumbling
over a length of track hidden in the snow even though
he had been prepared for it. He stepped onto where
the ties would be between the tracks and walked up to
the entrance, peering in at the tall thick timbers that
had been used for supports along the walls and across
the ceiling. He tugged hard at one just at the entrance,
ready to leap back if it gave way and the ceiling shattered down, but it held, and taking a breath he walked
carefully in, footsteps echoing as he tested the next
supports farther down, not tugging as heavily but
using enough strength all the same to be able to tell if
they were secure. He tested them like that all the
way along, walking carefully, hardly breathing, until
about thirty feet from the entrance, just where the dim
light from the air out there was giving out, he came
up against a solid wall of rock and timber and debris
from where there had been a cave-in, pausing, turning,
looking, walking out.

"It's all right," he told her, feeling the wind again
after the absolute stillness of the mine. He was helping
her dismount, leading the two horses over the hidden
track and up along the ties into the mine where they
could see the uncertain footing exposed and manage it
better. The air was still again.

"Is this where we'll be staying?" Sarah asked.

He looked at her. It was one of the few things she had said since the day before when Claire had died. Her face was spiritless but there was a faint edge in her voice as if she were hoping that this would be the end, that after this there would be some kind of security and order.

"No," he said. "That's what they'll be expecting us to do. From the map this is the only obvious shelter anywhere around." His voice was echoing. "But they won't be sure until they follow our tracks up here and I'm counting on that wind to cover the tracks and make it hard for them. I figure we've got maybe half a day before they get here. That's time enough."

She didn't understand.

"What's the matter, aren't you hungry? Food. We may not have much, but while we've got the chance, we're going to make a feast."

And for the first time in a while her eyes had light in them, not much but it was a start, and her face changed a little, hard to tell but it looked like the effort at a smile.

He loosened the cinches on the horses, not wanting to take their saddles off in case somebody came after all and they had to get out of here fast. He started to untie the sleeping bag from the back of the pinto, wanting to wrap it around her, and then thought better.

"I've got some work for you to do."

He didn't mean it to sound abrupt, but it came out that way, and instead of putting her off, the thought of something to do only made her seem more interested.

"What is it?"

"There's been a cave-in down at the end. I want you to be very careful. I want you to go back there and get some wood. I don't want you to take any from the cave-in itself. There's plenty of bits and pieces lying around back there without your having to touch the cave-in. You do and you just might start the whole thing coming down on you."

She looked reluctant now.

"There isn't any danger. Just stay away from the rocks and you'll be fine."

She looked at him, unconvinced, nodded slowly, and turned reluctantly to go down. He tied the reins of the horses in under the ties between the tracks and went outside.

3

THE SHED WAS FIRST, but even as he was passing it, he found what he was looking for, a piece of corrugated metal leaning half covered by snow against the side. It was about two feet square, exactly the right size for what he needed, and picking it up, the thin metal difficult to keep a grip on through the woolen gloves that he was wearing, he went around to the door of the shed, trying it.

The thing was padlocked, and he didn't want to break it in, didn't want to make it obvious that they'd been here. Even with the wind as reduced as it was, their tracks were filling in all the same, and with luck the tracks would be completely gone by the time the others came. Blinking, eyes watering from concentration in the wind, he worked around the shed, no windows, coming to a corner where the sheets of metal had begun to separate from the post that they were anchored to. He pried at one, pulling it farther from the post until there was space enough to edge through, and squeezing, he ripped the shoulder of his coat on a nail as he went in.

The place was close to five feet by eight feet, the crack he had come through giving him light enough to look around. There was a workbench that took up one wall, nothing on it. There was a motor, he didn't know what kind or what for, that took up one corner, long since rusted over. A pile of refuse in another corner, more of it under the bench. The place had obviously been for making repairs or storing equipment. The men who worked the tunnel had probably lived in cabins or tents down in the trees, leaving as soon as the vein played out.

He couldn't put off looking at the rip in his coat anymore, afraid that the nail had gone clean through and that the coat wouldn't keep out the cold any longer, but it was only the outer layer of wool, the inner layer was still all right, and feeling better, he stooped to sort through the refuse in the corner. Rusty cans, their labels faded, illegible, empty liquor bottles, cogs and wheels, the head of a hammer. And he picked that up, putting it in his pocket, sorting lower. A dry brittle nest at the bottom, probably from a field mouse, but no sign that it had been back this year or ever, a few specks of gray fur in among the twigs and yellowed grass. He put everything back the way he had found it.

The pile under the workbench wasn't much better,

more pieces of machinery, more cans and bottles, a pair of cracked leather boots with open toes. Except that underneath everything, close to the wall, there was an old pot with a hole rusted through, and he took that as well, replacing everything, gripping the piece of metal he had found outside and slipping through the crack in the corner out into the wind, careful not to rip his coat again as he eased past the nail.

Sarah was just setting down a pile of wood and starting back for more when he came up past the mounds of rock into the tunnel. "What's that for?" she told him, pointing toward the piece of metal.

"That's our fireplace."

He meant it to sound like a joke, but it wasn't. Just as he had not wanted to break the lock on the shed and make it obvious that they'd been here, so he couldn't very well build a fire in the tunnel and scorch the rock and maybe burn some ties. He had to leave this place looking the same as when they'd found it.

"Here," he said, setting the metal on the rock floor between the tracks and the wall. "We'll build a fire on this and when we're done we'll bury the ashes in the snow. They'll never know we cooked anything, so they'll think we're weaker than we are, and maybe they won't push after us as hard. Hand me some of that wood. While I think of it, why don't you get down your sleeping bag as well, and that'll give us something soft to sit on."

He was hunkered down, breaking the dry splintered wood into little pieces, making a small pile of them on the metal, leaving a small hole at the bottom to let air in.

"Matches," he told himself, taking them out of his

pocket. Like the salt he now carried on him, they were one thing he'd been careful about, never to be without them. He lit one, reaching it into the hole in the wood, waiting for it to catch, but it didn't. He heard Sarah standing beside him, breathing. He struck another, and another. The third one caught, a tiny flame that licked at the wood and curled one thin end and spread along it, licking at another end, spreading along it as well until flames were darting faintly through the top. The horses tugged at their reins to get back from it, and he shifted the metal a little away from them, putting on more wood.

"But not too much," he told her. "Just a few pieces at a time and not very big at that. We don't need a fire to warm thousands, just one to cook on."

The wood was crackling now, a faint gray-white haze rising up, vaguely pungent.

"In the summer this place is damp. The wood must have started to rot. Now that the cold is coming out of it, the rot must be what we're smelling."

He watched the smoke drift up and waft toward the back of the tunnel, then rise a little more and drift toward the opening.

"Good," he said, taking off his gloves and rubbing his hands, holding them palms down over the flames. "Good. Here, get closer to the fire while I fix our supper."

Three cans in the pack he had taken from the hotel. He held them up. "Which one?"

She said she didn't care.

"Well, pick one just the same."

"The bean with bacon soup."

"Sounds fine to me."

He pulled out his knife and the head from the hammer, sitting down beside her.

"Hold the can. Be careful I don't cut you."

He pressed the knife point down on the edge of the lid of the can, raising the hammer, slamming down, puncturing the metal. He held up the knife and inspected the tip. Then with a series of quick raps he had the knife worked all around the lid and it was open. He checked the knife again, setting the open can on one corner of the metal, close enough to the fire to get warm without burning. Then he put another piece of wood on the fire, picked up the pot from the shed, and scraped the knife against the rust in it, tipping the pot so the specks fell out.

"Well, it might not be very sanitary and there might be a hole in it, but at least it's a pot," he said, and standing he went outside to pack some snow in it.

The wind was stronger outside, and he was grateful to come back to the fire, tipping the pot against a rock so the melted snow would collect in a corner away from the hole in the bottom.

"I think this batch we'll throw out and say we sterilized the thing."

The second batch was warm and gritty, leaving the taste of pennies in his mouth. Even so, it was water and he waited a bit to make sure it wasn't going to make him sick before he handed it to Sarah. She took a sip and made a face, but she didn't say anything and she finished it.

"Now some salt," he said, and he was so dehydrated that when he licked a handful out of his palm he didn't taste it.

They had to put their gloves on to pass the can of

soup back and forth, blowing on it, sipping, and once he took too much, burning the roof of his mouth, but the sauce was thick and the beans were something solid to chew and there were little specks of brownish-red bacon floating on top. They finished the soup before it seemed they even got started.

"I'm still hungry," Sarah said.

"So am I," he said, knowing they ought to save their food for as long as they could but not caring. "Which one this time? The tomato soup or the peas?"

"I hate tomato soup."

"Sure, but you hate peas too. Which one?"

"I guess the tomato soup."

"It's all the same to me."

And while she held the can, he hammered the knife around it.

4

THE FOOD made a difference. His head felt clearer, his body more alert as he carried the square of metal with the wood coals on it out into the open, the wind scattering some of the coals even before he chose a snowdrift well away from the tunnel and buried them. The wind had changed direction now, gusting up the draw rather than across it, so that their tracks were filling faster, and once he had made sure that the horses hadn't left any droppings, once he had taken the rest of the wood back to the cave-in, arranging it in among the rocks so that it looked as if it hadn't been touched, he was fairly certain that the others would have a hard time telling if he and Sarah had been around or not. He cinched the horses tight again, untied their reins from the ties between the tracks and led them out of the tunnel into the wind, helping Sarah onto the pinto, then getting on the bay himself. The wind was at their backs as they turned left, passing the metal shed, crossing the rest of the pass and starting down the opposite draw.

The rocks gave way under the snow and blended into ground and dead grass and pine needles under there. Then they passed a tree and another tree and they were in the forest again, riding past two roof-collapsed tumbled cabins, snow seeping into them, that he had guessed would be down here from the men who worked the mine, the snow deeper again, drifted up almost to the horses' knees. He decided to angle to his right across the slope rather than down it, wanting to stay up where the snow wouldn't be as deep, where the close rise of the bluff behind them would give them some kind of shelter from the wind. Then their progress became monotonous again, the good feeling from the fire and the warm food slowly disappearing almost as if it had never been, his mind and body growing numb again from the cold and the snow and the wind. There had been the goal of the tunnel behind him and the fire and the food. With no other vivid goal in front of him, he found himself concentrating solely on the pattern of his horse's hooves, one footfall after the other, his coat clutched tightly around him, his hands bunched up inside his gloves.

They went on like that through the rest of the afternoon and into the evening, and he couldn't tell when the change of light was from the sun going down or from the high thin gray clouds that grew lower and thicker and darker as they went along. He just realized that the trees seemed to be gathering denser around him as he worked along the slope, that his range of visibility had got shorter, grayer, and he was going to have to make some decision where to spend the night. There really wasn't much choice anyhow, a hollow in among the trees or a spot where dead fallen timber had jumbled together to form some kind of hutch, one as good as the other and second-rate at best, but he couldn't afford to go on any farther and maybe lose so much visibility that he couldn't make any choice at all, so he just arbitrarily chose the fallen timber, dismounting where the trees had fallen together in a V, tying the horses, unsaddling them and placing the saddles in under the trees at the wide end of the V to form a windbreak, packing down the snow behind them, laying the saddle blankets on top of the packed-down snow, putting the sleeping bag on top of the blankets, helping Sarah crawl in. Then using rope he retied the horses so they were closer to the wide end of the V, giving them room enough that they could paw at the snow for whatever grass might be under there, but still close enough to where he and Sarah would be sleeping that they would act as a further windbreak.

He didn't sleep much anyway. He crawled into the sleeping bag with Sarah, zipping it shut, feeling the soft insulation of the bag above him and beneath him and the harder saddle blankets under that and the snow at the bottom, cold seeping up, and he snuggled close to

Sarah, arms around her, giving heat. It felt strange and awkward to have his big snow-stiffened boots pressing down against the bottom lining of the sleeping bag, Sarah's own hard against his knees whenever either of them moved, but he couldn't take the chance of removing them in the cold and never getting them on again, and the best he could do was loosen them, letting the blood circulate, hoping for as much comfort as he could. Which wasn't much. As the wind rose and fell, growing stronger, night gathering all around them, they hunched down farther into the sleeping bag, their heads totally muffled against the cold, their breath vapor collecting damply along the top lining of the bag, the close suffocating dampness becoming so much for him that he put his head out into the air again, and the sharp bitter cold stung the inside of his nostrils, froze the mucus in there so that he had to duck his head back in under the warm close folds of the sleeping bag again.

The wolves woke him, first a few, then what seemed a whole pack of them howling right on top of him. Then they didn't sound very close at all, and he realized that the wind must be carrying their commotion to him, but the horses were skittering nervously just the same. He thought about crawling out and tying them more securely, but he had already done the best he could with them, and he couldn't stay up all night cut there with them.

"What is it?" Sarah said, half asleep.

"The wind."

"The other thing. What is it?"

"Wolves, but they're far. There's nothing to worry about."

He had his gun out, though, and he kept it next to him all through the night, dozing, waking with a start, listening to the nervous snorting of the horses, dozing again. The snow had drifted up over the saddles onto the sleeping bag when he finally wakened. He felt the pressure on him before he knew what it was, and fumbling to get his head out from under the sleeping bag he saw the several inches of snow weighing down on him. He kicked with his knees to get it off, rousing Sarah, crawling out over the saddles into the bitter cold morning air, still no sun, everything dull and gray, needing to squint anyhow as he looked to see if the drift of snow on the sleeping bag meant another storm in the night, but the levels looked the same all around him, and it must have been the wind, and then turning to check the horses, he saw that the pinto was gone. He didn't know when or how. The thick branch of fallen timber he had tied the pinto to wasn't broken and he knew that his knot had been good enough that it should have held solid, but the rope was gone clean, and then he saw where the pinto tugging at the rope must have snapped off another smaller branch that had projected up and kept the rope from slipping off the bigger one. It didn't matter. The horse was gone, and the wind had drifted its tracks so that he couldn't follow it and the wolves would have got it by now anyway.

Then looking off through the forest he saw movement in under the low-hanging branches of a pine tree as one of the wolves crawled out from between a snowdrift and the trunk, and he had his gun up aimed to fire before he recognized the old man's dog. Even so, he almost shot it anyway. The only thing that stopped

him was his fear that someone following them would
hear the shot.

"My horse is gone."

"And we've got company," he told Sarah, pointing.
"Stay away from it. Give me a hand. Roll up the sleeping bag."

He was setting the two saddle blankets onto the
bay while she did what she was told. Then he was
burying one saddle in the snow, hefting the other one
onto the bay, cinching it, and all the while the air was
totally still in contrast with the wind in the night, and
the dog stood fifty yards away over there under the
low-slung branches of the pine tree, watching them. It
hardly breathed or blinked or otherwise moved a muscle, just stood there, waiting. He coiled up the rope he
had used to tether the horse and secured it to the saddle. He picked up the saddle bags from the pinto and
tied them over the ones on the bay. Then he tied the
rolled-up sleeping bag over them, lifted Sarah onto the
saddle, got on behind her and started off. They had
deliberately not eaten the night before, figuring that
the soup they had eaten at the mine was enough for
one day. Now he pulled out some dried beef that he
had saved from the meal they had eaten with the old
man back in town, gave some to Sarah, bit into some
himself, cold and brittle, taking a while to soften it in
his mouth, and looking back he saw where the dog
was coming out from under the pine branches, struggling through the chest deep snow, bounding, stumbling, finally reaching the depression of their tracks and
following slowly after.

5

IT KEPT THE SAME DISTANCE, fifty yards behind them. He looked back once, and it was gone. He looked back another time, and it was following them again.

"What are you stopping for?" Sarah asked.

And the dog stopped too, easing down its back haunches, legs straight out in front of it.

He nudged the horse forward. The dog stood up and followed. He nudged the horse faster, and the dog kept pace. Then fearful of draining the horse's strength, he reined the horse slower, and the dog eased up as well, still following after.

In time the wind returned, coming from the right, gusting snow across in front and back of him. But the snow never rose more than four feet off the ground, it just kept streaking along the ground, the thick green boughs of the pine trees clear all around him above it but everything hidden below, and glancing back he couldn't see the dog anymore. He imagined it darting closer to them under the cover of the gusting snow, imagined it leaping, his hand on his gun in its holster, riding faster, and then the wind eased off and he looked quickly back and the dog wasn't there anymore.

Then it was.

The procession went on like that, the dog sometimes there, sometimes not, sometimes hidden by the gusting

snow but always the same distance behind whenever
he saw it. He was forced to stop that night in a hollow
among the trees, the only half-decent spot that he
could find, and he couldn't let himself sleep, lying there
in the sleeping bag, keeping watch over Sarah, gun by
his hand, the rope that tethered the horse wound several times around a tree and then around his wrist so
that he could tell in the dark if anything was happening to it out there.

He must have dozed, but if he did, he didn't know
it, day suddenly and the horse all right and the dog
the same distance over there in under a tree. He saddled
the horse again and they started off again, the dog
following, and this time the wind returned much earlier,
not just picking up snow and blowing it along but
bringing flakes down with it from the sky, sporadic at
first, then thin and constant, by late afternoon a regular snowfall, and this was what? the third day, he
wasn't sure anymore, since the horse had eaten anything and it was moving slower, more awkwardly, and
he didn't see how it could keep on much longer. Once
it stumbled to its knees, and he was barely able to urge
it up.

That was when the dog moved a little closer.

Or maybe it was before that. Since the snowfall
shortened the distance that he could see but he could
still see the dog behind them, the dog must have been
moving closer all the while, keeping them in sight in
the gathering snowfall.

The white-out settled everything, the wind so strong,
the snow coming down so thick around them that sky,
earth, air, everything was the same gray washed-out
color, and trees which they bumped into weren't vis-

ible even a foot away, their faces crusted with ice and snow, the horse hardly moving, every way the same and likely a chasm right in front of them, and when the horse finally tumbled down, he knew that they were finished. The horse just kept tumbling down and he and Sarah were falling over, rolling in the snow, him tugging at Sarah to keep her free from the weight of the horse as it rolled, and then they were lying motionless, him still gripping the reins of the fallen horse but as close as it was to him, unable to see it. He struggled to his feet, waist-deep in snow, fighting to get the horse up, shouting at it, the wind driving his words back into his throat. He got it up and it rolled again, and he realized that he couldn't see Sarah, clutching for her in the blinding snow, finding her, dragging her with him into the depression that the horse's body had made, sinking down exhausted, for one brief moment thinking of the dog again before he noticed that the wind had lessened.

No, it hadn't. It just seemed that way from where they were collapsed in the snow. They were in a kind of trench, sheltered by the walls, the white-out whipping over them, and this was maybe the last idea he would ever have but he had to try it, cursing, rousing himself into motion, fumbling at the snow.

"Dig!"

"My hands."

"God damn it, dig!"

He was clawing at the snow, grabbing Sarah's hands and working them, scooping with his arms, burrowing into the side of the drift. "Dig!" he kept telling her, squirming farther in, the wind lessening the more he worked, and in a moment he had a hollow in there

for her, pushing her in, and he was clawing at the snow
beside her, scooping, digging, worming in next to her.
The hollow was maybe four feet by six feet, just room
enough for the two of them scrunched up on their sides
in there, but the wind was less and he could breathe
again and if snow was still coming in on them it wasn't
so much that he couldn't keep pushing it away.

He crawled out, groping for the horse.

He couldn't find it. Then he had it, almost drifted
over by the snow, breathing weakly, trembling under
his touch, and he was sure that the horse was going
to die anyway and he couldn't let it stand somehow
and wander off and get buried by the snow where he
would never find it again, so he slipped off his glove,
fumbling for his gun. In the blinding snow he couldn't
see the horse's head, he had to feel along until he
touched where its massive jaw bones curved up at the
back of its head toward its ears and pressing the barrel
of his gun against the soft spot just behind the ears, he
cocked and fired. The horse jerked against him, knocking him back down into the snow. Sarah screamed, and
he almost let it go at that, but he couldn't bear the
thought that he might not have killed it, that it still
might be alive and suffering, so he struggled to stand
and felt and fired, the shot almost muffled soundless
in the storm, and this time when the horse jerked, it
was just from the impact of the bullet and he was
satisfied.

Sarah was only a few feet in back of him. Even so,
when he uncinched the saddle from the horse and
worked it free, he almost didn't find his way back to
her.

"You shot the horse."

"I had to. It was suffering."

And something else, and he didn't know how she was going to take it, but he had to be honest with her.

"We're going to eat it. It's what's going to keep us alive up here."

He was scooping out more snow to make room for the saddle and the saddle bags and the sleeping bag, glancing at her, and the idea of eating the horse didn't seem to matter to her one way or the other. It might be food, but it wasn't food now, and she just settled back against the low wall of the hollow, holding herself.

He made one more trip out, groping for the saddle blankets off the horse, finding his way back, spreading the blankets under them, covering themselves with the sleeping bag, leaning back with his head against the saddle.

One more thing. Always one more thing.

"Here," he said. "Use these saddle bags for a headrest. Here's some jerky."

It was the last two pieces he had left, one for her, one for him, and they nibbled at them in silence, him sucking on a piece in his mouth while he waited for it to soften so he could chew it.

<hr>

6

HE DIDN'T KNOW when he fell asleep, but the close stale air woke him, and he couldn't see, and he realized that the snow had blocked up the entrance. He pushed to clear it, and then he was out into darkness and the wind was shrieking in his face and he ducked back down, registering that it was night out there, that the snow was still coming, him sucking huge gulps of fresh air, crawling back down to where the air was warm from their breathing. He didn't hear anything from Sarah, touching her, slumping back satisfied that she was breathing. He snuggled in under the sleeping bag, heat from his body still lingering in its folds to comfort him. The entrance blocked up once more in the night, and he woke, crawling to clear it, only this time when he burst through, the snow blinded him in a different way, the storm gone, not night but day, the sky deep blue and cloudless and the sun arcing off the snow so brilliantly that after the darkness of their hollow he had to close his eyes and duck his head.

He crawled back to Sarah.

"Wake up. It's morning."

She didn't move.

"Wake up I said."

But she still didn't move, and suddenly frightened he reached under her arms, dragging her to the entrance, nudging her, watching as her nostrils opened in the sharp cold air, seeing her eyelids flicker. The air down there must have half-poisoned her. Or maybe she was simply exhausted. No matter. He had to wake her. He tapped at her face, pried at one eyelid, and then her arm was up, pushing weakly to get his hand away.

"I know," he said. "It's hard to see. But we can fix that. Right now we've got to get some water in you. We're going to be all right. Do you understand?"

She did and she nodded weakly, but it was obvious that she didn't believe him.

"No, it's true. Listen. As long as we've got water, we can stay alive. There's a rule of numbers that some-body made up once for people who get lost up here. You can only go three days maybe without water, but you can go for as much as three weeks without food. You might not look like much after all that time, you might not have very much flesh on you, but you can stay alive that long, and as it is we've got plenty of water, all this snow around here, God knows we've got plenty of that, and we've got the horse for food, and we're going to be all right, do you understand me?"

She nodded again, and this time her nod was a little more convincing as she took a handful of snow and brought it toward her mouth.

He had to stop her. "No, that isn't what I meant. I told you, it takes too much heat to melt the snow in your mouth. We've got to fix up that hole down there. We've got to widen it, find a way to make it stronger, warmer, get it big enough to build a fire."

And that did it. The idea of a fire began to brighten her, and as soon as she had rested longer, as soon as he had made sure she was fine, they crawled back in, him rounding the ceiling so there wouldn't be as much stress on it, digging at the walls, widening them while she pushed the snow out of the opening, piling it on either side the way he had shown her to form a windbreak. He wasn't worried about the others coming after them now. The snow had fallen so deep that nothing could move around up here for very far or long, he wasn't even worried about the dog anymore, and he was bet-ting that the others assumed he and Sarah had died in the storm.

Certainly they should have. It was only the merest chance that they hadn't. But now they were going to be all right, he told himself, convincing himself. It was just going to take a lot of work. He didn't dare think about how long the winter could be up here, how deep the snow could fall, how little meat there would be on the horse after everything he had put it through. He just fought to concentrate on widening the burrow, sculpting the walls and the roof, wondering if he shouldn't have built a fire out there right away and melted snow for Sarah to drink, deciding he was right, that another storm could come up anytime, and they needed shelter before a fire and they needed to do everything at once or not at all.

He crawled out, groping through the snow before he came upon the frozen-solid horse, deciding that since everything had to be done and the horse was immediately before him, he would do this first.

But he didn't know how, chipping at the hide with his knife, barely penetrating it. He saw how one leg stuck out like some dead limb from a tree, and that gave him the idea, mustering his energy as he stood and jumped down on it, trying to break it at the knee. He tried three times before he heard a crack in it and saw a split in the hide at the joint. Then he sat patiently cutting at it, not sure how much of this his knife could take without dulling, unable to do much about that anyway. It seemed to take an hour before he jumped once more and the lower part of the leg broke off. When he picked it up, it felt like a club in his hand, the horseshoe and the hoof unnatural as he held it.

"Take this inside," he told her.

She didn't want to touch it.

"Take it. I've got to get some wood."

They were in a hollow laced with pine trees. The nearest was fifteen feet, but the snow was so deep as he struggled over that it might as well have been a hundred. The snow wedged up under his pant legs and his coat. He tried scooping the snow from in front of him, leaning into it to pack it down and give him footing. Nothing worked.

Dear God, I'm going to have to dig a trench.

But he didn't have the strength.

Then rocking back and forth to shift the snow, determined to get to that tree, he felt his coat snag against something under there, and digging down he saw the tip of a branch. No, it wasn't the tip, it was the jagged end from where the rest of it had already broken off, and digging farther down he came to the massive fallen trunk.

It had been there all along, just a few feet ahead of him, and leaning forward, grabbing it, he drew himself up out of the snow onto it, close enough to stand and touch the nearest ends of the pine boughs.

But these were all green, he needed to get over to the inside branches of the tree where he could snap off dead limbs and twigs and dead needles to help get the fire started. Leaning out as far as he could without falling, he grasped the thickest branch he could reach and swung out into the snow, so underestimating his weakness that he almost lost his grip, fighting to keep hold as he pulled himself hand over hand along the branch through the snow toward where the drift was not as deep. By then he was in among the other branches, and easing himself down, the snow just up to his thighs here, he began snapping off the wood he needed, twigs and clumps of needles that he put in his pockets, one stout dead branch that took all his effort to tug and break. It had other smaller branches projecting from it, and plenty of twigs and dead needles as well, and it would be enough to get a small fire started that would last for quite a while, but he didn't want to have to make this trip anymore than he had to, and moving around the trunk of the tree he found more branches to break off. Then climbing a short way, he broke off more branches, but he didn't have the strength to climb any higher, and when he found himself gripping the trunk of the tree, fighting to breathe, he knew he had to stop. He slipped down, almost falling, into the snow, gathering the branches, tossing them one at a time toward the entrance to the burrow. The smaller ones made it easily, Sarah over there watching him, gathering them in a pile, but the bigger wider ones with shorter branches projecting from them seemed to float in the air and only made it half way. He had to wade over to them, throwing them again, reaching the fallen trunk hidden in the snow, stepping onto it and over it into the trough he had already made and working his way toward Sarah. She already had most of them together, and he was so lightheaded and tired from his effort that all he could do was just sit there by the entrance and struggle to catch his breath, feeling his sweat beneath his clothes, his throat burning, while Sarah broke off the smaller branches from the bigger ones, setting them in a pile, carrying them in as he told her, and then he had strength enough to stand and jump onto the bigger branches, snapping them.

The sun was well down across from them, the air colder when they finished, his sweat freezing on him, making him shiver, and he was grateful to have this over, to be able to crawl back into the burrow and start to build the fire, anticipating the warmth, the smell of food.

But there was always something more to do, he told himself. Always. He would never be finished. Because as soon as he had set down the square of metal, putting dead needles in a pile onto it, setting twigs on top of that and then a few finger-thick bits of wood, he realized that he had not made allowance for the smoke. There might not be much, but it would be enough to choke them out, and he had to find a way to clear it.

At first he thought of pushing two straight branches up through the roof of the burrow, leaving a small space between them and poking the snow free from there to form a kind of chimney. But he had already broken the branches too short and he couldn't get himself to go out again for more and there was too much risk of bringing down the roof.

There had to be another way.

He had been looking at it all the time. The tree that helped form the back wall of the burrow. He crawled over to it, grabbing a branch from the pile he had gathered and digging a small hole up through the snow at its side. The branch was three feet long, and when he had gone its length, he had to crawl in closer, turning onto his back and looking up toward the hole as he raised his arm and dug even higher. The snow fell on his face and he kept wiping it away, blinking it out of his eyes, digging higher, and then before he expected, he was through, daylight filtered by the needled branches of the tree showing greenish-gray up there.

He crawled back to the pile of kindling, striking a match under the thickest part of the pine needles, watching them catch and crackle and spread all too fast, the twigs themselves barely catching.

But they did, and their slight flames spread to the

finger-thick chunks of wood, and in a moment he had the start of a fire going. Now if the chimney only worked, and he watched as a trail of gray smoke drifted up, gathering in the dome at the top, spreading. The smoke was sweet from the dried streaks of pine resin on the surface of the wood, and it took too long to build up so he could see if it was drifting toward the chimney. He added more twigs, more bits of wood to the fire, tensing as he set down two larger bits of wood and in a moment they were burning as well and he knew that the fire itself was going to be all right, he was just going to take a while before he had enough solid wood on it that he wouldn't have to keep feeding it all the time.

But sweet or not, the smoke was making him cough a little, and Sarah was coughing as well, and he saw now that the dome of the burrow was higher than the entrance to the chimney so that the smoke was spreading low around them before it drifted away. He was so lightheaded from fatigue and hunger that he had to think for what seemed too long before he knew what to do, taking a piece of wood and scooping a channel from the top of the dome to the chimney, and the smoke was drifting freely out now, the burrow clearing. It was only as he put a few more bits of wood on the fire that he thought of the extra advantage of using the tree. If the others were out looking for him, they would not be able to spot the smoke very well, hidden by the branches of the tree.

He couldn't let himself think about it.

"How are you feeling?" he asked Sarah.

"Fine." But she didn't look well at all. She was warming her hands close over the fire, face pale, shivering, and he imagined how her earlier sickness plus the strain of the last few days must have weakened her.

"You'll feel better when you eat." He crawled over to her saddle bags, taking out the can of peas, grateful that they had saved it, wishing now that they had saved one of the cans of soup as well. He punched two holes in the top with his knife while she held it, and the lid punctured easily enough but the frozen liquid underneath held back the knife and he had to set the can close by the fire, waiting for the liquid inside to melt enough that he could finish with the lid and get it off.

He set the part of the horse's leg that he had broken off near the fire, close enough that it would start to thaw, far enough that the hide wouldn't start to burn. In a while the liquid inside the can of peas was half-melted, and he got the lid off, sprinkling some salt in of them in the burrow, and taking them a little farther with the liquid. He kept turning the horse's leg, testing it with his fingers to see how much it had thawed. Then the peas were bubbling, steam rising, the sweet smell from the fire so they could cool, he whittled two flat spoons from some pieces of wood, and dipping the spoons into the can, balancing the peas on them, they blew gently at the peas, brought their mouths down and started chewing them. The spoons didn't do much good. They were even a nuisance, but they gave him and Sarah something to fool with while they waited for the liquid in the can to cool just enough for them to drink it, and anyway he didn't want to eat too fast.

"I want you to make these peas last quite a while," he told Sarah. "Not because we want to save our food, though that's a good idea, but we haven't eaten in so long that we'll bring these up if we don't chew them properly. Chew them until they're just a liquid in your mouth. Swallow a few and wait a while."

He checked the hide on the horse's leg again. It had softened enough for him to cut it with his knife. Making a slit all the way down from where the knee had been to just above the hoof, he started prying at the flaps of hide, separating them from the flesh, what there was of it. Then he came to a place where the hide was still fairly frozen and he set it near the fire again.

"I think the juice from the peas is cool enough that we can drink some. You first." And he watched as she took a sip and rinsed it around her mouth and finally swallowed it. "That's right. Take your time. We've got all the time in the world."

Then the leg was thawed enough that he could pry the hide off. He spread it out on the snow by the fire, flesh side up.

"Have another drink," he told her.

Then he took one himself.

7

THE MEAL LASTED well into the night. He felt the juice from the peas warm in his stomach. The cave itself was warming pleasantly, his chill leaving him, and he opened his coat, brushing the snow away from in there, loosening his boots, reaching up his pant cuffs to get the snow out from there as well. He ate a few peas. He put more wood on the fire, got the two empty cans from the soup they had eaten at the mine, filled them with snow, and set them near the fire. Then he ate a few more peas and drank more juice. He slit strips of flesh, muscle really, off the horse's leg as it thawed, setting them near the fire. Then drinking some of the melted snow, giving some to Sarah, taking some salt, he stretched out on the saddle blankets near the fire, Sarah's head down near his feet so that they shared the fire evenly. He warmed the sleeping bag and opened it, wrapping it around and above them. In time he slept.

When he woke, Sarah was asleep as well, and the fire was out. It took him a while to get it going again, waking Sarah to give her the last of the juice from the peas, forcing her to take more salt. She slept almost immediately. The entrance was dark from the night out there, and he started to doze, but he kept himself awake long enough to cut a few more strips from the horse leg, and he woke periodically after that, worried about the fire.

The day was warm, another cloudless sky, the sun so stark it melted the surface of the snow. He was afraid that the top of the drift might soften enough to tumble the roof of the burrow, but there wasn't anything he could do about that, and he took advantage of the weather to work toward another tree and gather more wood.

He cooked a strip of horsemeat each for them, spitting them on the end of a stick and holding them over the fire, watching them curl and drip grease and darken, their smell a little like lamb or rabbit, he couldn't decide which, sweet on the one hand, on the other somewhat wild. They spent the morning on the one strip each, first sucking the juices out, softening the meat with their teeth, mulching it, biting off little bits and chewing them into liquid and swallowing them.

By midday they had dysentery. Not because the meat was bad, he was sure it wasn't, or because they weren't used to the idea of eating horsemeat, by then they were both ready to eat anything, but simply because they had not eaten solid food in so long that their system was rejecting it, their excrement flecked with bits of undigested peas which even chewed as well as they had chewed them still had not been accepted. Once he didn't think he was going to make it to the tree that they had selected for a latrine, and he must have had more than enough salt in him by now because his intestinal tract was loose and burning, sometimes nothing but pale mucus-clouded water coming out, the salt acting as a purgative.

They sat weakly by the entrance to the burrow, holding themselves. He didn't want to, but he had to keep him and Sarah eating, not much, just a little to help build their strength, and as soon as he could manage it, he crawled back into the burrow, cooking two more strips, then changing his mind and letting Sarah cook her own, testing it for her to make sure it was done, nibbling at his own. By evening the spasms had passed, and they drank melted snow, a little at a time, to replace the liquid they had lost. Night brought freezing cold, and they slept huddled close to the fire. Morning, the melted surface of the snow had turned to ice, slippery but solid, and he found that by crawling he could easily get to nearby trees for wood.

THEY WERE JUST EXPERIMENTING with a thick green-needled pine bough for a sled when they heard the helicopter. He had got the idea from the slippery ice-surface of the snow, and after they had cooked more meat and eaten it, he had taken a stout piece of wood and chopped steps through the ice into the snow all the way up one angle of the hollow, stopping at a pine tree near the top. They hung on one of the branches until they cracked it, and twisting it off, they sat on the matted part of the bough, Sarah behind him, arms around his waist while he pointed the branch end toward the bottom, and lifting it so he could steer, released his footing, gliding fast down in among the trees blurring past, reaching the bottom and part way up the opposite slope before they stopped and slid on back.

They sat there laughing, and after the dysentery he didn't want them to use much strength but Sarah wanted him to do it just once more, so they climbed up the steps to the top again, and halfway down, distinct above the rush of the wind and the scratching of the needles on the ice, he heard it. He wrenched the branch to one side, sliding sideways toward a pine tree, spilling off and scrambling to grab Sarah and drag her under, but she had heard it as well and she didn't need any guiding.

They lay on their stomachs in under there, peering up through the needles toward the direction of the motor. He couldn't see it. It might be to their right as much as their left, above as well as below. There might be two of them, any moment swooping down over the hollow, spotting the pattern of their tracks.

No, there was only one. He saw it now. Down there at the bottom of the valley, sweeping across from left to right, a small glistening speck that turned back to the left now, the chugging of its motor coming several seconds after it went whirling out of sight. Then it was back again, moving to the right again, out of sight then and in a moment working back. It was obvious what they were doing. They were assuming that he had done what in fact he had almost done, which was to follow the line of least resistance and head down into the valley instead of working along its slope, stopping at the bottom, and instead of struggling up the other slope, following the direction of the watershed down there. They had waited this long so that in case he survived the storm he would have had plenty of time to dig himself out and leave obvious signs in the snow. They had waited to give him confidence that they were no longer after him, so he could make mistakes.

Which he had, although the tracks around the burrow weren't a mistake, they were a necessity, but they amounted to the same, and as soon as that helicopter had crisscrossed far enough up this slope, the people in there could not help but see the tracks he had made in the snow to get firewood from the trees. The people in there might not be certain at first. They would assume the possibility that a few larger animals like deer and elk had stayed in the high ground and somehow survived, leaving tracks, but they would certainly check this hollow out, and when they did, he didn't see what chance his revolver would stand against a rifle. He watched as the helicopter crisscrossed higher up the slope. It was closer now, larger. He could dimly make out its tail propeller and its bubbled dome. The periods when he saw it were less now as his angle of vision reduced the higher it came, and each time he saw it again, it was closer, more distinct, the sun glinting off its whirling blades, noise coming to him in a roar. He could make out the bulk of two men in the bubble, and he was thinking, there must be something I can do, I can't just lie here waiting, there must be something I can do.

But there wasn't. He had no way to camouflage the deep sets of tracks, not with the snow frozen the way it was, and even if the snow had been soft he would only have made more tracks covering up the first ones. He looked down at the horse's flank showing clearly through the snow where he had dug for it. There was no way they could miss that, and while he might be able to chip some frozen snow and cover it, he didn't have the time, the helicopter crisscrossing less than a hundred yards down from them now, the roar no longer several seconds behind the helicopter but right onto it. He drew his gun, feeling Sarah tense beside him. He looked toward the helicopter, testing his aim, calculating how close the helicopter would have to come before he would have a possibility of hitting anyone in the bubble. He didn't want to do it. He didn't want to give his position away or let on they were still alive. But he didn't see what choice he had. The helicopter could not fail to see his tracks, and his only option was surprise.

Then he realized that if by some chance he did manage to shoot them that would be as obvious a sign as any that he was out here. When the helicopter didn't come back, the people who were after him would just send more men out here, another helicopter, and he didn't see how he could convincingly hide the wreckage of the first one. Pine boughs wouldn't work. A huge pile of them in among the trees would be the first thing they would notice, not to mention the trees it would bring down with it when it crashed. So there wasn't any point in firing to keep them from finding him, only for defense, and he waited as the helicopter crisscrossed closer, and then it was out of sight again, and he waited, and it didn't come back.

It's just a trick of perspective, he thought.

Plus you're waiting, and that makes it seem longer for them to come back.

But they weren't. He could hear the motor quite clearly over there to his left, but it wasn't getting any louder or softer, just hovering at the same pitch as if it were watching something, and then it was loud again as it came toward him, and he thought this is it, cocking his revolver as it came in sight, heading to his right.

But not across the slope, down it in the direction it had first come, down toward the bottom of the valley and the water shed, and he didn't understand, and then he did as the darkness floated over them, shutting out the sun.

He crawled out from under the pine boughs, realizing that he must have been registering the slight increase of wind all along, staring up behind him at the clouds. The lowest, blackest, thickest he had seen, taking up the whole sky from left to right, already one-third over the valley and rushing to complete it, their underbellies swirling, churning, the temperature dropping abruptly, wind rising, snow onto him even as he turned and grabbed Sarah and slid down the rest of the hollow to the burrow. It was like day suddenly become night, and in the little time they took to slide down toward the burrow, the storm was already so thick around them that they had to squint to find the tunnel.

*

9

THEY CRAWLED IN out of the storm to the still, close, warm air of the burrow, fighting to catch their breath while the storm raged past the entrance out there, gusting snow in at them. He had to take the saddle and block off the tunnel, anchoring a saddle blanket over and around it to close off the remaining spaces. Then he felt secure.

"It's only a storm," he told her.

But he wasn't fooling anybody. He had never seen anything like it, not just dropping snow, but dumping it, unloading it, and if the wind was that bad at the start, what was it going to be like when it really had a chance to start blowing. It was shrieking out there, pushing at the saddle and the blanket, wailing to get in.

"Daddy, I'm scared."

So am I, he thought. "It's all right. Believe me, there's nothing to be afraid of."

He drew her to him and held her, staring at the blanket flapping sharply, at the saddle fidgeting under it as if the saddle were alive, listening to the constant high-pitched screaming of the wind.

Then the wind came to them muffled and the blanket stopped and the saddle, and he couldn't stop from saying what had happened.

"The entrance is blocked. The storm's filled it in."

His words were flat, muffled in the burrow, and for a moment she relaxed in his arms, grateful to be separated from the storm, suddenly tensing, turning to him as she realized.

"We won't be able to breathe."

"Sure we will. We've still got the airspace for the smoke. The branches up there will droop down and keep it from filling in."

But it's too small, he knew. No room for the cold air to come down and displace the warm. Already he could see where the fire was flickering, dimming, and they were either going to have air or heat, but not both, and he was grabbing a piece of wood, crawling over to the tree at the back wall of the burrow, digging out snow from the side of the tree opposite the chimney, crawling in under there, digging up, the snow falling on his face as he finally poked through. Or at least thought he did. The storm was so dark up there that he couldn't see a change in light, but he felt a rush of wind on his face, and looking over at the fire he saw it blaze a little brighter now and then a little brighter after that, cold air coming down upon him, breath easier now. That was why they had been breathing so hard before, not from fright but because the oxygen was going.

He relaxed and crawled back to her.

"See. Everything's going to be fine."

Sure. Except if the storm dumped enough snow on the drift up there, the weight of it all might push the whole thing down. They'd never be able to fight their way out. They'd suffocate and die.

He couldn't think about it, breath already difficult again.

"We've just got to relax and let it pass."

He was thinking of the layer of ice up there, wondering if it was strong enough to hold.

"It has to."

"What?"

"Nothing. Let's get ourselves something to eat."

They had plenty of meat anyhow. The day before, when it had been warm and they had not yet developed dysentery, he had broken off the other limbs from the horse, skinning them and cutting them into strips and putting them deep into the walls of the burrow before they had a chance to spoil. He had not been able to get at the bottom side of the horse, but the top side he had skinned as well and cut off meat, and he had set Sarah to gathering wood, so that on those terms at least, they had nothing to worry about.

He thought he heard a cracking noise from the roof of the burrow, looked up at it, watching for stress lines, but there weren't any, and rather than frighten Sarah, he gave her a strip of meat to cook, spitting one on the end of a stick himself, holding it over the fire. Their stomachs had adjusted well enough to food now that they didn't have to eat as slowly, and in a while they were cooking again, wiping the grease off their mouths, the thick wild aftertaste of the meat clinging to the back of his tongue.

His eyes hurt. At first he thought that was from the wind but then he understood that it was from the sharp reflection of the sun, and for something to do, he set to work cutting a strip of horsehide into what looked like a blindfold, narrow tongs of leather coming around on both sides to where he could tie them in back of his head. Then he cut thin slits where his eyes would be and he had a pair of snow goggles. He cut a pair for Sarah as well, measuring them against her head as he went along, making jokes about mustaches and bandits. He had often thought of cutting his own mustache and beard off with his knife, but he had decided that it gave him protection from the wind, and thinking of that, he looked at Sarah's wind-angered face, skin peeling off her cheeks, furious at himself for being so stupid that he hadn't thought of wiping grease from the horsemeat over her face before they went out into the sun.

Next time.

And then he heard the crack in the roof again.

Sarah heard it too. She didn't need to ask. All she had to do was look at him.

"I don't know," he said. "Maybe it will. But I can't let myself worry. There's nothing I can do about it."

The air grew foul from their breath and the smell of the fire and the horsemeat. They took turns crawling over to the second airspace he had dug and breathing under it. He worked to keep the fire going, worried at the same time that the heat might start the walls to soften. He got hungry and cooked again. He slept and woke and slept again. It seemed the storm out there would never end.

10

"I NEVER KNEW HIM. There were pictures, snapshots that my mother had saved, but no wedding pictures and no pictures of the two of them together. I'm not sure if she destroyed those or if she just put them away somewhere, determined never to look at them again. But the snapshots of him alone she kept in a photo album, and sometimes she'd bring them out for me to look at. I think the idea was that, if she didn't want the pictures of her and him around to put her through the pain again, she still figured that I ought to have some notion of what my father had looked like, so once in a while she'd bring them out for me and she'd stand beside me looking at them for a little and then she'd go away and do something. They were all the same, him standing by a flower bed at the side of a house or next to some rosebushes or in among a rock garden, and I asked my mother once if that was where they lived when they were married, and she said no, that they lived in an apartment, the house had belonged to some friends of theirs. In New Jersey. Near the flight school where he taught. And he was always standing there in his uniform, pants perfectly pressed, a crease down each sleeve of his jacket, his wing insignia on his jacket, on his cap. He wasn't very tall, and he was a little on the slight side, his hair not dark like mine but sandy like yours, and he had a kind of young man's look, I guess he was twenty-eight or so then, my mother never told me, his cheeks smooth, his face oval. He was killed shoftly after in the war."

"Daddy?" Sarah asked him.

"What's the matter, sweetheart?"

"I don't want to die."

"Neither do I," he told her, disgusted with himself for letting the story take the direction it had. All he had wanted to do was ease her mind off things, and here he'd only reminded her. "That's why we're not going to."

But the storm out there wouldn't end. Even with the close thick walls of snow around and above them, they could still hear the shrieking of the wind out there, and they didn't have enough to do. Eating, watching the fire, sleeping, these things repeated themselves over and over. With no distinction between day and night, the numbers on his watch became meaningless. It could have been noon or midnight. They could have slept two hours or fourteen. The storm could have been one day or five. There was no way of knowing. He told her all the stories he could think of, about how when she was very little she had nearly lost one of her fingers on a broken pane of glass, how she had used to have nightmares about clowns, how she had loved to look at dump trucks. Then his head became so clouded that he couldn't think of any stories anymore, and he just sat watching the fire, and then he couldn't even do that any longer, and he mostly slept.

11

THE STORM must have been over for quite a while before he realized it, the cave so still that his mind was automatically supplying the muffled shrieking of the wind he had become so used to hearing that even when he crawled over to the breathing hole by the tree and saw the light up through there he did not at first register its significance. He just lay there, looking, breathing, blinking, and then at last he understood.

"It's over."

But his words were weak and he could hardly move.

"Did you hear me?"

She nodded weakly.

"Then let's go."

But neither of them moved.

What's the matter with us?

The air. The air must be so bad we're nearly dead.

It was all he could do to crawl over to where the tunnel had been and push away the saddle and the blanket and paw once at the snow.

Christ, I don't even have the strength to get out. We're going to die in here.

He could barely lift his hand to paw again at the snow. He slumped down exhausted, fighting to breathe, and he suddenly couldn't stand this place, the walls so thick that they were smothering him. His hands began working on their own. He was fascinated by them. He decided to help them.

The dog was waiting for him. He never understood how it had managed to live through the storm out there, but it had, crawling out from under the branches of a pine tree twenty yards away this time instead of fifty. It shook itself, head and shoulders above a drift in front of the tree, looking at him, and he was so grateful to be out in the clear bright open air again that he didn't care whether the dog was there or not. He just lay on the icy wind-packed snow, gulping breaths, sheltering his eyes, and then all he could think of was Sarah and he was crawling back in, dragging her out, and the two of them were breathing.

Then the dog became important to him, not as a threat but as a chance for more food, and he suddenly didn't care if anybody heard the shot or not, drawing his gun, aiming, as the dog turned and ducked under the level of the drift, disappearing beneath the branches of the pine tree. Later when he had strength enough to work his way through the snow over there, he saw where the dog had dug a burrow of its own in under the snow by the tree and where it had used the cover of the tree to wade out away from him, a deep belly-drawn track leading off down the slope through the trees. He almost went after it, but he couldn't leave Sarah, and anyway he was certain it would be back.

But it always came back at night, and even when he tried staying up in wait for it, he always missed it, crawling out in the morning to see where it had dug up a bone that he had finished with and buried, where it had dug down to get at the carcass of the horse but hadn't been able to nibble away much of the frozen meat.

In the meantime there was the painful process of gathering more wood, working out farther and farther away as he used up all the dead branches on the trees nearest him, all the while sensing that the dog was somewhere nearby watching him. And something else. Sarah. It was as if their long stay in the burrow had shown her what the winter would be like and her mind could no longer sustain her. There wasn't anything to do, she simply told him, and he knew what she meant. There was a constant attention to themselves to keep from dying, but each day was the same as the next, and she was losing her interest. He invented games for her, jokes, riddles. He sang songs with her. He gave her more chores to do. But what was the use, they didn't have enough food, she told him. They had used up the last of the strips he had cut from the horse carcass before the weather froze the flesh so hard that he couldn't cut anymore, and he could see the carcass out there from where the dog had dug down to it, and he couldn't accept the physical necessity that kept him from somehow getting a portion of it into the burrow where he could cook it. The food was right there before him, yet they were going to starve.

He was a day before he realized the answer. If he couldn't bring the meat to the fire, he would bring the fire to the meat, and he was gripping the metal with his gloves, feeling its heat through the wool, easing it out of the tunnel and onto the carcass of the horse, building up the fire until the heat through the bottom of the metal would cook the meat underneath. He used a stick to push the metal to another portion of the carcass, cutting off the square that he had cooked. It was only an inch down and the top was badly charred, but he had the answer and when he had cooked another square, he built the fire low again and shifted it back into the burrow. She ate the meat gladly, but her joy was only temporary as the pattern repeated itself and she could see where there was less meat on the horse each day and there hadn't been much on it to begin with and soon they were down on this side to the bones. They could see where the dog had been nibbling at them in the night. One morning there were tracks where the dog had eased past the saddle into the burrow while they slept and taken the last bits of meat that they had saved. Once he heard Sarah coughing in the night.

The end came shortly after. She just kept coughing longer, harder, drinking less, sleeping more. He chipped around where the horse was frozen solid to the snow, straining, flipping it over, showing her where there was still a lot of meat to cook. But she didn't even have the energy to look at it much, just wanted to get back into the sleeping bag, edging closer to the fire. He tried everything he could think of, shoving a thick-needled pine bough underneath the saddle blankets and the sleeping bag as insulation against the cold, forcing her to drink hot water, tying her hood closer around her head, huddling nearer to her. But there wasn't any use. It wasn't just the cold outside that was getting to her but something inside as well. It was as if the mountains had been against her from the start. You could get sick up here from not enough oxygen or too little salt or your blood just thinning out, but these were all chemical reactions to the height, and sickness in the sense of germs, disease, that hardly ever happened. This far up, there were hardly any germs to begin with, and what there were had very little strength.

But with Sarah everything had come together. Her earlier nausea had weakened her resistance, the ride up here had weakened her further, and now the germs were having their effect. Her coughing kept him up all night, not because of its loudness but because he knew what she was going through. From worry about keeping her warm, he now had to worry about the reverse, her temperature burning, him bathing her face with luke-warm strips of cloth from his shirt. He felt where her clothes were damp all through, heat conducting outward, cold conducting in, taking them one at a time and drying them, taking the fire outside to cook more squares of meat, knowing she shouldn't be without the fire too long, working as fast as he could, bringing the fire back in and warming her, then cooling her again. He forced her to eat, but she barely had the strength to chew. He bathed her face again. He heard the liquid murmur in her throat and chest, and wanting to ease her effort, turned her on her side, in time on her stomach, then on her other side, on her back again. But the relief was always temporary and with each sunrise her condition grew much worse. She spoke in her delirium as if she were back in their house before the start of everything, preparing for bed in her room, picking out her clothes for school the next morning. He recalled one night around that time when he had given her a bath, drying her, combing her hair, and they had made up rhymes then, mostly excremental, laughing, and looking now at the dirty tangles of her hair sticking out around the edges of her hood, remembering the smooth thin sandy-brown hair he had been combing that night, he had to turn away. Once she spoke as if it wasn't him but Claire beside her, saying "Mother, can I have a friend to stay the night?" One morning she was dead.

Even when he heard the dog outside, gnawing at the
carcass of the horse, he didn't move. He just kept looking at her, staring at her open eyes, staring into them,
amazed at the utter sense of lifelessness, the sightless
eyes a parody, in time closing them, in need of pretending she only was asleep. When the dog came back the
second time, he didn't move then either, just continued
staring at her, watching her face turn white, her body
settle, stiffen. He stayed like that until he sensed the
change in light outside and realized he hadn't moved
all day, and even then he only moved because he
needed to protect her, chipping a low chamber out of
the left side of the burrow, easing her into it, knowing
that if he kept her too long near the fire her body
would start to decompose.

He slept, and waking, took her out and looked at
her. Then worrying more about preserving her, he put
her back in, packing snow around her. He went out and
relieved himself, squinting from the sunlight off the
snow, day again, staring down at the two frozen
splashed-out circles in the snow near the one that he
was making, understanding he had come out twice
since this time yesterday, not recalling when. He
looked disinterestedly at where the dog had been gnawing at the carcass of the horse. He went back in, be-
grudging all the time he melted snow and drank it,
looking at her.

In time he worried even more about preserving her
and sealed her in, pushing away the snow each morning to look at her face, then sealing her in again. He
took the fire out, cooking more squares of meat, be-
grudging the need to eat as well but forcing himself,

little by little, tasteless in his mouth. He wandered farther and farther from the burrow to find wood for the fire, eating more now so he could keep up the strength to get the wood, coming back into the burrow, afraid the dog had come while he was gone and got at her. But the dog never did, and going out each morning after he had looked at Sarah's face, staring at where the dog had gnawed further at the carcass of the horse, he understood that if she hadn't died they both would have anyhow, not enough meat from the horse to last them both, not enough for the dog and him as well, and in need of occupying his mind, he spent his days and nights now on the problem of keeping the dog from the horse, rousing himself, pretending to go off for wood but hiding close by waiting for the dog so he could shoot it, staying awake as long as he could, listening for some sound of the dog out there working at the horse. But always the dog came when he really did have to go out for wood or when he dozed, and soon between the two of them the horse was hardly anything but bones. He broke the bones off from the frame, boiling them, drinking the broth, sucking at the marrow, getting every bit of food he could from them, and then thinking it through, wondering what further use he could make of them, he took two of the largest curving rib bones, used horsehide to tie them together at top and bottom, tied smaller bones across at spaces in the middle, and then threading horsehide through them from top to bottom, doing the same with another set of curving rib bones, he fashioned a pair of snowshoes. He thought what else he could do with the other bones and couldn't figure anything, eating what he could from them, leaving them outside for the dog.

And then there was nothing. He sat back in the burrow, hoarding a few last squares of meat that he had saved, looking occasionally at Sarah, thinking what more to do, figuring that he was going to have to use the snowshoes to walk down out of here. But he couldn't bring himself to leave Sarah, and he couldn't carry her, and even with the meat that he had saved, he knew he wouldn't have the strength to make it all the way, the first good storm would finish him, no game around, and he kept on sitting there. A series of warm days made him think that spring was on the way, but he only fooled himself he knew, it was too soon for spring yet, and then the cold returned, much harder than before, and he used up wood more quickly. Against his will he took Sarah's sweater from her, cutting it, wrapping it around his head and shoulders in under his coat, leaving her own coat on her, not able to bear the thought of the back of her head against the snow. He looked at his watch, but it was stopped. He scratched at the sores on his thighs, his arms, in under his beard. From not washing and no food.

The dog came right into the burrow this time, stopping just inside the entrance, staring at him. It must have been there quite a while, him half dozing, before he noticed it, stretched out on its stomach, staring at him. It looked at the meat he had sprinkled with snow next to him. It looked back at him and edged a little closer. He had his gun out without thinking. He cocked and raised it, aiming at one eye. The dog edged closer. He thought that when he shot it he'd have more food, a better chance to last the winter, but then he thought that it didn't matter, a week or two more food if that, it wouldn't make a difference, he'd only starve then anyhow, and perhaps it was because he was still a little dazed from sleeping, or maybe he just didn't care, but instead of firing he lowered the gun and chose a bit of meat and tossed it. The dog caught it, mouth open, biting. He regretted it instantly, and raising his gun to fire, he saw the dog was gone. He slumped back, cursing, then rousing himself, crawled to the entrance, aiming, but there wasn't anything. He cursed again, slumping flat at the entrance, blinking, dozing.

The meat was gone two days from then. He remembered what he had told Sarah about three days without water, three weeks without food, deciding he was going to have to walk out anyhow but didn't have the strength. He had visions of the dog coming back, shooting it, skinning it, eating it, had visions even of the square of meat that he had given to the dog. He remembered stories about people in plane crashes in the mountains, starving, finally eating corpses, thought of Sarah and shook his head. But maybe it would come to that. He couldn't pretend it wouldn't. The taboo against cannibalism lasted only as long as your mind controlled your body, and in time he knew he would be hardly more than some kind of animal, doing whatever it had to in order to stay alive. He would wake up some morning and uncover her, thinking of the possibility. Another morning he would tell himself that this was what she would want him to do. Some evening he would try to cut a sliver from her, stopping himself, then doing it anyhow, cooking it, tasting it, gagging but making himself chew anyhow, and in time he would be able to do it without much revulsion, perhaps even with reverence, justifying himself, thinking of communion.

He hardly bothered to go out for wood anymore, just sat there, drinking water, feeling his clothes going slack on him, imagining the dog, him raising the gun, firing, going for it with his knife, and he was some time before he registered that his vision of the dog wasn't just a vision, that the dog was really before him, standing there, staring at him from the entrance, and he already had the gun up, cocking, thinking this time if I don't kill it it'll come for me, aiming, finger tensing on the trigger as he recognized what it was holding in its mouth, and that second's hesitation was the difference.

A rabbit.

It was holding a rabbit in its mouth, coming forward, dropping it, and he didn't understand. If the dog had a rabbit, why didn't the damn thing eat it? What was it doing here with it, dropping it like that, backing off, not leaving, just settling down on its stomach like before, and then he realized. Meat. The dog had liked the taste of the roasted meat, and he was grabbing at the rabbit, slitting with his knife, gutting, skinning, spitting it onto a stick, cooking, and he almost forgot to give some to the dog, he was so hungry, but the dog growled at him as he raised it to his mouth and he ripped off a leg, throwing it, and they were eating. The dog brought him two more rabbits like that in the next few days. Then a squirrel, and in time they shared the burrow.

12

ON THE FIRST WARM DAY he came down off the mountain. He had gone up to the cliff wall high above the hollow he was in and pried away rocks and carried them down, taking Sarah out of the burrow and covering her with them. Still not satisfied, he had gone around to the trees below, working quite a ways down until he reached where he had not yet gone for firewood, breaking off thick dead limbs, digging up fallen timber in the snow, hauling up whatever he could and covering the rocks with them, twisting off rich green fir boughs from the trees nearby and setting them over the timber. Then finally certain that no animals would get to her, he looked once more inside the burrow for what he could save, taking the rusted pot and the three empty cans from the soup and the peas, putting them and the saddle blankets and the thin square of metal inside a sack that he had tied together made from animal fur. He hitched the sack over one shoulder, hitched the rolled-up sleeping bag over his other shoulder using thongs tied together from the horsehide, and adjusting his snow goggles over his eyes, he set off through the trees. His woolen gloves had long since worn through, replaced by mitts that he had made from fur, tying the hides together, skin to skin, so that he had fur on the inside and the out. His snowshoes were much stronger than he'd hoped, their lacing on occasion snapping, needing to be retied, but not so often that they bothered him, and he made a practice of each evening checking them.

He stood on a rim of high ground, looking down toward the country of the hollow he'd just left, staring toward what from this height he could only guess was the mound of rocks and timber and fir boughs that protected Sarah, and promising to come back, he turned, working farther up through the trees toward the pass that led up to the corrugated metal shack and the

mine. It took him four days getting there, retracing his
route as exactly as he could, him and the dog making
camp in the sheltering clump of trees where he and
Sarah once had slept, making camp the next night in
among the fallen V of timber, eating the cooked meat
that he had saved from the rabbits and squirrels that
the dog had been bringing to him. They slept together
in the sleeping bag, the saddle blankets under them,
him hardly ever speaking, waking and working on
through the trees while the dog on occasion darted off
somewhere and he kept moving, the dog catching up to
him with some animal to replenish their supply. They
finally made it to the pass, shuffling up through the
snow past the tumbled shacks from the miners, reaching the top where the snow had drifted bare enough
that he could take off his snowshoes for a time, walking
solidly on the floor of rock past the cliff walls on both
sides, and there it was, the corrugated metal shack and
the mine. They camped in the tunnel just as he and
Sarah had done, making a fire, cooking, warming
themselves. He looked around for any signs that they
had been here after him, but there were none, and he
woke the next morning, slipping on his snowshoes,
wading down toward the town.

It was drifted with snow, him passing the hollow
where he and Sarah had stopped after Claire had died,
taking the route down through the trees which as near
as he could guess was the way he had gone to look for
Claire that night, crossing the snow-blown meadow,
coming to where the town was nothing more than dips
and rises, apparently from irregularities in the plain as
much as anything, occasional burnt-out beams and
timbers standing up or showing through, black against

the sun-bright drifts to show what once had been. He made a shelter from charred boards, wading around to find a sign of the guy that the old man had knifed and they had thrown close to the fire, of the old man himself, of the guy that Claire had shotgunned in the stable, but there wasn't any of them either, nor of Claire whom he was really looking for. He knew that they would not have taken her with them, just some evidence that they had got her, burying her somewhere close around, burning her maybe, but the area was too much, she could have been anywhere, and promising he would come back here as well, he finally gave up.

There were occasional animal tracks in the snow, but nothing he could see to shoot, and the dog came back that night with another squirrel, the last it would have to bring because the next morning after they had gone to the river, him taking off his boots and tattered woolen socks, tucking them into the sack he had made and wading the ford, carrying the dog, the water numbing cold, him quickly drying his feet on the other side, he saw a rabbit as he was slipping on his socks and shot it, firing too quickly, hitting it in the shoulders, blowing its front half apart. But there was a little food from it, and after he had skinned it, gutted it, wrapping the meat in its fur, stuffing it into his sack, they worked along the river, up through the trees, to the break in the cliff that led through to the sheep desert. They were into their sixth day of unmistakable warm weather now, which was why the ice on the river had broken up and he had been forced to wade, and the niche in the cliff was narrow enough that not much snow had collected so that they did not have much trouble getting through, climbing over the boulders that he and the old man had tumbled down into it, him once making a wrong turn and coming to a dead end, going back, trying another, finally reaching through to the sheep desert, and he could see now the change that the weather was making, the snow melting loosely all around, still quite deep but rocks showing bare and wet all the same, them rounding the bottom of the canyon, coming to what would have been the dry rocky creek bed if the snow had been gone and he could see it.

They camped in a small box canyon, hunched in under a lip in the rock, building a fire that was bigger than any he had made so far, seeing that he was down to his last few matches, grateful that he had kept the fire going all the time back at the burrow, keeping it low but going all the same, and it didn't matter if he was down to his last few matches because they were getting closer to people all the time and if he ran out of matches before then, well he had gone without fire before and he could stand that a few more nights yet again. But he was going to have to start thinking about how he could go back among them, certainly not looking like this. There would be too many questions, too much attention toward him before he was ready for it, and he did what he could to make himself look clean, heating water and bathing near the fire, washing the sores on his face and his arms and his legs, rinsing his hair and his beard, trimming them as best he could with his knife. That was why he had made the fire so big, so he could get out of some of his clothes and clean them without freezing, looking now at his thighs and his chest, something he had not done since the start, stunned by the look of them, flesh used up, bones showing, pustules, sores. He couldn't clean his clothes very much. If he tried scrubbing them, he was afraid they might turn to rags, which was what they were close to being anyhow, and after he had done what he could, rinsing his woolen underwear and pants and coat, building the fire even larger and drying them, watching them steam, he put them back on, feeling their warmth again, sharing with the dog the last of their meat, crawling into the sleeping bag with the dog, and sleeping.

The next morning he shot another rabbit, this time properly, through the head, and after cooking it and eating it, he made his way out of the canyon, trying to decipher the intersecting slopes and ridges so they would lead him to the line shack. His contour maps were long since torn and crumbled, his only guide his compass which without the maps only gave him vague direction, and after a day and a half of searching he was sure he'd missed it when he came out on a stretch of rock and saw it. Down there in a clearing in the valley, close if he went straight down but a half day away since he had to work around off the cliff and down through the trees toward it. But he got there before nightfall, and after checking carefully around, certain that no one was near, he came up to the door, looking at where if they had come to the line shack after him they had replaced the broken lock the same as he had, opened the door, and stood there a moment staring at the shelves of food. No sign that anyone had been in, everything the same as he remembered it, and all he could think of was the cans of peaches and corn and beef, the Bisquick he could make bread with, and he spent three days there, cleaning himself further, fattening himself, knowing he was going to need all his strength before this would be finished, never staying too long in the cabin, certainly never sleeping there, camping without fire in among a rim of timber well up from the line shack, each day watching the snow melt, resting, soaking up the heat.

On the fourth day he left it, feeling better than he had in months, but his new-found luxuries, a fresh thick shirt, a store of bread and canned peaches and meat, a clean pair of socks, only made him feel the privation of the woods more, and he was grateful six days later when he finally came down through the wash of rocks and timber that he and Claire and Sarah had gone up that first day, hiking across the various levels down toward their cabin, always careful to stay inside the trees, reaching the corral and the equipment shed, coming more slowly in on an angle toward the cabin. The snow was thinner now, partly from the season, partly from the change in height, and there were spots of grass showing through as the cabin came in sight, its windows glinting in the sunlight. Exactly as he remembered it, as he had left it. The tower, the stoop at the back, the outhouse to the side. No tracks in the snow, no smoke from the chimney, no sign that anyone had been there for some time. He circled far off, coming in on a different angle toward the front. The well, the porch and door, the rocks around the foundation, the logs above them, all as he remembered them, and he camped far off in sight for a day before he felt safe enough to approach them.

He came in through the back, checking the downstairs rooms, the cupboards even, leaving the dog below while he went up to the upstairs bedrooms, the closets, finally up to the tower and there was no one.

The window up there was still open, its top panes still shattered from where they had shot at him, snow drifted in, and he left it all just as he had found it. He didn't understand. Nothing had changed at all. It was as if no one had been here since they had gone. Downstairs he found the lamp on the living room table just where he had left it, top off, core out, where he had been putting a new wick in. Everything was perfectly the same. He didn't understand it. Surely the owner would have come around, or the real-estate man when the rent wasn't paid. There was a mirror by one cupboard, and he trimmed his hair and beard even better. He finished the food that he had brought with him from the line shack and started in on the store in the cabin, heating stew and rice and tinned puddings, sharing everything with the dog, bathing, putting on a fresh set of clothes that were in the drawers in the downstairs bedroom. He kept checking outside, fearful of them coming up through the trees the way they had that first time, worrying all the time he bathed, grateful at least that the dog was by the front door watching. He got back up to his campsite in the trees as fast as he could, watching, going back to the cabin the next day to eat some more, and he worked it like that for a week until he thought that he was ready. He had considered shaving off his beard entirely, letting the sun get in at the sores on his face, but he didn't want to look too different, he wanted to be recognized.

"Hello again, haven't seen you in a while."

"I've been away."

"Well, what can I do for you this time?"

"I want that rifle up there, the six-point-five, and a high-powered scope and two boxes of those shells."

"Just the thing. How'd you do anyway?"

"Excuse me?"

"Hunting. How many did you get?"

"Not as many as I'd like."

"Yeah, that's what everyone's been saying."

Then he had gone to the real-estate man, and the guy had said the same. "No need to worry, though. Your friends have been coming in, just like you told them, every month to pay the rent."

Which was what he'd figured. It was the only reason why the place would not have been touched. They were very thorough. If he lived, they were thinking that he might come back and he was telling the guy not to let them know he was. They'd be coming in just once more to pay the rent and then they'd go on up to check the cabin for him, and he didn't want them to know he was, he wanted to surprise them. Which meant the guy would let it slip. He'd better anyhow. From the un-tracked snow around the cabin they hadn't been going up to look for him yet. But they obviously were plan-ning to go on up once the snow was nearly gone. That would be the only reason they kept paying for the place, just to be careful, to keep things neat. The trouble was, the snow was melting slower now than he hoped. They might not come back looking for him until next month, and he didn't want to wait that long. So they'd either go up on a chance the day they paid, or else the guy would let it slip, he likely would, and they'd go up for certain. In any case, in time they'd be there. Sooner or later, in one sense it was the same. He checked the calendar in the office. April 25. A few more days if everything worked out right. He bought a ground sheet for under the sleeping bag, went back to the cabin, laid up in the woods, and waited for them.

Where he lay was on some high ground to the left of the front of the cabin. From his point of view he could see the shed, the side of the house, part of the front porch and the well. He had a good view of the open slope and of the road up through the trees. If they came up that way as they had before, he certainly would spot them. The only problem was if they came up from his direction through the woods, and he was counting on the dog sensing them before they did. He had taken trouble back-tracking, circling far off into the woods and then back again, so that his footprints wouldn't show them where he was. He had made tracks around the cabin as well, but these he didn't worry about, wanting to advertise he'd returned. He built a fire in the cabin, smoke coming from the chimney, to make it seem that he was in there, and after the moon set each night he went back in, putting more rags and damp wood on the flames to keep up the smoke.

He counted the days, the twenty-ninth now, going in through the back that night and hearing a sound, a scratch in one corner that made hin think that they were there, tensing, lunging to one corner, but no shots, and he never did know what made the scratch, a small animal perhaps. But his fright made him even more careful, coming down to the cabin once the dark set in after that, wanting to be close enough to hear if they came close, knowing he never would be able to see them from his campsite if they came at night.

The thirtieth and then the first, and he was beginning to think that he'd misjudged. Maybe the real-estate guy had kept the secret after all. Maybe they weren't going to come. Maybe he was going to have to wait a few

weeks more, or even a month, when something bothered
him. Just before sunset on the second. He heard a car
far off on the road down there, and then it stopped.
It could be nothing. It could be just some people visiting another cabin a mile across over there or visiting
the old man with the horses, his place was in that direction too, but it could be them as well, and if they
were coming up through the trees at night, he couldn't
go down near the house this time. They might be down
there by then, waiting for him. He lay still listening.
No one and no warning from the dog. He lay still all
the same. He listened for the sound of the car to start
up, but it didn't, although that didn't mean much either.
If the car really was people visiting, they could have
chosen to stay the night. Sometime around three, he
guessed, he heard a snap down in the trees. A broken
branch settling, an animal moving. It could be anything.
Or it could be them and so he waited.

There were three of them, one in the trees at the
back, two others stretched out just below the top of the
slope in front. He could see them clearly in the first
bright light of day. They were wearing light brown
nylon padded jackets, warm-up pants the same, as
near as he could tell not the same three he had seen the
fall before in town, and he wanted them together and
he wanted to see what they were going to do anyhow, so
he waited. They kept checking their watches, and then
as if they had all agreed on a time they started shooting,
shotguns blowing out the windows, blasts echoing, re-
coils jerking, except for the guy in back who wasn't
shooting at all, just standing there in among the trees,
tensed and ready, as if the plan were to scare him
from in front and drive him out the back where the

guy would be there waiting for him. And they kept on shooting like that from in front until they'd each used up one magazine and then another and still no sign of him in there and then they stopped. They lay there, undecided, poking their heads up, one and then the other, to check for any movement in there. And of course there wasn't any, and the two guys in front had been some distance apart to begin with but now they moved even farther apart and as if on signal one jumped up running on an angle toward the front door while the other covered him. When the first guy ducked out of sight against the door, the second guy jumped up then running in on his own angle as if the other guy were covering him now. And the guy in back never moved. He imagined them cracking in the front door, one going in under cover of the other, then the second guy going in, them checking the place, and then he heard the crack from the door and he knew that was what they were doing.

They'd be going through the house upstairs and down and then out the back door to talk to the third guy and that's when they would be together and he was crawling back from sight, running with the dog through the trees, slowing as he thought that they might hear him, working toward a spot where he could see down to the back and the third man and then he was in position. He was about sixty yards up, the guy's back to him, the door in sight, easing down, sighting in with his scope, the cross hairs clearly focused just between the shoulder blades. Then he shifted his aim from the guy to the back door and it opened and the two of them were coming out, talking, shrugging. The third one lowered his shotgun, saying something indistinct, walk-

ing toward them on the stoop and then Bourne fired,
bringing down the third man easily, shifting quickly to
the men on the stoop, firing, bringing down another,
and the last of them was gone, ducked back into the
house.

He couldn't wait. He had to run around to the high
ground on the side in case the one in there got out the
front and down the slope. He slipped and fell, running,
reached the side, mud soaking through his clothes, and
had a good view of anyone who might come out the
front or back. There was always the chance that the
guy in there might already have got out, but he himself
had moved quite fast, and in any case the guy down
there would likely have turned cautious, wanting to
know exactly where he was being shot at from before
he made his move.

He didn't want to prolong it, firing at the lantern
he had put on the sill of the bedroom window on this
side in case he trapped them in the cabin, blasting it
apart, chipping the phosphorus strips he had taped to
the glass, the phosphorus open to the air now, burning,
igniting the spilled-out kerosene. At least it was supposed to work that way. But he saw no sign of fire and
he was beginning to think that he'd been wrong when
the flames shot up to fill the window. Now all he had
to do was wait. There were no windows on the other
side, the stove and cupboards against that wall in the
kitchen, the fireplace against it in the living room, so
when the fire got too close the guy in there was going
to have to come out either front or back.

The flames were all through the bedroom now, smoke
rising clearly through the windows in the upper rooms.
He could see smoke coming from the front now too

and it wouldn't be long, the guy would have to come out, but he stayed in as long as he could just the same, flames spreading all through the upstairs and reaching for the tower when the guy dove out the back. He almost missed him, glancing once at the tower, then at the back and the guy was running past the two men spread out on the ground, racing toward the cover of the trees when Bourne fired, missed, fired again and the guy's leg whipped out from under him. He flew sideways, cracking against a tree, lying there, shaking his head, starting to crawl into cover when Bourne fired again just ahead of him, shouting "Don't move or you're dead!"

The impact of the bullet ahead of the guy had stopped him anyway, scaring him back into the clearing, and the guy was holding his leg now, craning his neck to look around.

"Get rid of the shotgun!" Bourne yelled at him, and almost as if the thing were alive, the guy threw the shotgun away.

"Now stay where you are!" Bourne told him, starting down through the trees.

The guy was huddled holding his leg at the edge of the clearing, pale, blood soaking into the snow around his leg as Bourne reached the edge of the trees and looked around. The flames were licking through the roof of the house and the tower, smoke rising thick and white and black, the sound of the flames like a furnace, crackling in there, whooshing. He could see where the snow was melting all around the house and where the moisture on the jacket of the one guy close to the house had started steaming. He looked carefully at the other guy and then started for the third.

He searched him, taking away a knife and a .38 handgun, putting a tourniquet on his leg, giving him a handful of aspirins and forcing him to stand. Looking around the trees, he saw a fallen branch with a crook where the guy could put it under his arm and a shaft that was stiff enough that it wouldn't break if the guy put his weight on it, and then forcing him up into the trees toward where he had camped, he collected his gear, slipping it into his sack, shoving his rifle into the sleeping bag, rolling the bag up and hitching it over his shoulder, then pushing the guy up toward the hills.

The guy was in shock quite soon. It didn't matter. He had to keep him on the move. He let him rest when it seemed he couldn't go any farther for a while, giving him more aspirin, feeding him, letting him drink, then forcing him on again. He kept looking back toward the direction they'd just come from. No one was after him, although for a time there he did hear the sound of a siren. He looked up toward the cliff wall they were approaching, and he knew he would never get the guy over to the wash that led up to the top of it, would never be able to make him climb, so he finally chose a flat circle of snow-free ground near the base of it, thick trees encircling, pushed him down and waited.

"Take your clothes off," he finally told him.

"What?"

"You heard me. Take your clothes off."

"Why?"

He kicked him in the leg, and the guy took his clothes off.

"Lie down flat. Spread out your arms and legs."

The guy didn't move, and he kicked him again, and the guy spread out his arms and legs. His skin was white against the cold brown ground, his leg red-caked and swollen. The hole in his leg was just below the knee, the bone untouched, a black hole through the flesh, and Bourne had been loosening the tourniquet and tightening it as they came up through the trees, and now he loosened it and tightened it again.

"I don't want you to lose much strength."

He made four stakes and shoved them into the ground, secure enough that they wouldn't come free, tying the guy's arms and legs to them so that he was spread out chest and privates to the sky. Then drawing his knife, he sliced once thinly from his nipple to his navel. The guy had started screaming even before he did it, flesh spreading, blood swelling, dripping, and Bourne looked at him, grabbing his face so that he could look him directly in the eyes.

"Now I'm only going to ask this once. Were you with the others at the town they burned up there?"

The guy's eyes were wide and darting. "I don't know what you mean."

Bourne cut another stroke. The guy screamed and nodded violently. "Yes. Yes, I was with them."

"That's very good. You don't know how good. If you hadn't been with them, you might have been useless to me and then I would have had to kill you. All right now, here's another one. What did they do to the woman they shot?"

"They buried her."

"That's not what I mean. What did they do to her?"

"Took an ear."

"And then what?"

"Nothing. They just buried her."

"Where?"

"I don't know. Two others did it."

"But where did they say?"

"In a cabin across from the river."

"Which one?"

"I don't know."

"All right, I believe you. Here's another one. I want to know who it is you're responsible to."

And little by little, it came out, sometimes reluctantly, sometimes in obvious lies, Bourne cutting, probing, digging at the wound or at his chest or his arms or his other leg, sometimes staring at his privates and the guy talked faster after that, about who had told him what to do when and who that other guy might be responsible to and what might be the structure of command, and they were an hour at it that way, the guy crisscrossed with gashes, Bourne learning everything he could, the names of the other guys that this one had worked with, forcing the guy to keep talking so that he could remain alive. And then Bourne was finished. He couldn't think of anything more he needed to learn, and he just sat back looking at the guy, working through a litany of all that had been done to him, unable to stand it anymore, plunging in his knife and twisting.

EPILOGUE

IT TOOK HIM a year. He went back to the house in the town where everything had started, standing in the dark between the two fir trees, looking toward the place. He went back to the cemetery where Ethan was buried, staring at the tombstone. Then he made his way back toward the hills, hiking carefully up into them, up through the break in the cliff, past the line shack and the sheep desert to the town again, and he found where Claire was, where the guy had said, in a shallow grave in one of the tumbled cabins on the tree-side of the river, and she had one ear gone as the guy had said and he quickly covered her again. Then he hiked up toward the corrugated metal shack and the mine, across the pass and down toward the country of the mound, and the mound was as he'd left it, green boughs turned to brown but otherwise the same, and he didn't want to bother her, just sprinkled the dust he had gathered from the graves of Ethan and Claire over it, scooping up dirt from underneath one side of the mound, starting back toward Claire, sprinkling the dirt from the mound and some from Ethan's grave upon the soil that covered her, and weeks later, standing again in the dark in the cemetery, staring down toward Ethan's grave, he sprinkled the dirt together.

And then he started.

HE LAY ON HIS CHEST in among a line of trees that looked down on a fertile valley. Of the year, it had taken him the summer, fall, and winter getting there. He had gone around to the people the guy had mentioned when he was torturing him, and he had made them talk before they died as well, getting other names, higher ones, and finally he had got a lead and then another one, working back and forth across the country, using different names, sometimes with a beard, sometimes without, taking jobs on farms, in lumber camps, mending fences, painting barns, anything for which he didn't need a social security number, angling southwest as the weather changed from warm to cold but needing to go that way anyhow, the dog always with him, through Kansas, Colorado, Arizona, California, spring again, and he was lying in among the line of trees, looking down toward the valley.

There was a farm down there, a big wide spreading house and a barn and sheds and everything was white against the green of the growing crops, a family down there eating at a backyard table, Kess, his wife, two daughters, and a son, eating, talking, smiling he could see as he sighted in with his scope.

They were far enough from the house that only a few of them would have a chance to make it there before he would have to stop. Maybe he would get them all. Maybe they'd be so confused, looking around, trying to help each other, that none of them would make it to the house.

And now that he looked closer he could see the bodyguard by the corner of the garage and the other one just inside the screen door of the house, but they didn't matter. By the time they figured where he was he'd be gone, and if he got a chance he would get them too and the cat that was playing in the flower bed, that would make a balance, and his only question now was how to go about it.

He sighted in on the man, but that would be too easy. He'd be dead and he'd never know the feelings he had caused, and the only way to do this was to do it the way the man down there had started. But he wouldn't take the cat, not at first at any rate, that would give them too much chance for some of them to make it to the house. He'd start in on the people, youngest to oldest, take the cat when he couldn't take anything else, and if in working up he gave the guy a chance to get away, well that would be all right as well. He would hound him then, hunt him just as he had been, let him know the way it felt, and his only question now was which one was the youngest.

The girl on this end to the right was surely twelve, which left the girl and the boy beside her, and the boy looked older than the other girl, so he centered in on the farthest girl, long hair fine and sandy, freckled, smiling, and he shook his head.

He aimed again and saw the same and shook his head. Every time he sighted in on her, the child blurred into Sarah. He switched to the boy and thought of Ethan and the woman was Claire and he could see them all down there, Claire, Sarah, Ethan, eating, laughing, and he couldn't do it.

He told himself that he was being foolish. So what if the girl down there reminded him of Sarah. So what if the family reminded him of his. All the more reason to continue.

Even so he couldn't do it.

He thought of shooting the man. There had been no sense of doubling in his case at least, no image of himself down there, but it wasn't any good. All he could think of was his position in the reverse, of himself being killed and Claire and Sarah and Ethan looking at him, and he couldn't do it.

He told himself that if he didn't do it the man down there would just keep sending others after him. He told himself that if he didn't end it now he would never feel safe, never stop running. It didn't matter. It was too much, had been too much. He simply couldn't do it.

3

HE SITS in his room in a town that he does not identify, sometimes goes out, mostly doesn't. The dog stays with him, wondering why he doesn't. He thinks of his passage up through the graves from Ethan to Claire and Sarah and then back down again, sprinkling dust over them, wakes from dreams of them, and sometimes it seems those grains of dust falling through his hands, like these words, will never end.

"One of the finest
chase novels you will ever read."
—*Minneapolis Tribune*

FIRST BLOOD

by David Morrell

2-2976-9 $1.75

Here's the novel that critics couldn't find enough enthusi-
astic words for. The tough, rough story of Rambo, the
stranger who had just come back from Vietnam, honed to
kill, ready to prove it. Nobody in the small Kentucky town
knew who he was. They just knew he looked like trouble.
Unfortunately for them, they tried to get rid of him. And
the army had trained Rambo in the art of killing, an art he
couldn't seem to stop practicing.

"A terrific thriller."—*Saturday Review*

FAWCETT CREST
BESTSELLERS